Sidney Sheldon is the author of *The* *Midnight*, *A Stranger in the Mirror*, *Bloodline*, *Rage of Angels*, *Master of the Game*, *If Tomorrow Comes*, *Windmills of the Gods*, *The Sands of Time*, *Memories of Midnight*, *The Doomsday Conspiracy*, *The Stars Shine Down*, *Nothing Lasts Forever*, *Morning, Noon and Night*, *The Best Laid Plans* and *Tell Me Your Dreams*, all number one international bestsellers. His first book, *The Naked Face*, was acclaimed by the *New York Times* as 'the best first mystery novel of the year'. Mr Sheldon has won a Tony Award for Broadway's *Redhead* and an Academy Award for *The Bachelor and the Bobby Soxer*. *Rage of Angels*, *Master of the Game*, *Windmills of the Gods* and *Memories of Midnight* have been made into highly success- ful television miniseries.

He has written the screenplays for twenty-three motion pictures including *Easter Parade* (with Judy Garland) and *Annie Get Your Gun*. He also created four long-running television series, including *Hart to Hart* and *I Dream of Jeannie*, which he produced. He was awarded the 1993 Prix Littéraire de Deauville, from the Deauville Film Festival, and is now included in the *Guinness Book of Records* as 'The Most Translated Author'. Mr Sheldon and his wife live in Southern California and London.

For more about Sidney Sheldon, see his website at http://www.sidneysheldon.com.

SIDNEY SHELDON

Morning, Noon & Night

HarperCollins*Publishers*

HarperCollins*Publishers*
77–85 Fulham Palace Road,
Hammersmith, London W6 8JB

www.**fire**and**water**.com

Special overseas edition 1996
This paperback edition 1996
24

First published in Great Britain by
HarperCollins*Publishers* 1995

ISBN 0 00 649806 X

Set in Times Roman by
Rowland Phototypesetting Ltd,
Bury St Edmunds, Suffolk

Printed in Great Britain by
Clays Ltd, St Ives plc

To Kimberly
with love

Allow the morning sun to warm
Your heart when you are young
And let the soft winds of noon
Cool your passion,
But beware the night
For death lurks there,
Waiting, waiting, waiting.

ARTHUR RIMBAUD

MORNING

Chapter One

Dmitri asked, 'Do you know we're being followed, Mr Stanford?'

'Yes.' He had been aware of them for the past twenty-four hours.

The two men and the woman were dressed casually, attempting to blend in with the summer tourists strolling along the cobbled streets in the early morning, but it was difficult to remain inconspicuous in a place as small as the fortified village of St-Paul-de-Vence.

Harry Stanford had first noticed them because they were *too* casual, trying *too* hard not to look at him. Wherever he turned, one of them was in the background.

Harry Stanford was an easy target to follow. He was six feet tall, with white hair lapping over his collar and an aristocratic, almost imperious face. He was accompanied by a strikingly lovely young brunette, a pure-white German shepherd, and Dmitri Kaminsky, a six-foot four-inch bodyguard with a bulging neck and sloping forehead. *Hard to lose us*, Stanford thought.

He knew who had sent them and why, and he was filled with a sense of imminent danger. He had learned long ago to trust his instincts. Instinct and intuition had helped make him one of the wealthiest men in the world. *Forbes* magazine estimated the value of Stanford Enterprises at six billion dollars, while the *Fortune* 500 appraised it at seven billion. The *Wall Street Journal, Barron's,* and the *Financial Times* had all done profiles on Harry Stanford, trying to explain his mystique, his amazing sense of timing, the ineffable acumen that had created the giant Stanford Enterprises. None had fully succeeded.

What they all agreed on was that he had an almost palpable, manic energy. He was inexhaustible. His philosophy was simple: A day without making a deal was a day wasted. He wore out his competitors, his staff, and everyone else who came in contact with him. He was a phenomenon, larger than life. He thought of himself as a religious man. He believed in God, and the God he believed in wanted him to be rich and successful, and his enemies dead.

Harry Stanford was a public figure, and the press knew everything about him. Harry Stanford was a private figure, and the press knew nothing about him. They had written about his charisma, his lavish life-style, his private plane and his yacht, and his legendary homes in Hobe Sound, Morocco, Long Island, London, the South of France, and of course his magnificent estate, Rose Hill, in the Back Bay area of Boston. But the real Harry Stanford remained an enigma.

'Where are we going?' the woman asked.

He was too preoccupied to answer. The couple on the other side of the street was using the cross-switch technique, and they had just changed partners again. Along with his sense of danger, Stanford felt a deep anger that they were invading his privacy. They had dared come to him in this place, his secret haven from the rest of the world.

St-Paul-de-Vence is a picturesque, medieval village, weaving its ancient magic on a hilltop in the Alps Maritimes, situated inland between Cannes and Nice. It is surrounded by a spectacular and enchanting landscape of hills and valleys covered with flowers, orchards, and pine forests. The village itself, a cornucopia of artists' studios, galleries and wonderful antique shops, is a magnet for tourists from all over the world.

Harry Stanford and his group turned onto the Rue Grande.

Stanford turned to the woman Sophia, 'Do you like museums?'

'Yes, *caro.*' She was eager to please him. She had never met anyone like Harry Stanford. *Wait until I tell my girlfriends about him. I didn't think there was anything left for me to learn about sex, but my God, he's so creative! He's wearing me out!*

They went up the hill to the Fondation Maeght art museum, and browsed through its renowned collection of paintings by Bonnard and Chagall and many other contemporary artists. When Harry Stanford casually glanced around, he observed the woman at the other end of the gallery, earnestly studying a Miró.

Stanford turned to Sophia. 'Hungry?'

'Yes. If you are.' *Must not be pushy.*

'Good. We'll have lunch at La Colombe d'Or.'

La Colombe d'Or was one of Stanford's favorite restaurants, a sixteenth-century house at the entrance to the old village, converted into a hotel and restaurant. Stanford and Sophia sat at a table in the garden, by the pool, where Stanford could admire the Braque and Calder.

Prince, the white German shepherd, lay at his feet, ever watchful. The dog was Harry Stanford's trademark. Where Stanford went, Prince went. It was rumored that at Harry Stanford's command, the animal would tear out a person's throat. No one wanted to test that rumor.

Dmitri sat by himself at a table near the hotel entrance, carefully observing the other patrons as they came and went.

Stanford turned to Sophia. 'Shall I order for you, my dear?'

'Please.'

Harry Stanford prided himself on being a gourmet. He ordered a green salad and *fricassée de lotte* for both of them.

As they were being served their main course, Danielle Roux, who ran the hotel with her husband, François, approached the table and smiled. '*Bonjour*. Is everything all right, Monsieur Stanford?'

'Wonderful, Madame Roux.'

And it was going to be. *They are pygmies, trying to fell a giant. They're in for a big disappointment.*

Sophia said, 'I've never been here before. It's such a lovely village.'

Stanford turned his attention to her. Dmitri had picked her up for him in Nice a day earlier.

'Mr Stanford, I brought someone for you.'

'Any problem?' Stanford had asked.

Dmitri had grinned. 'None.' He had seen her in the lobby of the Hotel Negresco, and had approached her.

'Excuse me, do you speak English?'

'Yes.' She had a lilting Italian accent.

'The man I work for would like you to have dinner with him.'

She had been indignant. 'I'm not a *puttana*! I'm an actress,' she had said haughtily. In fact, she had had a walk-on part in Pupi Avati's last film, and a role with two lines of dialogue in a Giuseppe Tornatore film. 'Why would I have dinner with a stranger?'

7

Dmitri had taken out a wad of hundred-dollar bills. He pushed five into her hand. 'My friend is very generous. He has a yacht, and he is lonely.' He had watched her expression go through a series of changes from indignation, to curiosity, to interest.

'As it happens, I'm between pictures.' She smiled. 'It would probably do no harm to have dinner with your friend.'

'Good. He will be pleased.'

'Where is he?'

'St-Paul-de-Vence.'

Dmitri had chosen well. Italian. In her late twenties. A sensuous, catlike face. Full-breasted figure. Now, looking at her across the table, Harry Stanford made a decision.

'Do you like to travel, Sophia?'

'I adore it.'

'Good. We'll go on a little trip. Excuse me a moment.'

Sophia watched as he walked into the restaurant and to a public telephone outside the men's room.

Stanford put a *jeton* in the slot and dialed.

'Marine operator, please.'

Seconds later, a voice said, '*C'est l'opératrice maritime.*'

'I want to put in a call to the yacht *Blue Skies.* Whiskey bravo lima nine eight zero . . .'

The conversation lasted five minutes, and when

8

Stanford was finished, he dialed the airport at Nice. The conversation was shorter this time.

When Stanford was through talking, he spoke to Dmitri, who rapidly left the restaurant. Then he returned to Sophia. 'Are you ready?'

'Yes.'

'Let's take a walk.' He needed time to work out a plan.

It was a perfect day. The sun had splashed pink clouds across the horizon and rivers of silver light ran through the streets.

They strolled along the Rue Grande, past the Église, the beautiful twelfth-century church, and stopped at the *boulangerie* in front of the Arch to buy some fresh baked bread. When they came out, one of the three watchers was standing outside, busily studying the church. Dmitri was also waiting for them.

Harry Stanford handed the bread to Sophia. 'Why don't you take this up to the house? I'll be along in a few minutes.'

'All right.' She smiled and said softly, 'Hurry, *caro*.'

Stanford watched her leave, then motioned to Dmitri.

'What did you find out?'

'The woman and one of the men are staying at Le Hameau, on the road to La Colle.'

Harry Stanford knew the place. It was a

whitewashed farmhouse with an orchard a mile west of St-Paul-de-Vence. 'And the other one?'

'At Le Mas d'Artigny.'

Le Mas d'Artigny was a Provençal mansion on a hillside two miles west of St-Paul-de-Vence.

'What do you want me to do with them, sir?'

'Nothing. I'll take care of them.'

Harry Stanford's villa was on the Rue de Casette, next to the *mairie*, in an area of narrow cobblestone streets and very old houses. The villa was a five-level house made of old stone and plaster. Two levels below the main house were a garage and an old *cave* used as a wine cellar. A stone staircase led to upstairs bedrooms, an office, and a tiled-roof terrace. The entire house was furnished in French antiques and filled with flowers.

When Stanford returned to the villa, Sophia was in his bedroom, waiting for him. She was naked.

'What took you so long?' she whispered.

In order to survive, Sophia Matteo often picked up money between film assignments as a call girl, and she was used to faking orgasms to please her clients, but with this man, there was no need to pretend. He was insatiable, and she found herself climaxing again and again.

When they were finally exhausted, Sophia put her

arms around him and murmured happily, 'I could stay here forever, *caro*.'

I wish I could, Stanford thought, grimly.

They had dinner at Le Café de la Place in Plaza du General-de-Gaulle, near the entrance to the village. The dinner was delicious, and for Stanford the danger added spice to the meal.

When they were finished, they made their way back to the villa. Stanford walked slowly, to make certain his pursuers followed.

At one A.M., a man standing across the street watched the lights in the villa being turned off, one by one, until the building was in total darkness.

At four thirty in the morning, Harry Stanford went into the guest bedroom where Sophia slept. He shook her gently. 'Sophia . . . ?'

She opened her eyes and looked up at him, a smile of anticipation on her face, then frowned. He was fully dressed. She sat up. 'Is something wrong?'

'No, my dear. Everything is fine. You said you liked to travel. Well, we're going to take a little trip.'

She was wide awake now. 'At this hour?'

'Yes. We must be very quiet.'

'But . . .'

'Hurry.'

Fifteen minutes later, Harry Stanford, Sophia, Dmitri, and Prince were moving down the stone

11

staircase to the basement garage where a brown Renault was parked. Dmitri quietly opened the garage door and looked out onto the street. Except for Stanford's white Corniche, parked in front, it seemed deserted. 'All clear.'

Stanford turned to Sophia. 'We're going to play a little game. You and I are going to get in the back of the Renault and lie down on the floor.'

Her eyes widened. 'Why?'

'Some business competitors have been following me,' he said earnestly. 'I'm about to close a very large deal, and they're trying to find out about it. If they do, it could cost me a lot of money.'

'I understand,' Sophia said. She had no idea what he was talking about.

Five minutes later, they were driving past the gates of the village on the road to Nice. A man seated on a bench watched the brown Renault as it sped through the gates. At the wheel was Dmitri Kaminsky and beside him was Prince. The man hastily took out a cellular telephone and began dialing.

'We may have a problem,' he told the woman.

'What kind of problem?'

'A brown Renault just drove out of the gates. Dmitri Kaminsky was driving, and the dog was in the car, too.'

'And Stanford wasn't in the car?'

'No.'

'I don't believe it. His bodyguard never leaves him

at night, and that dog never leaves him, ever.'

'Is his Corniche still parked in front of the villa?' asked the other man sent to follow Harry Stanford.

'Yes, but maybe he switched cars.'

'Or it could be a trick! Call the airport.'

Within minutes, they were talking to the tower.

'Monsieur Stanford's plane? *Oui*. It arrived an hour ago and has already refueled.'

Five minutes later, two members of the surveillance team were on their way to the airport, while the third kept watch on the sleeping villa.

As the brown Renault passed through La Coalle-sur-Loup, Stanford moved onto the seat. 'It's all right to sit up, now,' he told Sophia. He turned to Dmitri, 'Nice airport. Hurry.'

Chapter Two

Half an hour later, at Nice airport, a converted Boeing 727 was slowly taxiing down the runway to the take-off point. Up in the tower, the flight controller said, 'They certainly are in a hurry to get that plane off the ground. The pilot has asked for a clearance three times.'

'Whose plane is it?'

'Harry Stanford. King Midas himself.'

'He's probably on his way to make another billion or two.'

The controller turned to monitor a Learjet taking off, then picked up the microphone. 'Boeing eight nine five Papa, this is Nice departure control. You are cleared for takeoff. Five left. After departure, turn right to a heading of one four zero.'

Harry Stanford's pilot and copilot exchanged a relieved look. The pilot pressed the microphone button. 'Roger. Boeing eight nine five Papa is cleared for takeoff. Will turn right to one four zero.'

A moment later, the huge plane thundered down the runway and knifed into the gray dawn sky.

The copilot spoke into the microphone again. 'Departure, Boeing eight nine five Papa is climbing out of three thousand for flight level seven zero.'

The copilot turned to the pilot. 'Whew! Old Man Stanford was sure anxious for us to get off the ground, wasn't he?'

The pilot shrugged. 'Ours not to reason why, ours but to do and die. How's he doing back there?'

The copilot rose and stepped to the door of the cockpit, and looked into the cabin. 'He's resting.'

They telephoned the airport tower from the car.

'Mr Stanford's plane . . . Is it still on the ground?'

'*Non*, monsieur. It has departed.'

'Did the pilot file a flight plan?'

'Of course, monsieur.'

'To where?'

'The plane is headed for JKF.'

'Thank you.' He turned to his companion. 'Kennedy. We'll have people there to meet him.'

When the Renault passed the outskirts of Monte Carlo, speeding toward the Italian border, Harry Stanford said, 'There's no chance that we were followed, Dmitri?'

'No, sir. We've lost them.'

'Good.' Harry Stanford leaned back in his seat and relaxed. There was nothing to worry about. They would be tracking the plane. He reviewed the situation in his mind. It was really a question of what they knew and when they knew it. They were jackals following the trail of a lion, hoping to bring him down. Harry Stanford smiled to himself. They had underestimated the man they were dealing with. Others who had made that mistake had paid dearly for it. Someone would also pay this time. He was Harry Stanford, the confidant of presidents and kings, powerful and rich enough to make or break the economies of a dozen countries.

The 727 was in the skies over Marseilles. The pilot spoke into the microphone. 'Marseilles, Boeing eight nine five Papa is with you, climbing out of flight level one nine zero for flight level two three zero.'

'Roger.'

The Renault reached San Remo shortly after dawn. Harry Stanford had fond memories of the city, but it had changed drastically. He remembered a time when it had been an elegant town with first-class hotels and restaurants, and a casino where black tie was required and where fortunes could be lost or won in an evening. Now it had succumbed to tourism, with loud-mouthed patrons gambling in their shirtsleeves.

The Renault was approaching the harbor, twelve miles from the French-Italian border. There were two marinas at the harbor, Marina Porto Sole to the east, and Porto Communale to the west. In Porto Sole, a marine attendant directed the berthing. In Porto Communale, there was no attendant.

'Which one?' Dmitri asked.

'Porto Communale,' Stanford directed. *The fewer people around, the better.*

'Yes, sir.'

A few minutes later, the Renault pulled up next to the *Blue Skies*, a sleek hundred-and-eighty-foot motor yacht. Captain Vacarro and the crew of twelve were lined up on deck. The captain hurried down the gangplank to greet the new arrivals.

'Good morning, Signor Stanford,' Captain Vacarro said. 'We'll take your luggage, and . . .'

'No luggage. Let's shove off.'

'Yes, sir.'

'Wait a minute.' Stanford was studying the crew. He frowned. 'The man on the end. He's new, isn't he?'

'Yes, sir. Our cabin boy got sick in Capri, and we took on this one. He's highly –'

'Get rid of him,' Stanford ordered.

The captain looked at him, puzzled. 'Get . . . ?'

'Pay him off. Let's get out of here.'

Captain Vacarro nodded. 'Right, sir.'

Looking around, Harry Stanford was filled with an increasing sense of foreboding. He could almost reach out and touch it. He did not want any strangers near him. Captain Vacarro and his crew had been with him for years. He could trust them. He turned to look at the girl. Since Dmitri had picked her up at random, here was no danger there. And as for Dmitri, his faithful bodyguard had saved his life more than once. Stanford turned to Dmitri. 'Stay close to me.'

'Yes, sir.'

Stanford took Sophia's arm. 'Let's go aboard, my dear.'

Dmitri Kaminsky stood on deck, watching the crew prepare to cast off. He scanned the harbor, but he saw nothing to be alarmed about. At this time of the morning, there was very little activity. The yacht's huge generators burst into life, and the vessel got under weigh.

The captain approached Harry Stanford. 'You didn't say where we were heading, Signor Stanford.'

'No, I didn't, did I, captain?' He thought for a moment. 'Portofino.'

'Yes, sir.'

'By the way, I want you to maintain strict radio silence.'

Captain Vacarro frowned. 'Radio silence? Yes, sir, but what if . . . ?'

Harry Stanford said, 'Don't worry about it. Just do it. And I don't want anyone using the satellite phones.'

'Right, sir. Will we be laying over in Portofino?'

'I'll let you know, captain.'

Harry Stanford took Sophia on a tour of the yacht. It was one of his prized possessions, and he enjoyed showing it off. It was a breathtaking vessel. It had a luxuriously appointed master suite with a sitting room and an office. The office was spacious and comfortably furnished with a couch, several easy chairs, and a desk, behind which was enough equipment to run a small town. On the wall was a large electronic map with a small moving boat showing the current position of the yacht. Sliding glass doors opened from the master suite onto an outside veranda deck furnished with a chaise longue and a table with four chairs. A teak railing ran along the outside. On balmy days, it was Stanford's custom to have breakfast on the veranda.

There were six guest staterooms, each with hand-painted silk panels, picture windows, and a bath with a Jacuzzi. The large library was done in koa wood.

The dining room could seat sixteen guests. A fully equipped fitness salon was on the lower deck. The yacht also contained a wine cellar and a theater that was ideal for running films. Harry Stanford had one of the world's greatest libraries of pornographic movies. The furnishings throughout the vessel were exquisite, and the paintings would have made any museum proud.

'Well, now you've seen most of it,' Stanford told Sophia at the end of the tour. 'I'll show you the rest tomorrow.'

She was awed. 'I've never seen anything like it! It's . . . it's like a city!'

Harry Stanford smiled at her enthusiasm. 'The

steward will show you to your cabin. Make yourself comfortable. I have some work to do.'

Harry Stanford returned to his office and checked the electronic map on the wall for the location of the yacht. *Blue Skies* was in the Ligurian Sea, heading northeast. *They won't know where I've gone*, Stanford thought. *They'll be waiting for me at JFK. When we get to Portofino, I'll straighten everything out.*

Thirty-five thousand feet in the air, the pilot of the 727 was getting new instructions. 'Boeing eight nine five Papa, you are cleared directly to Delta India November upper route forty as filed.'

'Roger. Boeing eight nine five Papa is cleared direct Dinard upper route forty as filed.' He turned to the copilot. 'All clear.'

The pilot stretched, got up, and walked to the cockpit door. He looked into the cabin.

'How's our passenger doing?' the copilot asked.

'He looks hungry to me.'

Chapter Three

The Ligurian coast is the Italian Riviera, sweeping in a semicircle from the French-Italian border around to Genoa, and then continuing down to the Gulf of La Spezia. The beautiful long ribbon of coast and its sparkling waters contain the storied ports of Portofino, Vernazza, and beyond them Elba, Sardinia, and Corsica.

Blue Skies was approaching Portofino, which even from a distance was an impressive sight, its hillsides covered with olive trees, pines, cypresses and palms. Harry Stanford, Sophia, and Dmitri were on deck, studying the approaching coastline.

'Have you been to Portofino often?' Sophia asked.

'A few times.'

'Where is your main home?'

Too personal. 'You'll enjoy Portofino, Sophia. It's really quite beautiful.'

Captain Vacarro approached them. 'Will you be having lunch aboard, Signor Stanford?'

'No, we'll have lunch at the Splendido.'

'Very good. And shall I be prepared to weigh anchor right after lunch?'

'I think not. Let's enjoy the beauty of the place.'

Captain Vacarro studied him, puzzled. One moment Harry Stanford was in a terrible hurry, and the next moment he seemed to have all the time in the world. And the radio shut down? Unheard of! *Pazzo*.

When *Blue Skies* dropped anchor in the outer harbor, Stanford, Sophia and Dmitri took the yacht's launch ashore. The small seaport was charming, with a variety of amusing shops and outdoor *trattorie* lining the single road that led up to the hills. A dozen or so small fishing boats were pulled up onto the pebbled beach.

Stanford turned to Sophia. 'We'll be lunching at the hotel on top of the hill. There's a lovely view from there.' He nodded toward a taxi stopped beyond the docks. 'Take a taxi up there, and I'll meet you in a few minutes.' He handed her some *lire*.

'Very well, *caro*.'

His eyes followed her as she walked away; then he turned to Dmitri. 'I have to make a call.'

But not from the ship, Dmitri thought.

The men went to the two phone booths at the side of the dock. Dmitri watched as Stanford stepped inside one of them, picked up the receiver, and inserted a token.

'Operator, I would like to place a call to someone at the Union Bank of Switzerland in Geneva.'

A woman was approaching the second phone booth.

Dmitri stepped in front of it, blocking her way.

'Excuse me,' she said. 'I . . .'

'I'm waiting for a call.'

She looked at him in surprise. 'Oh.' She glanced hopefully at the phone booth Stanford was in.

'I wouldn't wait,' Dmitri grunted. 'He's going to be on the telephone for a long time.'

The woman shrugged and walked away.

'Hello?'

Dmitri was watching Stanford speaking into the mouthpiece.

'Peter? We have a little problem.' Stanford closed the door to the booth. He was speaking very fast, and Dmitri could not hear what he was saying. At the end of the conversation, Stanford replaced the receiver and opened the door.

'Is everything all right, Mr Stanford?' Dmitri asked.

'Let's get some lunch.'

The Splendido is the crown jewel of Portofino, a hotel with a magnificent panoramic view of the emerald bay below. The hotel caters to the very rich, and jealously guards its reputation. Harry Stanford and Sophia had lunch out on the terrace.

'Shall I order for you?' Stanford asked. 'They have some specialties here that I think you might enjoy.'

'Please,' Sophia said.

Stanford ordered the *trenette al pesto*, the local pasta, veal, and *focaccia*, the salted bread of the region.

23

'And bring us a bottle of Schram Eighty-eight.' He turned to Sophia. 'It received a gold medal in the International Wine Challenge in London. I own the vineyard.'

She smiled. 'You're lucky.'

Luck had nothing to do with it. 'I believe that man was meant to enjoy the gustatory delights that have been put on the earth.' He took her hand in his. 'And other delights, too.'

'You're an amazing man.'

'Thank you.'

It excited Stanford to have beautiful women admiring him. This one was young enough to be his daughter and that excited him even more.

When they had finished lunch, Stanford looked at Sophia and grinned. 'Let's get back to the yacht.'

'Oh, yes!'

Harry Stanford was a protean lover, passionate and skilled. His enormous ego made him more concerned about satisfying a woman than about satisfying himself. He knew how to excite a woman's erotic zones, and he orchestrated his lovemaking in a sensuous symphony that brought his lovers to heights they had never achieved before.

They spent the afternoon in Stanford's suite, and when they were finished making love, Sophia was exhausted. Harry Stanford dressed and went to the bridge to see Captain Vacarro.

'Would you like to go on to Sardinia, Signor Stanford?' the captain asked.

'Let's stop off at Elba first.'

'Very good, sir. Is everything satisfactory?'

'Yes,' Stanford said. 'Everything is satisfactory.' He was feeling aroused again. He went back to Sophia's stateroom.

They reached Elba the following afternoon and anchored at Portoferraio.

As the Boeing 727 entered North American airspace, the pilot checked in with ground control.

'New York Center, Boeing eight nine five Papa is with you, passing flight level two six zero for flight level two four zero.'

The voice of New York Center came on. 'Roger, you are cleared to one two thousand, direct JFK. Call approach on one two seven point four.'

From the back of the plane came a low growl.

'Easy, Prince. That's a good boy. Let's get this seat belt around you.'

There were four men waiting when the 727 landed. They stood at different vantage points so they could watch the passengers descend from the plane. They waited for half an hour. The only passenger to come out was a white German shepherd.

* * *

Portoferraio is the main shopping center of Elba. The streets are lined with elegant, sophisticated shops, and behind the harbor, the eighteenth-century buildings are tucked under the craggy sixteenth-century citadel built by the Duke of Florence.

Harry Stanford had visited the island many times, and in a strange way, he felt at home here. This was where Napoleon Bonaparte had been sent into exile.

'We're going to look at Napoleon's house,' he told Sophia. 'I'll meet you there.' He turned to Dmitri. 'Take her to the Villa dei Mulini.'

'Yes, sir.'

Stanford watched Dmitri and Sophia leave. He looked at his watch. Time was running out. His plane would already have landed at Kennedy. When they learned that he was not aboard, the manhunt would begin again. *It will take them a while to pick up the trail*, Stanford thought. *By then, everything will have been settled.*

He stepped into a phone booth at the end of the dock. 'I want to place a call to London,' Stanford told the operator. 'Barclays Bank. One seven one . . .'

Half an hour later, he picked up Sophia and brought her back to the harbor.

'You go aboard,' Stanford told her. 'I have another call to make.'

She watched him stride over to the telephone booth

beside the dock. *Why doesn't he use the telephones on the yacht?* Sophia wondered.

Inside the telephone booth, Harry Stanford was saying, 'The Sumitomo Bank in Tokyo . . .'

Fifteen minutes later, when he returned to the yacht, he was in a fury.

'Are we going to be anchoring here for the night?' Captain Vacarro asked.

'Yes,' Stanford snapped. 'No! Let's head for Sardinia. Now!'

The Costa Smeralda in Sardinia is one of the most exquisite places along the Mediterranean coast. The little town of Porto Cervo is a haven for the wealthy, with a large part of the area dotted with villas built by Aly Khan.

The first thing Harry Stanford did when they docked was to head for a telephone booth.

Dmitri followed him, standing guard outside the booth.

'I want to place a call to Banca d'Italia in Rome . . .' The phone booth door closed.

The conversation lasted for almost half an hour. When Stanford came out of the phone booth, he was grim. Dmitri wondered what was going on.

Stanford and Sophia had lunch at the beach of Liscia di Vacca. Stanford ordered for them. 'We'll start with *malloreddus*.' Flakes of dough made of hard-grain wheat. 'Then the *porceddu*.' Little suckling pig, cooked with myrtle and bay leaves. 'For a wine, we'll have the Vernaccia, and for dessert, we'll have *sebadas*.' Fried fritters filled with fresh cheese and grated lemon rind, dusted with bitter honey and sugar.

'*Bene, signor*.' The waiter walked away, impressed.

As Stanford turned to talk to Sophia, his heart suddenly skipped a beat. Near the entrance to the restaurant two men were seated at a table, studying him. Dressed in dark suits in the summer sun, they were not even bothering to pretend they were tourists. *Are they after me or are they innocent strangers? I mustn't let my imagination run away with me*, Stanford thought.

Sophia was speaking. 'I've never asked you before. What business are you in?'

Stanford studied her. It was refreshing to be with someone who knew nothing about him. 'I'm retired,' he told her. 'I just travel around, enjoying the world.'

'And you're all by yourself?' Her voice was filled with sympathy. 'You must be very lonely.'

It was all he could do not to laugh aloud. 'Yes, I am. I'm glad you're here with me.'

She put her hand over his. 'I, too, *caro*.'

Out of the corner of his eye, Stanford saw the two men leave.

When luncheon was over, Stanford and Sophia and Dmitri returned to town.

Stanford headed for a telephone booth. 'I want the Crédit Lyonnais in Paris . . .'

Watching him, Sophia spoke to Dmitri. 'He's a wonderful man, isn't he?'

'There's no one like him.'

'Have you been with him long?'

'Two years,' Dmitri said.

'You're lucky.'

'I know.' Dmitri walked over and stood guard right outside the telephone booth. He heard Stanford saying, 'René? You know why I'm calling . . . Yes . . . Yes . . . You will? . . . That's wonderful!' His voice was filled with relief. 'No . . . not there. Let's meet in Corsica. That's perfect. After our meeting, I can return directly home. Thank you, René.'

Stanford put down the receiver. He stood there a moment, smiling, then dialed a number in Boston.

A secretary answered. 'Mr Fitzgerald's office.'

'This is Harry Stanford. Let me talk to him.'

'Oh, Mr Stanford! I'm sorry, Mr Fitzgerald is on vacation. Can someone else . . . ?'

'No. I'm on my way back to the States. You tell him I want him in Boston at Rose Hill at nine o'clock Monday morning. Tell him to bring a copy of my will and a notary.'

'I'll try to –'

'Don't try. Do it, my dear.' He put down the receiver and stood there, his mind racing. When he stepped out of the telephone booth, his voice was calm. 'I have a little business to take care of, Sophia. Go to the Hotel Pitrizza and wait for me.'

'All right,' she said flirtatiously. 'Don't be too long.'

'I won't.'

The two men watched her walk away.

'Let's get back to the yacht,' Stanford told Dmitri. 'We're leaving.'

Dmitri looked at him in surprise. 'What about . . . ?'

'She can screw her way back home.'

When they returned to the *Blue Skies*, Harry Stanford went to see Captain Vacarro. 'We're heading for Corsica,' he said. 'Let's shove off.'

'I just received an updated weather report, Signor Stanford. I'm afraid there's a bad storm. It would be better if we waited it out and –'

'I want to leave now, captain.'

Captain Vacarro hesitated. 'It will be a rough voyage, sir. It's a *libeccio* – the southwest wind. We'll have heavy seas and squalls.'

'I don't care about that.' The meeting in Corsica was going to solve all his problems. He turned to Dmitri. 'I want you to arrange for a helicopter to pick us up in Corsica and take us to Naples. Use the public telephone on the dock.'

'Yes, sir.'

Dmitri Kaminsky walked back to the dock and entered the telephone booth.

Twenty minutes later, *Blue Skies* was under weigh.

Chapter Four

His idol was Dan Quayle, and he often used the name as his touchstone.

'I don't care what you say about Quayle, he's the only politician with real values. Family – that's what it's all about. Without family values, this country would be up the creek even worse than it is. All these young kids are living together without being married, and having babies. It's shocking. No wonder there's so much crime. If Dan Quayle ever runs for president, he's sure got my vote.' It was a shame, he thought, that he couldn't vote because of a stupid law, but, regardless, he was behind Quayle all the way.

He had four children: Billy, eight, and the girls – Amy, Clarissa, and Susan, ten, twelve, and fourteen. They were wonderful children, and his greatest joy was spending what he liked to call quality time with them. His weekends were totally devoted to the children. He barbecued for them, played with them, took them to movies and ball games, and helped them with their homework. All the youngsters in the neighborhood adored him. He repaired their bikes and toys, and invited them on picnics with his family. They gave him the nickname of Papa.

On a sunny Saturday morning, he was seated in the bleachers, watching the baseball game. It was a picture-perfect day, with warm sunshine and fluffy cumulus clouds dappling the sky. His eight-year-old son, Billy, was at bat, looking very professional and grown up in his Little League uniform. Papa's three girls and his wife were at his side. *It doesn't get any better than this*, he thought happily. *Why can't all families be like ours?*

It was the bottom of the eighth inning, the score was tied, with two outs and the bases loaded. Billy was at the plate, three balls and two strikes against him.

Papa called out, encouragingly, 'Get 'em, Billy! Over the fence!'

Billy waited for the pitch. It was fast and low, and Billy swung wildly and missed.

The umpire yelled, 'Strike three!'

The inning was over.

There were groans and cheers from the crowd of parents and family friends. Billy stood there disheartened, watching the teams change sides.

Papa called out, 'It's all right, son. You'll do it next time!'

Billy tried to force a smile.

John Cotton, the team manager, was waiting for Billy. 'You're outta the game!' he said.

'But, Mr Cotton . . .'

'Go on. Get off the field.'

Billy's father watched in hurt amazement as his son left the field. *He can't do that*, he thought. *He has to give Billy another chance. I'll have to speak to Mr Cotton and explain*. At that instant, the cellular phone he carried rang. He let it ring four times before he answered it. Only one person had the number. *He knows I hate to be disturbed on weekends*, he thought angrily.

Reluctantly, he lifted the antenna, pressed a button, and spoke into the mouthpiece. 'Hello?'

The voice at the other end spoke quietly for several minutes. Papa listened, nodding from time to time. Finally he said, 'Yes. I understand. I'll take care of it.' He put the phone away.

'Is everything all right, darling?' his wife asked.

'No. I'm afraid it isn't. They want me to work over the weekend. I was planning a nice barbecue for us tomorrow.'

His wife took his hand and said lovingly, 'Don't worry about it. Your work is more important.'

Not as important as my family, he thought stubbornly. *Dan Quayle would understand*.

His hand began to itch fiercely and he scratched it. *Why does it do that?* he wondered. *I'll have to see a dermatologist one of these days*.

John Cotton was the assistant manager at the local supermarket. A burly man in his fifties, he had agreed to manage the Little League team because his son was a ballplayer. His team had lost that afternoon because of young Billy.

The supermarket had closed, and John Cotton was in the parking lot, walking toward his car, when a stranger approached him, carrying a package.

'Excuse me, Mr Cotton.'

'Yes?'

'I wonder if I could talk to you for a moment?'

'The store is closed.'

'Oh, it's not that. I wanted to talk to you about my son. Billy is very upset that you took him out of the game and told him he couldn't play again.'

'Billy is your son? I'm sorry he was even *in* the game. He'll never be a ballplayer.'

Billy's father said earnestly, 'You're not being fair, Mr Cotton. I know Billy. He's really a fine ballplayer. You'll see. When he plays next Saturday –'

'He isn't *going* to play next Saturday. He's out.'

'But . . .'

'No buts. That's it. Now, if there's nothing else . . .'

'Oh, there is.' Billy's father had unwrapped the package in his hand, revealing a baseball bat. He said pleadingly, 'This is the bat that Billy used. You can see that it's chipped, so it isn't fair to punish him because –'

'Look, mister, I don't give a damn about the bat. Your son is out!'

Billy's father sighed unhappily. 'You're sure you won't change your mind?'

'No chance.'

As Cotton reached for the door handle of his car, Billy's father swung the bat against the rear window, smashing it.

Cotton stared at him in shock. 'What . . . what the hell are you doing?'

'Warming up,' Papa explained. He raised the bat and swung it again, smashing it against Cotton's kneecap.

John Cotton screamed and fell to the ground, writhing in pain. 'You're crazy!' he yelled. 'Help!'

Billy's father knelt beside him and said softly, 'Make one more sound, and I'll break your other kneecap.'

Cotton stared up at him in agony, terrified.

'If my son isn't in the game next Saturday, I'll kill you and I'll kill your son. Do I make myself clear?'

Cotton looked into the man's eyes and nodded, fighting to keep from screaming with pain.

'Good. Oh, and I wouldn't want this to get out. I've got friends.' He looked at his watch. He had just enough time to catch the next flight to Boston.

His hand began to itch again.

At seven o'clock Sunday morning, dressed in a vested suit and carrying an expensive leather briefcase, he walked past Vendome, through Copley Square, and on to Stuart Street. A half block past the Park Plaza Castle, he entered the Boston Trust Building and approached the guard. With dozens of tenants in the huge building, there would be no way the guard at the reception desk could identify him.

'Good morning,' the man said.

'Good morning, sir. May I help you?'

He sighed. 'Even God can't help me. They think I have nothing to do but spend my Sundays doing the work that someone else should have done.'

The guard said, sympathetically, 'I know the feeling.' He pushed a log book forward. 'Would you sign in, please?'

He signed in and walked over to the bank of elevators. The office he was looking for was on the fifth floor. He took the elevator to the sixth floor, walked down a flight, and moved down the corridor. The legend on the door read, RENQUIST, RENQUIST & FITZGERALD, ATTORNEYS AT LAW. He looked around to make certain the corridor was deserted, then opened his briefcase and took out a small pick and a tension tool. It took him five seconds to open the locked door. He stepped inside and closed the door behind him.

The reception room was furnished in old-fashioned, conservative taste, as befitted one of Boston's top law firms. The man stood there a moment, orienting himself, then moved toward the back, to a filing room where records were kept. Inside the room was a bank of steel cabinets with alphabetical labels on the front. He tried the cabinet marked *R-S*. It was locked.

From his briefcase, he removed a blank key, a file, and a pair of pliers. He pushed the blank key inside the small cabinet lock, gently turning it from side to side. After a moment, he withdrew it and examined the black markings on it. Holding the key with the pair of pliers, he carefully filed off the black spots. He put the key into the lock again, and repeated the procedure. He was humming quietly to himself as he picked the lock, and he smiled as he suddenly realized what he was humming: 'Far Away Places'. I'll take my family on vacation, he thought happily. *A real vacation. I'll bet the kids would love Hawaii.*

The cabinet drawer came open, and he pulled it toward him. It took only a moment to find the folder he wanted. He removed a small Pentax camera from his briefcase and went to work. Ten minutes later he was finished. He took several pieces of Kleenex from the briefcase, walked over to the water cooler, and wet them. He returned to the filing room and wiped up the steel shavings on the floor. He locked the file cabinet, made his way out to the corridor, locked the front door to the offices, and left the building.

Chapter Five

~~~~

At sea, later that evening, Captain Vacarro came to Harry Stanford's stateroom.

'Signor Stanford . . .'

'Yes?'

The captain pointed to the electronic map on the wall. 'I'm afraid the winds are getting worse. The *libeccio* is centered in the Strait of Bonifacio. I would suggest that we take shelter in a harbor until –'

Stanford cut him short. 'This is a good ship, and you're a good captain. I'm sure you can handle it.'

Captain Vacarro hesitated. 'As you say, signor. I will do my best.'

'I'm sure you will, captain.'

Harry Stanford sat in the office of his suite, planning his strategy. He would meet René in Corsica and get everything straightened out. After that, the helicopter would fly him to Naples, and from there he would charter a plane to take him to Boston. *Everything is going to be fine*, he decided. *All I need is forty-eight hours. Just forty-eight hours.*

* * *

He was awakened at 2 A.M. by the wild pitching of the yacht and a howling gale outside. Stanford had been in storms before, but this was one of the worst. Captain Vacarro had been right. Harry Stanford got out of bed, holding on to the nightstand to steady himself, and made his way to the wall map. The ship was in the Strait of Bonifacio. *We should be in Ajaccio in the next few hours*, he thought. *Once we're there, we'll be safe.*

The events that occurred later that night were a matter of speculation. The papers strewn around the veranda suggested that the strong wind had blown some of the others away, and that Harry Stanford had tried to retrieve them, but because of the pitching yacht he had lost his balance and fallen overboard. Dmitri Kaminsky saw him fall into the water and immediately grabbed the intercom.

'Man overboard!'

Chapter Six

Capitaine François Durer, *chef de police* in Corsica, was in a foul mood. The island was overcrowded with stupid summer tourists who were incapable of holding onto their passports, their wallets, or their children. Complaints had come streaming in all day long to the tiny police headquarters at 2 Cours Napoléon off Rue Sergent Casalonga.

'A man snatched my purse.'

'My ship sailed without me. My wife is on board.'

'I bought this watch from someone on the street. It has nothing inside.'

'The drugstores here don't carry the pills I need.'

The problems were endless, endless, endless.

And now it seemed that the capitaine had a body on his hands.

'I have no time for this now,' he snapped.

'But they're waiting outside,' his assistant informed him. 'What shall I tell them?'

Capitaine Durer was impatient to get to his mistress. His impulse was to say, 'Take the body to some other island,' but he was, after all, the chief police official on the island.

'Very well.' He sighed. 'I'll see them briefly.'

A moment later, Captain Vacarro and Dmitri Kaminsky were ushered into the office.

'Sit down,' Capitaine Durer said, ungraciously.

The two men took chairs.

'Tell me, please, exactly what occurred.'

Captain Vacarro said, 'I'm not sure exactly. I didn't see it happen.' He turned to Dmitri Kaminsky. 'He was an eyewitness. Perhaps he should explain it.'

Dmitri took a deep breath. 'It was terrible. I work . . . worked for the man.'

'Doing what, monsieur?'

'Bodyguard, masseur, chauffeur. Our yacht was caught in the storm last night. It was very bad. He asked me to give him a massage to relax him. Afterward, he asked me to get him a sleeping pill. They were in the bathroom. When I returned, he was standing out on the veranda, at the railing. The storm was tossing the yacht around. He had been holding some papers in his hand. One of them flew away, and he reached out to grab for it, lost his balance, and fell over the side. I raced to save him, but there was nothing I could do. I called for help. Captain Vacarro immediately stopped the yacht, and through the captain's heroic efforts, we found him. But it was too late. He had drowned.'

'I am very sorry.' He could not have cared less.

Captain Vacarro spoke up. 'The wind and the sea carried the body back to the yacht. It was pure luck, but now we would like permission to take the body home.'

'That should be no problem.' He would still have time to have a drink with his mistress before he went home to his wife. 'I will have a death certificate and an exit visa for the body prepared at once.' He picked up a yellow pad. 'The name of the victim?'

'Harry Stanford.'

Capitaine Durer was suddenly very still. He looked up. 'Harry Stanford?'

'Yes.'

'*The* Harry Stanford?'

'Yes.'

And Capitaine Durer's future suddenly became much brighter. The gods had dropped manna in his lap. Harry Stanford was an international legend! The news of his death would reverberate around the world, and he, Capitaine Durer, was in control of the situation. The immediate question was how to manipulate it for the maximum benefit to himself. Durer sat there, staring into space, thinking.

'How soon can you release the body?' Captain Vacarro asked.

He looked up. 'Ah. That's a good question.' *How much time will it take for the press to arrive? Should I ask the yacht's captain to participate in the interview? No. Why share the glory with him? I will handle this alone*. 'There is much to be done,' he said regretfully. 'Papers to prepare . . .' He sighed. 'It could well be a week or more.'

Captain Vacarro was appalled. 'A week or more? But you said –'

'There are certain formalities to be observed,' Durer said sternly. 'These matters can't be rushed.' He picked up the yellow pad again. 'Who is the next of kin?'

Captain Vacarro looked at Dmitri for help.

'I guess you'd better check with his attorneys in Boston.'

'The names?'

'Renquist, Renquist & Fitzgerald.'

Chapter Seven

Although the legend on the door read RENQUIST, RENQUIST & FITZGERALD, the two Renquists had been long deceased. Simon Fitzgerald was still very much alive, and at seventy-six, he was the dynamo that powered the office, with sixty attorneys working under him. He was perilously thin, with a full mane of white hair, and he walked with the sternly straight carriage of a military man. At the moment, he was pacing back and forth, his mind in a turmoil.

He stopped in front of his secretary. 'When Mr Stanford telephoned, didn't he give any indication of what he wanted to see me about so urgently?'

'No, sir. He just said he wanted you to be at his house at nine o'clock Monday morning, and to bring his will and a notary.'

'Thank you. Ask Mr Sloane to come in.'

Steve Sloane was one of the bright, innovative attorneys in the office. A Harvard Law School graduate in his forties, he was tall and lean, with blond hair, amusedly inquisitive blue eyes, and an easy, graceful presence. He was the troubleshooter for the firm, and Simon Fitzgerald's choice to take over one day. *If I had had a son*, Fitzgerald thought, *I would have wanted him to be like Steve.* He watched as Steve Sloane walked in.

'You're supposed to be salmon fishing up in Newfoundland,' Steve said.

'Something came up. Sit down, Steve. We have a problem.'

Steve sighed. 'What else is new?'

'It's about Harry Stanford.'

Harry Stanford was one of their most prestigious clients. Half a dozen other law firms handled various Stanford Enterprises subsidiaries, but Renquist, Renquist & Fitzgerald handled his personal affairs. Except for Fitzgerald, none of the members of the firm had ever met him, but he was a legend around the office.

'What's Stanford done now?' Steve asked.

'He's gotten himself dead.'

Steve looked at him, shocked. 'He's *what*?'

'I just received a fax from the French police in Corsica. Apparently Stanford fell off his yacht and drowned yesterday.'

'My God!'

'I know you've never met him, but I've represented him for more than thirty years. He was a difficult man.' Fitzgerald leaned back in his chair, thinking about the past. 'There were really two Harry Stanfords – the

45

public one who could coax the birds off the money tree, and the sonofabitch who took pleasure in destroying people. He was a charmer, but he could turn on you like a cobra. He had a split personality – he was both the snake charmer and the snake.'

'Sounds fascinating.'

'It was about thirty years ago – thirty-one, to be exact – when I joined this law firm. Old Man Renquist handled Stanford then. You know how people use the phrase "larger than life"? Well, Harry Stanford was really larger than life. If he didn't exist, you couldn't have invented him. He was a colossus. He had an amazing energy and ambition. He was a great athlete. He boxed in college and was a ten-goal polo player. But even when he was young, Harry Stanford was impossible. He was the only man I've ever known who was totally without compassion. He was sadistic and vindictive, and he had the instincts of a vulture. He loved forcing his competitors into bankruptcy. It was rumored that there was more than one suicide because of him.'

'He sounds like a monster.'

'On the one hand, yes. On the other hand, he founded an orphanage in New Guinea and a hospital in Bombay, and he gave millions to charity – anonymously. No one ever knew what to expect next.'

'How did he become so wealthy?'

'How's your Greek mythology?'

'I'm a little rusty.'

'You know the story of Oedipus?'

Steve nodded. 'He killed his father to get his mother.'

'Right. Well, that was Harry Stanford. Only he killed his father to get his mother's *vote*.'

Steve was staring at him. 'What?'

Fitzgerald leaned forward. 'In the early thirties, Harry's father had a grocery store here in Boston. It did so well that he opened a second one, and pretty soon he had a small chain of grocery stores. When Harry finished college, his father brought him into the business as a partner and put him on the board of directors. As I said, Harry was ambitious. He had big dreams. Instead of buying meat from packing houses, he wanted the chain to raise its own livestock. He wanted it to buy land and grow its own vegetables, can its own goods. His father disagreed, and they fought a lot.

'Then Harry had his biggest brainstorm of all. He told his father he wanted the company to build a chain of supermarkets that sold everything from automobiles to furniture to life insurance, at a discount, and charge customers a membership fee. Harry's father thought he was crazy, and he turned down the idea. But Harry didn't intend to let anything get in his way. He decided he had to get rid of the old man. He persuaded his father to take a long vacation, and while he was away, Harry went to work charming the board of directors.

'He was a brilliant salesman and he sold them on

his concept. He persuaded his aunt and uncle, who were on the board, to vote for him. He romanced the other members of the board. He took them to lunch, went fox hunting with one, golfing with another. He slept with a board member's wife who had influence over her husband. But it was his mother who held the largest block of stock and had the final vote. Harry persuaded her to give it to him and to vote against her husband.'

'That's unbelievable!'

'When Harry's father returned, he learned that his family had voted him out of the company.'

'My God!'

'There's more. Harry wasn't satisfied with that. When his father tried to get into his own office, he found that he was barred from the building. And, remember, Harry was only in his thirties then. His nickname around the company was the Iceman. But credit where credit is due, Steve. He single-handedly built Stanford Enterprises into one of the biggest privately held conglomerates in the world. He expanded the company to include timber, chemicals, communications, electronics, and a staggering amount of real estate. And he wound up with all the stock.'

'He must have been an incredible man,' Steve said.

'He was. To men – and to women.'

'Was he married?'

Simon Fitzgerald sat there for a long time, remembering. When he finally spoke he said, 'Harry Stanford was married to one of the most beautiful women I've ever seen. Emily Temple. They had three children, two boys and a girl. Emily came from a very social family in Hobe Sound, Florida. She adored Harry, and she tried to close her eyes to his cheating, but one day it got to be too much for her. She had a governess for the children, a woman named Rosemary Nelson. Young and attractive. What made her even more attractive to Harry Stanford was the fact that she refused to go to bed with him. It drove him crazy. He wasn't used to rejection. Well, when Harry Stanford turned on the charm, he was irresistible. He finally got Rosemary into bed. He got her pregnant, and she went to see a doctor. Unfortunately, the doctor's son-in-law was a columnist, and he got hold of the story and printed it. There was one hell of a scandal. You know Boston. It was all over the newspapers. I still have clippings about it somewhere.'

'Did she get an abortion?'

Fitzgerald shook his head. 'No. Harry wanted her to have one, but she refused. They had a terrible scene. He told her he loved her and wanted to marry her. Of course, he had told that to dozens of women. But Emily overheard their conversation, and in the middle of that same night she committed suicide.'

'That's awful. What happened to the governess?'

'Rosemary Nelson disappeared. We know that she had a daughter she named Julia, at St Joseph's Hospital in Milwaukee. She sent a note to Stanford, but I don't believe he even bothered to reply. By then, he was involved with someone new. He wasn't interested in Rosemary anymore.'

'Charming . . .'

'The real tragedy is what happened later. The children rightfully blamed their father for their mother's suicide. They were ten, twelve, and fourteen at the time. Old enough to feel the pain, but too young to fight their father. They hated him. And Harry's greatest fear was that one day they would do to him what he had done to his own father. So he did everything he could to make sure that never happened. He sent them away to different boarding schools and summer camps, and arranged for his children to see as little of one another as possible. They received no money from him. They lived on the small trust that their mother had left them. All their lives he used the carrot-and-stick approach with them. He held out his fortune as the carrot, then withdrew it if they displeased him.'

'What's happened to the children?'

'Tyler is a judge in the circuit court in Chicago. Woodrow doesn't do anything. He's a playboy. He lives in Hobe Sound and gambles on golf and polo. A few years ago, he picked up a waitress in a diner, got her pregnant, and to everyone's surprise, married her. Kendall is a successful fashion designer, married to a Frenchman. They live in New York.' He stood up. 'Steve, have you ever been to Corsica?'

'No.'

'I'd like you to fly there. They're holding Harry Stanford's body, and the police refuse to release it. I want you to straighten out the matter.'

'All right.'

'If there's a chance of your leaving today . . .'

'Right. I'll work it out.'

'Thanks. I appreciate it.'

On the Air France commuter flight from Paris to Corsica, Steve Sloane read a travel book about Corsica. He learned that the island was largely mountainous, that its principal port city was Ajaccio, and that it was the birthplace of Napoleon Bonaparte. The book was filled with interesting statistics, but Steve was totally unprepared for the beauty of the island. As the plane approached Corsica, far below he saw a high solid wall of white rock that resembled the White Cliffs of Dover. It was breathtaking.

The plane landed at Ajaccio airport and a taxi took Steve down the Cours Napoléon, the main street that stretched from Place General de Gaulle northward to the train station. He had made arrangements for a plane to stand by to fly Harry Stanford's body back to Paris, where the coffin would be transferred to a plane to Boston. All he needed was to get a release for the body.

Steve had the taxi drop him off at the Préfecture building on Cours Napoléon. He went up one flight of stairs and walked into the reception office. A uniformed sergeant was seated at the desk.

'*Bonjour. Puis-je vous aider?*'

'Who is in charge here?'

'Capitaine Durer.'

'I would like to see him, please.'

'And what is it of concern in relationship to?' The sergeant was proud of his English.

Steve took out his business card. 'I'm the attorney for Harry Stanford. I've come to take his body back to the States.'

The sergeant frowned. 'Remain, please.' He disappeared into Capitaine Durer's office, carefully closing the door behind him. The office was crowded, filled with reporters from television and news services from all over the globe. Everyone seemed to be speaking at the same time.

'Capitaine, why was he out in a storm when . . . ?'

'How could he fall off a yacht in the middle of . . . ?'

'Was there any sign of foul play?'

'Have you done an autopsy?'

'Who else was on the ship with . . . ?'

'Please, gentlemen.' Capitaine Durer held up his hand. 'Please, gentlemen. Please.' He looked around the room at all the reporters hanging on his every word, and he was ecstatic. He had dreamed of moments like this. *If I handle this properly, it will mean a big promotion and –*

The sergeant interrupted his thoughts. 'Capitaine.'

He whispered in Durer's ear and handed him Steve Sloane's card.

Capitaine Durer studied it and frowned. 'I can't see him now,' he snapped. 'Tell him to come back tomorrow at ten o'clock.'

'Yes, sir.'

Capitaine Durer watched thoughtfully as the sergeant left the room. He had no intention of letting anyone take away his moment of glory. He turned back to the reporters and smiled. 'Now, what were you asking . . . ?'

In the outer office, the sergeant was saying to Sloane, 'I am sorry, but Capitaine Durer is very busy immediately. He would like you to expose yourself here tomorrow morning at ten o'clock.'

Steve Sloane looked at him in dismay. 'Tomorrow morning? That's ridiculous – I don't want to wait that long.'

The sergeant shrugged. 'That is of your chosen, monsieur.'

Steve frowned. 'Very well. I don't have a hotel reservation. Can you recommend a hotel?'

'*Mais oui*. I am pleased to have recommended the Colomba, eight Avenue de Paris.'

Steve hesitated. 'Isn't there some way . . . ?'

'Ten o'clock tomorrow morning.'

Steve turned and walked out of the office.

In Durer's office, the capitaine was happily coping with the barrage of reporters' questions.

A television reporter asked, 'How can you be sure it was an accident?'

Durer looked into the lens of the camera. 'Fortunately, there was an eyewitness to this terrible event. Monsieur Stanford's cabin has an open veranda. Apparently some important papers flew out of his hand, onto the terrace, and he ran to retrieve them. When he reached out, he lost his balance and fell into the water. His bodyguard saw it happen and immediately called for help. The ship stopped, and they were able to retrieve the body.'

'What did the autopsy show?'

'Corsica is a small island, gentlemen. We are not properly equipped to do a full autopsy. However, our medical examiner reports that the cause of death was drowning. We found seawater in his lungs. There were no bruises or any signs of foul play.'

'Where is the body now?'

'We are keeping it in the cold storage room until authorization is given for it to be taken away.'

One of the photographers said, 'Do you mind if we take a picture of you, capitaine?'

Capitaine Durer hesitated for a dramatic moment. 'No. Please, gentlemen, do what you must.'

And the cameras began to flash.

He had lunch at La Fontana on Rue Nôtre Dame, and with the rest of the day to kill, started exploring the town.

Ajaccio was a colorful Mediterranean town that still basked in the glory of having been Napoleon Bonaparte's birthplace. *I think Harry Stanford would have identified with this place*, Steve thought.

It was the tourist season in Corsica, and the streets were crowded with visitors chatting away in French, Italian, German and Japanese.

That evening Steve had an Italian dinner at Le Boccaccio and returned to his hotel.

'Any messages?' he asked the room clerk, optimistically.

'No, monsieur.'

He lay in bed haunted by what Simon Fitzgerald had told him about Harry Stanford.

Did she get an abortion?

No. Harry wanted her to have one, but she refused. They had a terrible scene. He told her he loved her and wanted to marry her. Of course, he had told that to dozens of women. But Emily overheard their conversation, and in the middle of that same night she committed suicide.

Steve wondered how she had done it.

He finally fell asleep.

At ten o'clock the following morning, Steve Sloane appeared again at the Préfecture. The same sergeant was seated behind the desk.

'Good morning,' Steve said.

'*Bonjour*, monsieur. Can I help to assist you?'

Steve handed the sergeant another business card. 'I'm here to see Capitaine Durer.'

'A moment.' The sergeant got up, walked into the inner office, and closed the door behind him.

Capitaine Durer, dressed in an impressive new uniform, was being interviewed by an RAI television crew from Italy. He was looking into the camera. 'When I took charge of the case, the first thing I did was to make certain that there was no foul play involved in Monsieur Stanford's death.'

The interviewer asked, 'And you were satisfied that there was none, capitaine?'

'Completely satisfied. There is no question but that it was an unfortunate accident.'

The director said, '*Bene*. Let us cut to another angle and a closer shot.'

The sergeant took the opportunity to hand Capitaine Durer Sloane's business card. 'He is outside.'

'What is the matter with you?' Durer growled. 'Can't you see I'm busy? Have him come back tomorrow.' He had just received word that there were a dozen more reporters on their way, some from as far away as Russia and South Africa. '*Demain*.'

'*Oui*.'

'Are you ready, capitaine?' the director asked.

Capitaine Durer smiled. 'I'm ready.'

The sergeant returned to the outer office. 'I am sorry, monsieur. Capitaine Durer is out of business today.'

'So am I,' Steve snapped. 'Tell him that all he has to do is sign a paper authorizing the release of Mr Stanford's body, and I'll be on my way. That's not too much to ask, is it?'

'I am afraid, yes. The capitaine has many responsibilities, and –'

'Can't someone else give me the authorization?'

'Oh, no, monsieur. Only the capitaine can do the authority.'

Steve Sloane stood there, seething. 'When can I see him?'

'I suggest if you try again tomorrow morning.'

The phrase 'try again' grated on Steve's ears.

'I'll do that,' he said. 'By the way, I understand there was an eyewitness to the accident – Mr Stanford's bodyguard, a Dmitri Kaminsky.'

'Yes.'

'I would like to talk to him. Could you tell me where he's staying?'

'Australia.'

'Is that a hotel?'

'No, monsieur.' There was pity in his voice. 'It is a country.'

Steve's voice rose an octave. 'Are you telling me that the only witness to Stanford's death was allowed by the police to leave here before anyone could interrogate him?'

'Capitaine Durer interrogated him.'

Steve took a deep breath. 'Thank you.'

'No problems, monsieur.'

When Steve returned to his hotel, he reported back to Simon Fitzgerald.

'It looks like I'm going to have to stay another night here.'

'What's going on, Steve?'

'The man in charge seems to be very busy. It's the tourist season. He's probably looking for some lost purses. I should be out of here by tomorrow.'

'Stay in touch.'

In spite of his irritation, Steve found the island of Corsica enchanting. It had almost a thousand miles of coastline, with soaring, granite mountains that stayed snow-topped until July. The island had been ruled by the Italians until France took it over, and the combination of the two cultures was fascinating.

During his dinner at the Crêperie U San Carlu, he remembered how Simon Fitzgerald had described Harry Stanford. *He was the only man I've ever known who was totally without compassion . . . a sadistic and vindictive man.*

Well, Harry Stanford is causing a hell of a lot of trouble even in death, Steve thought.

On the way to his hotel, Steve stopped at a newsstand to pick up a copy of the *International Herald Tribune.* The headline read: WHAT WILL HAPPEN TO THE STANFORD EMPIRE? He paid for the newspaper, and as he turned to leave, his eye was caught by the headlines in some of the foreign papers on the stand. He picked them up and looked through them, stunned. Every single newspaper had front-page stories about the death of Harry Stanford, and in each one of them, Capitaine Durer was prominently featured, his photograph beaming from the pages. *So that's what's keeping him so busy! We'll see about that.*

At nine forty-five the following morning, Steve returned to Capitaine Durer's reception office. The sergeant was not at his desk, and the door to the inner office was ajar. Steve pushed it open and stepped inside. The capitaine was changing into a new uniform, preparing for his morning press interviews. He looked up as Steve entered.

'*Qu'est-ce que vous faites ici? C'est un bureau privé! Allez-vous-en!*'

'I'm with the *New York Times*,' Steve Sloane said.

Instantly, Durer brightened. 'Ah, come in, come in. You said your name is . . . ?'

'Jones. John Jones.'

'Can I offer you something, perhaps? Coffee? Cognac?'

'Nothing, thanks,' Steve said.

'Please, please, sit down.' Durer's voice became somber. 'You are here, of course, about the terrible tragedy that has happened on our little island. Poor Monsieur Stanford.'

'When do you plan to release the body?' Steve asked. Capitaine Durer sighed. 'Ah, I am afraid not for many, many days. There are a great number of forms to fill out in the case of a man as important as Monsieur Stanford. There are protocols to be followed, you understand.'

'I think I do,' Steve said.

'Perhaps ten days. Perhaps, two weeks.' *By then the interest of the press will have cooled down.*

'Here's my card,' Steve said. He handed Capitaine Durer a card.

The capitaine glanced at it, then took a closer look. 'You are an attorney. You are not a reporter?'

'No. I'm Harry Stanford's attorney.' Steve Sloane rose. 'I want your authorization to release his body.'

'Ah, I wish I could give it to you,' Capitaine Durer said, regretfully. 'Unfortunately, my hands are tied. I do not see how –'

'Tomorrow.'

'That is impossible! There is no way . . .'

'I suggest that you get in touch with your superiors in Paris. Stanford Enterprises has several very large factories in France. It would be a shame if our board of directors decided to close all of them down and build in other countries.'

Capitaine Durer was staring at him. 'I . . . I have no control over such matters, monsieur.'

'But *I* do,' Steve assured him. 'You will see that Mr

Stanford's body is released to me tomorrow, or you're going to find yourself in more trouble than you can possibly imagine.' Steve turned to leave.

'Wait! Monsieur! Perhaps in a few days, I can –'

'Tomorrow.' And Steve was gone.

Three hours later, Steve Sloane received a telephone call at his hotel.

'Monsieur Sloane? Ah, I have wonderful news for you! I have managed to arrange for Mr Stanford's body to be released to you immediately. I hope you appreciate the trouble . . .'

'Thank you. A private plane will leave here at eight o'clock tomorrow morning to take us back. I assume all the proper papers will be in order by then.'

'Yes, of course. Do not worry. I will see to –'

'Good.' Steve replaced the receiver.

Capitaine Durer sat there for a long time. *Merde! What bad luck! I could have been a celebrity for at least another week.*

When the plane carrying Harry Stanford's body landed at Logan International Airport in Boston, there was a hearse waiting to meet it. Funeral services were to be held three days later.

Steve Sloane reported back to Simon Fitzgerald.

'So the old man is finally home,' Fitzgerald said. 'It's going to be quite a reunion.'

61

'A reunion?'

'Yes. It should be interesting,' he said. 'Harry Stanford's children are coming here to celebrate their father's death. Tyler, Woody and Kendall.'

Chapter Eight

Judge Tyler Stanford had first seen the story on Chicago's station WBBM. He had stared at the television set, mesmerized, his heart pounding. There was a picture of the yacht *Blue Skies*, and a news commentator was saying, '. . . in a storm, in Corsican waters, when the tragedy occurred. Dmitri Kaminsky, Harry Stanford's bodyguard, was a witness to the accident, but was unable to save his employer. Harry Stanford was known in financial circles as one of the shrewdest . . .'

Tyler sat there, watching the shifting images, remembering, remembering . . .

It was the loud voices that had awakened him in the middle of the night. He was fourteen years old. He had listened to the angry voices for a few minutes, then crept down the upstairs hall to the staircase. In the foyer below, his mother and father were having a fight. His mother was screaming, and he watched his father slap her across the face.

*   *   *

The picture on the television set shifted. There was a scene of Harry Stanford in the Oval Office of the White House, shaking hands with President Ronald Reagan. 'One of the cornerstones of the president's new financial task force, Harry Stanford has been an important adviser to . . .'

They were playing football in back of the house, and his brother, Woody, threw the ball toward the house. Tyler chased it, and as he picked it up he heard his father, on the other side of the hedge. 'I'm in love with you. You know that!'

He stopped, thrilled that his mother and father were not fighting, and then he heard the voice of their governess, Rosemary. 'You're married. I want you to leave me alone.'

And he suddenly felt sick to his stomach. He loved his mother and he loved Rosemary. His father was a terrifying stranger.

The picture on the screen flashed to a series of shots of Harry Stanford posing with Margaret Thatcher . . . President Mitterrand . . . Mikhail Gorbachev . . . The announcer was saying, 'The legendary tycoon was equally at home with factory workers and world leaders.'

He was passing the door to his father's office when he heard Rosemary's voice. 'I'm leaving.' And then his father's voice, 'I won't let you leave. You've got to be reasonable, Rosemary! This is the only way that you and I can . . .'

'I won't listen to you. And I'm keeping the baby!'

Then Rosemary had disappeared.

The scene on the television set shifted again. There were old clips of the Stanford family in front of a church, watching a coffin being lifted into a hearse. The commentator was saying, '. . . Harry Stanford and the children beside the coffin . . . Mrs Stanford's suicide was attributed to her failing health. According to police investigators, Harry Stanford . . .'

In the middle of the night, he had been shaken awake by his father. 'Get up, son. I have some bad news for you.'

The fourteen-year-old boy began to tremble.

'Your mother had an accident, Tyler.'

It was a lie. His father had killed her. She had committed suicide because of his father and his affair with Rosemary.

The newspapers had been filled with the story. It was a scandal that rocked Boston, and the tabloids took full advantage of it. There was no way to keep the news from the Stanford children. Their classmates made their lives hell. In just twenty-four hours, the three young children had lost the two people they loved most. And it was their father who was to blame.

'I don't care if he is our father.' Kendall sobbed. 'I hate him.'

'Me, too!'

'Me, too!'

They thought about running away, but they had nowhere to go. They decided to rebel.

Tyler was delegated to talk to him. 'We want a different father. We don't want you.'

Harry Stanford had looked at him and said, coldly, 'I think we can arrange that.'

Three weeks later, they were all shipped off to different boarding schools.

As the years went by, the children saw very little of their father. They read about him in newspapers, or watched him on television, escorting beautiful women or chatting with celebrities, but the only time they were with him was on what he called 'occasions' – photo opportunities at Christmas time or other holidays – to show what a devoted father he was. After that, the children were sent back to their different schools and camps until the next 'occasion'.

Tyler sat hypnotized by what he was watching. On the television screen was a montage of factories in different parts of the world, with pictures of his father. '. . . one of the largest privately held conglomerates in the world. Harry Stanford, who created it, was a legend . . . The question in the minds of Wall Street experts is, What is going to happen to the family-owned company now that its founder is gone? Harry Stanford left three children, but it is not known who will inherit the multibillion-dollar fortune that Stanford left behind, or who will control the corporation . . .'

He was six years old. He loved roaming around the large house, exploring all the exciting rooms. The only place that was off-limits to him was his father's office. Tyler was aware that important meetings went on in there. Impressive-looking men dressed in dark suits were constantly coming and going, meeting with his father. The fact that the office was off-limits to Tyler made it irresistible.

One day when his father was away, Tyler decided to go into the office. The huge room was overpowering, awesome. Tyler stood there, looking at the large desk and at the huge leather chair that his father sat in. *One day I'm going to sit in that chair, and I'm going to be important like Father.* He moved over to the desk and examined it. There were dozens of official-looking papers on it. He moved around to the back of the desk and sat in his father's chair. It felt wonderful. *I'm important now, too!*

'*What the hell are you doing?*'

Tyler looked up, startled. His father stood in the doorway, furious.

'Who told you you could sit behind that desk?'

The young boy was trembling. 'I . . . I just wanted to see what it was like.'

His father stormed over to him. 'Well, you'll never know what it's like! *Never!* Now get the hell out of here and *stay out!*'

Tyler ran upstairs, sobbing, and his mother came to his room. She put her arms around him. 'Don't cry, darling. It's going to be all right.'

'It's . . . it's *not* going to be all right,' he sobbed. 'He . . . he hates me!'

'No. He doesn't hate you.'

'All I did was to sit in his chair.'

'It's *his* chair, darling. He doesn't want anyone to sit in it.'

He could not stop crying. She held him close and said, 'Tyler, when your father and I were married, he said he wanted me to be part of his company. He gave me one share of stock. It was kind of a family joke. I'm going to give you that share. I'll put it in a trust for you. So now you're part of the company, too. All right?'

There were one hundred shares of stock in Stanford Enterprises, and Tyler was now a proud owner of one share.

When Harry Stanford heard what his wife had done, he scoffed, 'What the hell do you think he's going to do with that one share? Take over the company?'

Tyler switched off the television set and sat there, adjusting to the news. He felt a deep sense of satisfaction. Traditionally, sons wanted to be successful to please their fathers. Tyler Stanford had longed to be a success so he could *destroy* his father.

As a child, he had a recurring dream that his father was charged with murdering his mother, and Tyler was the one who would pass sentence. *I sentence you to die in the electric chair!* Sometimes the dream would vary, and Tyler would sentence his father to be hanged or poisoned or shot. The dreams became almost real.

The military school he was sent to was in Mississippi, and it was four years of pure hell. Tyler hated the discipline and the rigid life-style. In his first year at school, he seriously contemplated committing suicide, and the only thing that stopped him was the determination not to give his father that satisfaction. *He killed my mother. He's not going to kill me.*

It seemed to Tyler that his instructors were particularly hard on him, and he was sure his father was responsible. Tyler refused to let the school break him. Although he was forced to go home on holidays, his visits with his father grew more and more unpleasant.

His brother and sister were also home for holidays, but there was no sense of kinship. Their father had destroyed that. They were strangers to one another, waiting for the holidays to be over so they could escape.

Tyler knew that his father was a multibillionaire but the small allowance that Tyler, Woody, and Kendall had came from their mother's estate. As he grew older,

Tyler wondered whether he was entitled to the family fortune. He was sure he and his siblings were being cheated. *I need an attorney.* That, of course, was out of the question, but his next thought was, *I'm going to become an attorney.*

When Tyler's father heard about his son's plans, he said, 'So, you're going to become a lawyer, huh? I suppose you think I'll give you a job with Stanford Enterprises. Well, forget it. I wouldn't let you within a mile of it!'

When Tyler was graduated from law school he could have practised in Boston, and because of the family name he would have been welcomed on the boards of dozens of companies, but he preferred to get far away from his father.

He decided to set up a law practice in Chicago. In the beginning, it was difficult. He refused to trade on his family name, and clients were scarce. Chicago politics were run by the Machine, and Tyler very quickly learned that it would be advantageous for a young lawyer to become involved with the powerful central Cook County Lawyers Association. He was given a job with the district attorney's office. He had a keen mind and was a quick study, and it was not long before he became invaluable to them. He prosecuted felons accused of every conceivable crime, and his record of convictions was phenomenal.

He rose rapidly through the ranks, and finally the

day came when he received his reward. He was appointed Cook County circuit court judge. He had thought his father finally would be proud of him. He was wrong.

'You? A circuit court judge? For God's sake, I wouldn't let you judge a baking contest!'

Judge Tyler Stanford was a short, slightly overweight man with sharp, calculating eyes and a hard mouth. He had none of his father's charisma or attractiveness. His outstanding feature was a deep, sonorous voice, perfect for pronouncing sentence.

Tyler Stanford was a private man who kept his thoughts to himself. He was forty years old, but he looked much older than his years. He prided himself on having no sense of humor. Life was too grim for levity. His only hobby was chess, and once a week he played at a local club, where he invariably won.

Tyler Stanford was a brilliant jurist, held in high esteem by his fellow judges, who often came to him for advice. Very few people were aware that he was one of *the* Stanfords. He never mentioned his father's name.

The judge's chambers were in the large Cook County Criminal Court Building at Twenty-sixth and California streets, a fourteen-storey stone edifice with steps leading up to the front entrance. It was in a dangerous neighborhood, and a notice outside stated: BY JUDICIAL

71

ORDER, ALL PERSONS ENTERING THIS BUILDING SHALL SUBMIT TO SEARCH.

This was where Tyler spent his days, hearing cases involving robbery, burglary, rape, shootings, drugs and murders. Ruthless in his decisions, he became known as the Hanging Judge. All day long he listened to defendants pleading poverty, child abuse, broken homes, and a hundred other excuses. He accepted none of them. A crime was a crime and had to be punished. And in the back of his mind, always, was his father.

Tyler Stanford's fellow judges knew very little about his personal life. They knew that he had had a bitter marriage and was now divorced, and that he lived alone in a small three-bedroom Georgian house on Kimbark Avenue in Hyde Park. The area was surrounded by beautiful old homes, because the great fire of 1871 that razed Chicago had whimsically spared the Hyde Park district. He made no friends in the neighborhood, and his neighbors knew nothing about him. He had a housekeeper who came in three times a week, but Tyler did the shopping himself. He was a methodical man with a fixed routine. On Saturdays, he went to Harper Court, a small shopping mall near his home, or to Mr G's Fine Foods or Medici's on Fifty-seventh Street.

From time to time, at official gatherings, Tyler would meet the wives of his fellow jurists. They sensed that he was lonely, and they offered to introduce him to women friends or invite him to dinner. He always declined.

'I'm busy that evening.'

His evenings seemed to be full, but they had no idea what he was doing with them.

'Tyler isn't interested in anything but the law,' one of the judges explained to his wife. 'And he's just not interested in meeting any women yet. I heard he had a terrible marriage.'

He was right.

After his divorce, Tyler had sworn to himself that he would never become emotionally involved again. And then he had met Lee, and everything had suddenly changed. Lee was beautiful, sensitive and caring – the one Tyler wanted to spend the rest of his life with. Tyler loved Lee, but why should Lee love him? A successful model, Lee had dozens of admirers, most of them wealthy. And Lee liked expensive things.

Tyler had felt that his cause was hopeless. There was no way to compete with others for Lee's affection. But overnight, with the death of his father, everything could change. He could become wealthy beyond his wildest dreams.

He could give Lee the world.

Tyler walked into the chambers of the chief judge. 'Keith, I'm afraid I have to go to Boston for a few

days. Family affairs. I wonder if you would have someone take over my caseload for me.'

'Of course. I'll arrange it,' the chief judge said.

'Thank you.'

That afternoon, Judge Tyler Stanford was on his way
to Boston. On the plane, he thought again about his
father's words on that terrible day: *I know your dirty
little secret.*

Chapter Nine

It was raining in Paris, a warm July rain that sent pedestrians racing along the street for shelter or looking for nonexistent taxis. Inside the auditorium of a large gray building on a corner of Rue Faubourg St Honoré, there was panic. A dozen half-naked models were running around in a kind of mass hysteria, while ushers finished setting up chairs and carpenters pounded away at last-minute bits of carpentry. Everyone was screaming and gesticulating wildly, and the noise level was painful.

In the eye of the hurricane, trying to bring order out of chaos, was the *maîtresse* herself, Kendall Stanford Renaud. Four hours before the fashion show was scheduled to begin, everything was falling apart.

Catastrophe: John Fairchild of *W* was unexpectedly going to be in Paris, and there was no seat for him.

Tragedy: the speaker system was not working.

Disaster: one of the top models was ill.

Emergency: two of the make-up artists were fighting backstage and were far behind schedule.

Calamity: all the seams on the cigarette skirts were tearing.

In other words, Kendall thought wryly, *everything is normal*.

Kendall Stanford Renaud could have been mistaken for one of the models herself, and at one time she had been a model. She exuded carefully plotted elegance from her golden chignon to her Chanel pumps. Everything about her – the curve of her arm, the shade of her nail polish, the timbre of her laugh – bespoke well-mannered chic. Her face, if stripped of its careful make-up, was actually plain, but Kendall took pains to see that no one ever realized this, and no one ever did.

She was everywhere at once.

'Who lit that runway, Ray Charles?'

'I want a blue backdrop . . .'

'The lining is showing. Fix it!'

'I don't want the models doing their hair and make-up in the holding area. Have Lulu find them a dressing room!'

Kendall's venue manager came hurrying up to her. 'Kendall, thirty minutes is too long! Too long! The show should be no more than twenty-five minutes.'

She stopped what she was doing. 'What do you suggest, Scott?'

'We could cut a few of the designs and –'

'No. I'll have the models move faster.'

She heard her name called again, and turned.

'Kendall, we can't locate Pia. Do you want Tami to switch to the charcoal gray jacket with the trousers?'

'No. Give that to Dana. Give the cat suit and tunic to Tami.'

'What about the dark gray jersey?'

'Monique. And make sure she wears the dark gray stockings.'

Kendall looked at the board holding a set of Polaroid pictures of the models in a variety of gowns. When they were set, the pictures would be placed in a precise order. She ran a practiced eye over the board. 'Let's change this. I want the beige cardigan out first, then the separates, followed by the strapless silk jersey, then the taffeta evening gown, the afternoon dresses with matching jackets . . .'

Two of her assistants hurried up to her.

'Kendall, we're having an argument about the seating. Do you want the retailers together, or do you want to mix them with the celebrities?'

The other assistant spoke up. 'Or we could mix the celebrities and press together.'

Kendall was hardly listening. She had been up for two nights, checking everything to make sure nothing would go wrong. 'Work it out yourselves,' she said.

She looked around at all the activity and thought about the show that was about to begin, and the famous names from all over the world who would be there to applaud what she had created. *I should thank my father for all this. He told me I would never succeed...*

She had always known that she wanted to be a designer. From the time she was a little girl, she had had a natural sense of style. Her dolls had the trendiest outfits in town. She would show off her latest creations for her mother's approval. Her mother would hug her and say, 'You're very talented, darling. Someday you're going to be a very important designer.'

And Kendall was sure of it.

In school, Kendall studied graphic design, structural drawing, spatial conceptions, and color coordination.

'The best way to begin,' one of her teachers had advised her, 'is to become a model yourself. That way, you will meet all the top designers, and if you keep your eyes open, you will learn from them.'

When Kendall had mentioned her dream to her father, he had looked at her and said, '*You?* A model! You must be joking!'

When Kendall finished school, she returned to Rose Hill. *Father needs me to run the house*, she thought. There were a dozen servants, but no one was really in charge. Since Harry Stanford was away a good deal of the time, the staff was left to its own devices. Kendall tried to organize things. She scheduled the household activities, served as hostess for her father's parties, and did everything she could to make him comfortable.

She was longing for his approval. Instead, she suffered a barrage of criticisms.

'Who hired that damned chef? Get rid of him.'

'I don't like the new dishes you bought. Where the hell is your taste . . . ?'

'Who told you you could redecorate my bedroom? Keep the hell out of there.'

No matter what Kendall did, it was never good enough.

It was her father's domineering cruelty that finally drove her out of the house. It had always been a loveless household, and her father had paid no attention to his children, except to try to control and discipline them. One night, Kendall overheard her father saying to a visitor, 'My daughter has a face like a horse. She's going to need a lot of money to hook some poor sucker.'

It was the final straw. The following day, Kendall left Boston and headed for New York.

Alone in her hotel room, Kendall thought, *All right. Here I am in New York. How do I become a designer? How do I break into the fashion industry? How do I get anyone even to notice me?* She remembered her teacher's advice. *I'll start as a model. That's the way to begin.*

The following morning, Kendall looked through the yellow pages, copied a list of modeling agencies, and began making the rounds. *I have to be honest with them*, Kendall thought. *I'll tell them that I can stay with them only temporarily, until I get started designing.*

She walked into the office of the first agency on her list. A middle-aged woman behind a desk said, 'May I help you?'

'Yes. I want to be a model.'

'So do I, dearie. Forget it.'

'What?'

'You're too tall.'

Kendall's jaw tightened. 'I'd like to see whoever is in charge here.'

'You're looking at her. I own this joint.'

The next half a dozen stops were no more successful.

'You're too short.'

'Too thin.'

'Too fat.'

'Too young.'

'Too old.'

'Wrong type.'

By the end of the week, Kendall was getting desperate. There was one more name on her list.

Paramount Models was the top modeling agency in Manhattan. There was no one at the reception desk.

A voice from one of the offices said, 'She'll be available next Monday. But you can have her for only one day. She's booked solid for the next three weeks.'

Kendall walked over to the office and peered inside.

A woman in a tailored suit was talking on the phone.

'Right. I'll see what I can do.' Roxanne Marinack replaced the receiver and looked up. 'Sorry, we aren't looking for your type.'

Kendall said desperately, 'I can be any type you want me to be. I can be taller or I can be shorter. I can be younger or older, thinner –'

Roxanne held up her hand. 'Hold it.'

'All I want is a chance. I really *need* this.'

Roxanne hesitated. There was an appealing eagerness about the girl and she did have an exquisite figure. She was not beautiful, but possibly with the right make-up . . . 'Have you had any experience?'

'Yes. I've been wearing clothes all my life.'

Roxanne laughed. 'All right. Let me see your portfolio.'

Kendall looked at her blankly. 'My portfolio?'

Roxanne sighed. 'My dear girl, no self-respecting model walks around without a portfolio. It's your bible. It's what your prospective clients are going to look at.' Roxanne sighed again. 'I want you to get two head shots – one smiling and one serious. Turn around.'

'Right.' Kendall began to turn.

'Slowly.' Roxanne studied her. 'Not bad. I want a photo of you in a bathing suit or lingerie, whatever is the most flattering for your figure.'

'I'll get one of each,' she said eagerly.

Roxanne had to smile at her earnestness. 'All right.

You're . . . er . . . different, but you might have a shot.'

'Thank you.'

'Don't thank me too soon. Modeling for fashion magazines isn't as simple as it looks. It's a tough business.'

'I'm ready for it.'

'We'll see. I'm going to take a chance on you. I'll send you out on some go-sees.'

'I'm sorry?'

'A go-see is where clients catch up on all the new models. There will be models from other agencies there, too. It's kind of a cattle call.'

'I can handle it.'

That had been the beginning. Kendall went on a dozen go-sees before a designer was interested in having her wear his clothes. She was so tense, she almost spoiled her chances by talking too much.

'I really love your dresses, and I think they would look good on me. I mean, they would look good on *any* woman, of course. They're wonderful! But I think they'll look especially good on me.' She was so nervous that she was stammering.

The designer nodded sympathetically. 'This is your first job, isn't it?'

'Yes, sir.'

He had smiled. 'All right. I'll try you. What did you say your name was?'

'Kendall Stanford.' She wondered if he would make

the connection between her and *the* Stanfords, but of course, there was no reason for him to.

Roxanne had been right. Modeling was a tough business. Kendall had to learn to accept constant rejection, go-sees that led nowhere, and weeks without work. When she did work, she was in make-up at six A.M., finished a shoot, went on to the next, and often didn't get through until after midnight.

One evening, after a long day's shoot with half a dozen other models, Kendall looked in a mirror and groaned, 'I won't be able to work tomorrow. Look how puffy my eyes are!'

One of the models said, 'Put cucumber slices over your eyes. Or you can put some camomile tea bags in hot water, let them cool, and put them over your eyes for fifteen minutes.'

In the morning, the puffiness was gone.

Kendall envied the models who were in constant demand. She would hear Roxanne arranging their bookings: 'I originally gave Scaasi a secondary on Michelle. Call and tell them that she will be available, so I'm moving them up to a tentative.'

Kendall quickly learned never to criticize the clothes she was modeling. She became acquainted with some of the top photographers in the business, and had a photo composite made to go with her portfolio. She carried a model's bag filled with necessities – clothes, make-up, a nail-care bag, and jewelry. She learned to blow-dry her hair upside down to give it more body, and to add curl to her hair with heated rollers.

There was a lot more to learn. She was a favorite of the photographers, and one of them pulled her aside to give her some advice. 'Kendall, always save your smiling shots for the end of the shoot. That way, your mouth will have less creasing.'

Kendall was becoming more and more popular. She was not the conventional drop-dead beauty that was the hallmark of most models, but she had something more, a graceful elegance.

'She's got class,' one of the advertising agents said.

And that summed it up.

She was also lonely. From time to time she went out on dates, but they were meaningless. She was working steadily, but she felt she was no nearer to her goal than she was when she had first arrived in New York. *I have to find a way to make contact with the top designers*, Kendall thought.

'I have you booked for the next four weeks,' Roxanne told her. 'Everybody loves you.'

'Roxanne . . .'

'Yes, Kendall?'

'I don't want to do this anymore.'

Roxanne stared at her disbelievingly. 'What?'

'I want to do runway modeling.'

Runway modeling was what most models aspired to. It was the most exciting and the most lucrative form of modeling.

Roxanne was dubious. 'That's almost impossible to break into and –'

'I'm going to.'

Roxanne studied her. 'You really mean it, don't you?'

'Yes.'

Roxanne nodded. 'All right. If you're serious about this, the first thing you have to do is learn to walk the beam.'

'What?'

Roxanne explained.

That afternoon, Kendall bought a six-foot narrow wooden beam, sandpapered it to avoid splinters, and placed it on her floor. The first few times she tried to walk on it, she fell off. *This is not going to be easy*, Kendall decided. *But I'm going to do it.*

Each morning she got up early and practiced walking the beam on the balls of her feet. *Lead with the pelvis. Feel with the toes. Lower the heel.* Day by day her balance improved.

She strode up and back in front of a full-length mirror, with music playing. She learned to walk with a book on her head. She practiced changing rapidly from sneakers and shorts to high heels and an evening gown.

85

When Kendall felt that she was ready, she went back to Roxanne.

'I'm sticking my neck out for you,' Roxanne told her. 'Ungaro is looking for a runway model. I recommended you. He's going to give you a chance.'

Kendall was thrilled. Ungaro was one of the most brilliant designers in the business.

The following week, Kendall arrived at the show. She tried to seem as casual as the other models.

Ungaro handed Kendall the first outfit she was to wear and smiled. 'Good luck.'

'Thanks.'

When Kendall went out on the runway, it was as though she had been doing it all her life. Even the other models were impressed. The show was a big success, and from that time on Kendall was a member of the elite. She started working with the giants of the fashion industry – Yves Saint Laurent, Halston, Christian Dior, Donna Karan, Calvin Klein, Ralph Lauren, St John. Kendall was in constant demand, traveling to shows all over the world. In Paris, the haute couture shows took place in January and July. In Milan, the peak months were March, April, May and June, while in Tokyo, shows peaked in April and October. It was a hectic, busy life, and she loved every minute of it.

* * *

Kendall kept working and she kept learning. She modeled the clothes of famous designers and thought about the changes she would make if *she* were the designer. She learned how clothes were supposed to fit, and how fabric was supposed to move and swing around the body. She learned about cuts and drapes and tailoring, and what body parts women wanted to hide, and what parts they wanted to show. She made sketches at home, and the ideas seemed to flow. One day, she took a portfolio of her sketches to the head buyer at I Magnin's. The buyer was impressed. 'Who designed these?' she asked.

'I did.'

'They're good. They're very good.'

Two weeks later, Kendall went to work for Donna Karan as an assistant and began to learn the business side of the garment trade. At home, she kept designing clothes. One year later, she had her first fashion show. It was a disaster.

The designs were ordinary and nobody cared. She gave a second show, and no one came.

I'm in the wrong profession, Kendall thought.

One day you're going to be a very famous designer.

What am I doing wrong? Kendall wondered.

The epiphany came in the middle of the night. Kendall awakened and lay in bed, thinking, *I'm designing dresses for models to wear. I should be designing for real women with real jobs and real families. Smart, but comfortable. Chic, but practical.*

It took Kendall about a year to get her next show on, but it was an instant success.

Kendall rarely returned to Rose Hill, and when she did, the visits were dreadful. Her father had not changed. If anything, he had gotten worse.

'Haven't hooked anybody yet, eh? Probably never will.'

It was at a charity ball that Kendall met Marc Renaud. He worked at the international desk of a New York brokerage house, where he dealt with foreign currencies. Five years younger than Kendall, he was an attractive Frenchman, tall and lean. He was charming and attentive, and Kendall was immediately attracted to him. He asked her to dine the next evening, and that night Kendall went to bed with him. They were together every night after that.

One evening, Marc said, 'Kendall, I'm madly in love with you, you know.'

She said softly, 'I've been looking for you all my life, Marc.'

'There is a serious problem. You are a big success. I don't make anywhere near as much money as you. Perhaps one day –'

Kendall had put her finger to his lips. 'Stop it. You've given me more than I could ever have hoped for.'

* * *

On Christmas Day, Kendall took Marc to Rose Hill to meet her father.

'You're going to marry *him*?' Harry Stanford exploded. 'He's a nobody! He's marrying you for the money he thinks you're going to get.'

If Kendall had needed any further reason to marry Marc, that would have been it. They got married in Connecticut the following day. And Kendall's marriage to Marc gave her happiness she had never known before.

'You mustn't let your father bully you,' he had told Kendall. 'All his life, he has used his money as a weapon. We don't need his money.'

And Kendall had loved him for that.

Marc was a wonderful husband – kind, considerate, and caring. *I have everything*, Kendall thought happily. *The past is dead.* She had succeeded in spite of her father. In a few hours, the fashion world was going to be focused on her talent.

The rain had stopped. It was a good omen.

The show was stunning. At its end, with music playing and flash bulbs popping, Kendall walked out onto the runway, took a bow and received an ovation. Kendall wished that Marc could have been in Paris with her to share her triumph, but his brokerage house had refused to give him the time off.

*   *   *

When the crowd had left, Kendall went back to her office, feeling euphoric. Her assistant said, 'A letter came for you. It was hand-delivered.'

Kendall looked at the brown envelope her assistant handed her, and she felt a sudden chill. She knew what it was about before she opened it. The letter read:

> *Dear Mrs Renaud,*
> *I regret to inform you that the Wild Animal Protection Association is short of funds again. We will need $100,000 immediately to cover our expenses. The money should be wired to account number 804072-A at the Crédit Suisse bank in Zurich.*

There was no signature.

Kendall sat there, staring at it, numb. *It's never going to stop. The blackmail is never going to stop.*

Another assistant came hurrying into the office. 'Kendall! I'm so sorry. I just heard some terrible news.'

I can't bear any more terrible news, Kendall thought. 'What . . . what is it?'

'There was an announcement on Radio-Télé Luxembourg. Your father is . . . dead. He drowned.'

It took Kendall a moment for it to sink in. Her first thought was, *I wonder what would have made him prouder? My success or the fact that I'm a murderer?*

Chapter Ten

Peggy Malkovich had been married to Woodrow 'Woody' Stanford for two years, but to the residents of Hobe Sound, she was still referred to as 'that waitress'.

Peggy had been waiting on tables at the Rain Forest Grille when Woody first met her. Woody Stanford was the golden boy of Hobe Sound. He lived in the family villa, had classical good looks, was charming and gregarious, and a target for all the eager debutantes in Hobe Sound, Philadelphia, and Long Island. It was therefore a seismic shock when he suddenly eloped with a twenty-five-year-old waitress who was plain-looking, a high-school dropout, and the daughter of a day laborer and a housewife.

It was even more of a shock because everyone had been expecting Woody to marry Mimi Carson, a beautiful, intelligent young heiress to a timber fortune who was madly in love with Woody.

As a rule, the residents of Hobe Sound preferred to gossip about the affairs of their servants rather than their peers, but in Woody's case, his marriage was so outrageous that they made an exception. The information quickly spread that he had gotten Peggy Malkovich pregnant and then married her. They were quite sure which was the greater sin.

'For God's sake, I can understand the boy getting her pregnant, but you don't marry a waitress!'

The whole affair was a classic case of *déjà vu*. Twenty-four years earlier, Hobe Sound had been rocked by a similar scandal involving the Stanfords. Emily Temple, the daughter of one of the founding families, had committed suicide because her husband had gotten the children's governess pregnant.

Woody Stanford made no secret of the fact that he hated his father, and the general feeling was that he had married the waitress out of spite, to show that he was a more honorable man than his father.

The only person invited to the wedding was Peggy's brother, Hoop, who flew in from New York. Hoop was two years older than Peggy and worked in a bakery in the Bronx. He was tall and emaciated, with a pock-marked face and a heavy Brooklyn accent.

'You're gettin' a great girl,' he told Woody after the ceremony.

'I know,' Woody said tonelessly.

'You take good care of my sister, huh?'

'I'll do my best.'

'Yeah. Cool.'

An unmemorable conversation between a baker and the son of one of the wealthiest men in the world.

Four weeks after the wedding, Peggy lost the baby.

Hobe Sound is a very exclusive community, and Jupiter Island is the most exclusive part of Hobe Sound. The island is bordered on the west by the Intercoastal Waterway and on the east by the Atlantic Ocean. It is a haven of privacy – wealthy, self-contained and protective, with more police per capita than almost any other place in the world. Its residents pride themselves on being understated. They drive Tauruses or station wagons, and own small sailboats, an eighteen-foot Lightning or a twenty-four-foot Quickstep.

If one was not born to it, one had to earn the right to be a member of this Hobe Sound community. After the marriage between Woodrow Stanford and 'that waitress', the burning question was, what were the residents going to do about accepting the bride into their society?

Mrs Anthony Pelletier, the doyenne of Hobe Sound, was the arbiter of all social disputes, and her devout mission in life was to protect her community against parvenus and the nouveaux riches. When newcomers arrived at Hobe Sound and were unfortunate enough to displease Mrs Pelletier, it was her custom to have delivered to them, by her chauffeur, a leather traveling case. It was her way of informing them that they were not welcome in the community.

Her friends delighted in telling the story of the garage mechanic and his wife who had bought a house in Hobe Sound. Mrs Pelletier had sent them her ritual traveling bag, and when the wife learned its significance, she laughed. She said, 'If that old harridan thinks she can drive me out of this place, she's crazy!'

But strange things began to happen. Workmen and repairmen were suddenly unavailable, the grocer was always out of items that she ordered, and it was impossible to become a member of the Jupiter Island Club or even to get a reservation at any of the good local restaurants. And no one spoke to them. Three months after receiving the suitcase, the couple sold their home and moved away.

So it was that when word of Woody's marriage got out, the community held its collective breath. Excommunicating Peggy Malkovich would also mean excommunicating her popular husband. There were bets being quietly made.

For the first few weeks, there were no invitations to dinners or to any of the usual community functions. But the residents liked Woody and, after all, his grandmother on his mother's side had been one of the founders of Hobe Sound. Gradually, people started inviting him and Peggy to their homes. They were eager to see what his bride was like.

'The old girl must have something special or Woody never would have married her.'

They were in for a big disappointment. Peggy was dull and graceless, she had no personality, and she dressed badly. *Dowdy* was the word that came to people's minds.

Woody's friends were baffled. 'What on earth does he see in her? He could have married *anyone*.'

One of the first invitations was from Mimi Carson. She had been devastated by the news of Woody's marriage, but she was too proud to reveal it.

When her closest friend had tried to console her by saying, 'Forget it, Mimi! You'll get over him,' Mimi had replied, 'I'll live with it, but I'll never get over him.'

Woody tried hard to make a success of the marriage. He knew he had made a mistake, and he did not want to punish Peggy for it. He tried desperately to be a good husband. The problem was that Peggy had nothing in common with him or with any of his friends.

The only person Peggy seemed comfortable with was her brother, and she and Hoop spoke on the telephone every day.

'I miss him,' Peggy complained to Woody.

'Would you like to have him come down and stay with us for a few days?'

'He can't.' And she looked at her husband and said spitefully, 'He's got a job.'

At parties, Woody attempted to bring Peggy into the conversations, but it was quickly apparent that she had nothing to contribute. She sat in corners, tongue-tied, nervously licking her lips, obviously uncomfortable.

Woody's friends were aware that even though he was staying at the Stanford villa, he was estranged from his father and that he was living off the small annuity that his mother had left him. His passion was polo and he rode the ponies owned by friends. In the world of polo, players are ranked by goals, with ten goals being the best. Woody was nine goals, and he had ridden with Mariano Aguerre from Buenos Aires, Wicky el Effendi from Texas, Andres Diniz from Brazil, and dozens of other top goals. There were only about twelve ten-goal players in the world, and Woody's driving ambition was to be the thirteenth.

'You know why, don't you?' one of his friends remarked. 'His father was ten goals.'

Because Mimi Carson knew that Woody could not afford to buy his own polo ponies, she purchased a string for him to play. When friends asked why, she said, 'I want to make him happy in any way I can.'

When newcomers asked what Woody did for a living, people just shrugged. In reality, he was living a secondhand life, making money playing skins at golf, betting on polo matches, borrowing other people's polo ponies and racing yachts, and on occasion, other people's wives.

The marriage with Peggy was deteriorating rapidly, but Woody refused to admit it.

'Peggy,' he would say, 'when we go to parties, please try to join in the conversation.'

'Why should I? Your friends all think they're too good for me.'

'Well, they're not,' Woody assured her.

Once a week, the Hobe Sound Literary Circle met at the country club for a discussion of the latest books, followed by a luncheon.

On this particular day, as the ladies were dining, the steward approached Mrs Pelletier. 'Mrs Woodrow Stanford is outside. She would like to join you.'

A hush fell over the table.

'Show her in,' Mrs Pelletier said.

A moment later, Peggy walked into the dining room. She had washed her hair and pressed her best dress. She stood there, nervously looking at the group.

Mrs Pelletier gave her a nod, then said pleasantly, 'Mrs Stanford.'

Peggy smiled eagerly, 'Yes, ma'am.'

'We won't need you. We already have a waitress.' And Mrs Pelletier turned back to her lunch.

When Woody heard the story, he was furious. 'How dare she do that to you!' He took her in his arms. 'Next time, ask me before you do a thing like that, Peggy. You have to be *invited* to that luncheon.'

'I didn't know,' she said sullenly.

'It's all right. Tonight we're having dinner at the Blakes', and I want –'

'I won't go!'

'But we've accepted their invitation.'

'You go.'

'I don't want to go without you.'

'I'm not going.'

Woody went alone, and after that, he began going to every party without Peggy.

He would come home at all hours, and Peggy was sure he had been with other women.

The accident changed everything.

It happened during a polo match. Woody was playing the number one position, and a member of the opposing team, trying to stroke the ball in close quarters, accidently hit the legs of the pony that Woody was riding. The pony went down and rolled on top of him. In the pile-up that followed, a second pony kicked Woody. At the emergency room of the hospital, the doctors diagnosed a broken leg, three fractured ribs, and a punctured lung.

Over the next two weeks, there were three separate operations, and Woody was in excruciating pain. The doctors gave him morphine to ease it. Peggy came to visit him every day. Hoop flew in from New York to console his sister.

*   *   *

His physical pain was unbearable, and the only relief Woody had was from the drugs the doctors kept prescribing for him. It was shortly after Woody got home that he seemed to change. He began to have violent mood swings. One minute he was his usual ebullient self, and the next minute he would go into a sudden rage or a deep depression. At dinner, laughing and telling jokes, Woody would suddenly become angry and abusive toward Peggy and storm out. In the middle of a sentence he would drift off into a deep reverie. He became forgetful. He would make dates and not show up; he would invite people to his home and not be there when they arrived. Everyone was concerned about him.

Soon, he became abusive to Peggy in public. Bringing a cup of coffee to a friend one morning, Peggy spilled some and Woody sneered, 'Once a waitress, always a waitress.'

Peggy also began to show signs of physical abuse, and when people asked her what happened, she would make excuses.

'I bumped into a door' or 'I fell down,' and she would make light of it. The community was outraged. Now it was Peggy they were feeling sorry for. But when Woody's erratic behavior offended someone, Peggy would defend her husband.

'Woody is under a lot of stress,' Peggy would insist. 'He isn't himself.' She would not allow anyone to say anything against him.

*   *   *

99

It was Dr Tichner who finally brought it out into the open. He asked Peggy to come see him in his office one day.

She was nervous. 'Is something wrong, doctor?'

He studied her a moment. She had a bruise on her cheek, and her eye was swollen.

'Peggy, are you aware that Woody is doing drugs?'

Her eyes flashed with indignation. 'No! I don't believe it!' She stood up. 'I won't listen to this!'

'Sit down, Peggy. It's about time you faced the truth. It's becoming obvious to everyone else. Surely you've noticed his behavior. One minute he's on top of the world, talking about how wonderful everything is, and the next minute he's suicidal.'

Peggy sat there, watching him, her face pale.

'He's addicted.'

Her lips tightened. 'No,' she said stubbornly. 'He's not.'

'He is. You've got to be realistic. Don't you want to help him?'

'Of course, I do!' She was wringing her hands. 'I'd do anything to help him. *Anything.*'

'All right. Then let's start. I want you to help me get Woody into a rehabilitation center. I've asked him to come in and see me.'

Peggy looked at him for a long time, then nodded. 'I'll talk to him,' she said quietly.

*   *   *

That afternoon, when Woody walked into Dr Tichner's office, he was in a euphoric mood. 'You wanted to see me, doc? It's about Peggy, isn't it?'

'No. It's about you, Woody.'

Woody looked at him in surprise. 'Me? What's my problem?'

'I think you know what your problem is.'

'What are you talking about?'

'If you go on like this, you're going to destroy your life and Peggy's life. What are you taking, Woody?'

'Taking?'

'You heard me.'

There was a long silence.

'I want to help you.'

Woody sat there, staring at the floor. When he finally spoke, his voice was hoarse. 'You're right. I've . . . I've tried to kid myself, but I can't any longer.'

'What are you on?'

'Heroin.'

'My God!'

'Believe me, I've tried to stop, but I . . . I can't.'

'You need help, and there are places where you can get it.'

Woody said wearily, 'I hope to God you're right.'

'I want you to go to the Harbor Group Clinic in Jupiter. Will you try it?'

There was a brief hesitation. 'Yes.'

'Who's supplying you with the heroin?' Dr Tichner asked.

Woody shook his head. 'I can't tell you that.'

'Very well. I'll make arrangements for you at the clinic.'

The following morning, Dr Tichner was seated in the office of the chief of police.

'Someone is supplying him with heroin,' Dr Tichner said, 'but he won't tell me who.'

Chief of Police Murphy looked at Dr Tichner and nodded. 'I think I know who.'

There were several possible suspects. Hobe Sound was a small enclave, and everyone knew everyone else's business.

A liquor store had opened recently on Bridge Road that made deliveries to their Hobe Sound customers at all hours of the day and night.

A doctor at a local clinic had been fined for overprescribing drugs.

A gymnasium had opened a year earlier, on the other side of the waterway, and it was rumored that the trainer took steroids and had other drugs available for his good customers.

But Chief of Police Murphy had another suspect in mind.

Tony Benedotti had served as a gardener for many of the homes in Hobe Sound for years. He had studied horticulture and loved spending his days creating beautiful gardens. The gardens and lawns he tended were the loveliest in Hobe Sound. He was a quiet man who kept to himself, and the people he worked for knew very little about him. He seemed to be too well educated to be a gardener, and people were curious about his past.

Murphy sent for him.

'If this is about my driver's license, I renewed it,' Benedotti said.

'Sit down,' Murphy ordered.

'Is there some kind of problem?'

'Yeah. You're an educated man, right?'

'Yes.'

The chief of police leaned back in his chair. 'So how come you're a gardener?'

'I happen to love nature.'

'What else do you happen to love?'

'I don't understand.'

'How long have you been gardening?'

Benedotti looked at him, puzzled. 'Have any of my customers been complaining?'

'Just answer the question.'

'About fifteen years.'

'You have a nice house and a boat?'

'Yes.'

'How can you afford all that on what you make as a gardener?'

Benedotti said, 'It's not that big a house, and it's not that big a boat.'

'Maybe you make a little money on the side.'

'What do you . . . ?'

'You work for some people in Miami, don't you?'

'Yes.'

'There's a lot of Italians there. Do you ever do them some little favors?'

'What kind of favors?'

'Like pushing drugs.'

Benedotti looked at him, horrified. 'My God! Of course not.'

Murphy leaned forward. 'Let me tell you something, Benedotti. I've been keeping an eye on you. I've had a talk with a few of the people you work for. They don't want you or your mafia friends here anymore. Is that clear?'

Benedotti squeezed his eyes shut for a second, then opened them. 'Very clear.'

'Good. I'll expect you out of here by tomorrow. I don't want to see your face again.'

Woody Stanford went into the Harbor Group Clinic for three weeks, and when he came out, he was the old Woody – charming, gracious, and delightful to be with. He went back to playing polo, riding Mimi Carson's ponies.

Sunday was the Palm Beach Polo & Country Club's eighteenth anniversary, and South Shore Boulevard was heavy with traffic as three thousand fans converged on the polo grounds. They rushed to fill the box seats on the west side of the field and the bleachers at the opposite end. Some of the finest players in the world were going to be in the day's game.

Peggy was in a box seat next to Mimi Carson, as Mimi's guest.

'Woody told me that this is your first polo match, Peggy. Why haven't you been to one before?'

Peggy licked her lips. 'I . . . I guess I've always been too nervous to watch Woody play. I don't want him to get hurt again. It's a very dangerous sport, isn't it?'

Mimi said thoughtfully, 'When you get eight players, each weighing about one hundred and seventy-five pounds, and their nine-hundred-pound ponies racing at each other over three hundred yards at forty miles an hour – yes, accidents can happen.'

Peggy shuddered. 'I couldn't stand it if anything happened to Woody again. I really couldn't. I go crazy worrying about him.'

Mimi Carson said gently, 'Don't worry. He's one of the best. He studied under Hector Barrantas, you know.'

Peggy was looking at her blankly. 'Who?'

'He's a ten-goal player. One of the legends of polo.'

'Oh.'

There was a murmur from the crowd as the ponies moved across the field.

'What's happening?' Peggy asked.

'They just finished a practice session before the game. They're ready to begin now.'

On the field, the two teams were starting to line up under the hot Florida sun, getting ready for the umpire's throw-in.

Woody looked wonderful, tan and fit and lithe – ready to do battle. Peggy waved and blew him a kiss.

Both teams were lined up now, side by side. The players held their mallets down for the throw-in.

'There are usually six periods of play, called chukkers,' Mimi Carson explained to Peggy. 'Each chukker lasts seven minutes. The chukker ends when the bell rings. Then there's a short rest. They change ponies every period. The team that scores the most goals wins.'

'Right.'

Mimi wondered just how much Peggy understood.

On the field, the players' eyes were fixed on the umpire, anticipating when the ball would be tossed. The umpire looked around at the crowd, then suddenly bowled the white plastic ball between the two rows of players. The game had begun.

The action was swift. Woody made the first play, getting possession of the ball and hitting an offside forehand. The ball sped toward a player on the opposing team. The player galloped down the field after it. Woody rode up to him and hooked his mallet to spoil his shot.

'Why did Woody do that?' Peggy asked.

Mimi Carson explained. 'When your opponent gets

the ball, it's legal to hook his mallet so he can't score or pass. Woody will use an offside stroke next to control the ball.'

The action was happening so fast that it was almost impossible to follow.

There were cries of, 'Center.'

'Boards.'

'Leave it . . .'

And the players were racing down the field at full speed. The ponies – usually pure or three-quarter thoroughbred – were responsible for seventy five percent of their riders' successes. The ponies had to be fast, and have what players call polo sense, being able to anticipate their rider's every move.

Woody was brilliant during the first three chukkers, scoring two goals in each one and being cheered on by the roaring crowd. His mallet seemed to be everywhere. It was the old Woody Stanford, riding like the wind, fearless. By the end of the fifth chukker, Woody's team was well ahead. The players went off the field for the break.

As Woody passed Peggy and Mimi, sitting in the front row, he smiled at both of them.

Peggy turned to Mimi Carson, excitedly. 'Isn't he wonderful?'

She looked over at Peggy. 'Yes. In every way.'

Woody's teammates were congratulating him.

'Right on the mark, old boy! You were fabulous!'

'Great plays!'

'Thanks.'

'We're going out there and rub their noses in it some more. They haven't got a chance!'

Woody grinned. 'No problem.'

He watched his teammates move out to the field, and he suddenly felt exhausted. *I pushed myself too hard*, he thought. *I wasn't really ready to go back to the game yet. I'm not going to be able to keep this up. If I go out there, I'll make a fool of myself.* He began to panic, and his heart started to pound. *What I need is a little pick-me-up. No! I won't do that. I can't. I promised. But the team is waiting for me. I'll do it just this once, and never again. I swear to God, this is the last time.* He went to his car and reached into the glove compartment.

When Woody returned to the field, he was humming to himself, and his eyes were unnaturally bright. He waved to the crowd, and joined his waiting team. *I don't even need a team*, he thought. *I could beat those bastards single-handedly. I'm the best damned player in the world.* He was giggling to himself.

The accident occurred during the sixth chukker, although some of the spectators were to insist later that it was no accident.

The ponies were bunched together, racing toward the goal, and Woody had control of the ball. Out of the corner of his eye he saw one of the opposing players closing in on him. Using a tail shot, he sent the ball to the rear of the pony. It was picked up by Rick Hamilton, the best player on the opposing team, who began racing toward the goal. Woody was after him at full speed. He tried to hook Hamilton's mallet and missed. The ponies were getting closer to the goal. Woody kept desperately trying to get possession of the ball, and failed each time.

As Hamilton neared the goal, Woody deliberately swerved his pony to crash into Hamilton and ride him off the ball. Hamilton and his pony went tumbling to the ground. The crowd rose to its feet, screaming. The umpire angrily blew the whistle and held up a hand.

The first rule in polo is that when a player has possession of the ball and is heading toward the goal, it is illegal to cut across the line in which the player is traveling. Any player who crosses that line creates a dangerous situation and commits a foul.

Play stopped.

The umpire approached Woody, anger in his voice. 'That was a deliberate foul, Mr Stanford!'

Woody grinned. 'It wasn't my fault! His damned pony –'

'The opponents will receive a penalty goal.'

The chukker turned into a disaster. Woody committed two more blatant violations within three minutes of each other. The penalties resulted in two more goals for the other team. In each case the opponents were awarded a free penalty shot on an unguarded goal. In the last thirty seconds of the game, the opposing team scored the winning goal. What had been an assured victory, had turned into a rout.

In the box, Mimi Carson was stunned by the sudden turn of events.

Peggy said timidly, 'It didn't go well, did it?'

Mimi turned to her. 'No, Peggy. I'm afraid it didn't.'

A steward approached the box. 'Miss Carson, may I have a word with you?'

Mimi Carson turned to Peggy. 'Excuse me a moment.'

Peggy watched them walk away.

After the game, Woody's team was very quiet.

Woody was too ashamed to look at the others. Mimi Carson hurried over to Woody.

'Woody, I'm afraid I have some terrible, terrible news.' She put a hand on his shoulder. 'Your father is dead.'

Woody looked up at her and shook his head from side to side. He began to sob. 'I'm . . . I'm responsible. It's m . . . my fault.'

'No. You mustn't blame yourself. It isn't your fault.'

'Yes, it is,' Woody cried. 'If it weren't for my penalties, we would have won the game.'

Chapter Eleven

~~~~~~

Julia Stanford had never known her father, and now he was dead, reduced to a black headline in the *Kansas City Star*: TYCOON HARRY STANFORD DROWNS AT SEA! She sat there, staring at his photograph on the front page of the newspaper, filled with conflicting emotions. *Do I hate him because of the way he treated my mother, or do I love him because he's my father? Do I feel guilty because I never tried to get in touch with him, or do I feel angry because he never tried to find me? It doesn't matter anymore*, she thought. *He's gone.*

Her father had been dead to her all her life, and now he had died again, cheating her out of something she had no words for. Inexplicably, she felt an overwhelming sense of loss. *Stupid!* Julia thought. *How can I miss someone I never knew?* She looked at the newspaper photograph again. *Do I have anything of him in me?* Julia stared into the mirror on the wall. *The eyes. I have the same deep gray eyes.*

Julia went into her bedroom closet, removed a battered cardboard box, and from it lifted a

111

leather-bound scrapbook. She sat on the edge of her bed and opened the box. For the next two hours, she pored over its familiar contents. There were countless photographs of her mother in her governess's uniform, with Harry Stanford and Mrs Stanford and their three young children. Most of the pictures had been taken on their yacht, at Rose Hill, or at the Hobe Sound villa.

Julia picked up the yellowed newspaper clippings recounting the scandal that had happened so many years before in Boston. The faded headlines were lurid:

LOVE NEST ON BEACON HILL
BILLIONAIRE HARRY STANFORD IN SCANDAL
TYCOON'S WIFE COMMITS SUICIDE GOVERNESS
ROSEMARY NELSON DISAPPEARS

There were dozens of gossip columns filled with innuendos.

Julia sat there for a long time, lost in the past.

She had been born at St Joseph's Hospital in Milwaukee. Her earliest memories were of living in dreary walk-up apartments and constantly moving from city to city. There were times when there was no money at all, and little to eat. Her mother was continually ill, and it had been difficult for her to find steady work. The young girl quickly learned never to ask for toys or new dresses.

Julia started school when she was five, and her classmates would mock her because she wore the same dress and scruffy shoes every day. When the other children teased her, Julia fought them. She was a rebel, and she was always being brought up before the principal. Her teachers didn't know what to do with her. She was in constant trouble. She might have been expelled except for one thing: she was the brightest student in her class.

Her mother had told Julia that her father was dead, and she had accepted that. But when Julia was twelve years old, she stumbled across a picture album filled with photographs of her mother with a group of strangers.

'Who are these people?' Julia asked.

And Julia's mother decided that the time had come.

'Sit down, my darling.' She took Julia's hand and held it tightly. There was no way to break the news tactfully. 'That is your father, and your half sister, and your two half brothers.'

Julia was looking at her, puzzled. 'I don't understand.'

The truth had finally come out, shattering Julia's peace of mind. Her father was alive! And she had a half sister and two half brothers. It was too much to comprehend. 'Why . . . why did you lie to me?'

'You were too young to understand. Your father and I . . . had an affair. He was married, and I . . . I had to leave, to have you.'

'I hate him!' Julia said.

'You mustn't hate him.'

'How could he have done this to you?' she demanded.

'What happened was my fault as much as his.' Each word was agony. 'Your father was a very attractive man, and I was young and foolish. I knew that nothing could ever come of our affair. He told me he loved me ... but he was married and had a family. And ... and then I became pregnant.' It was difficult for her to go on. 'A reporter got hold of the story and it was in all the newspapers. I ran away. I intended for you and me to go back to him, but his wife killed herself, and I ... I could never face him or the children again. It was my fault you see. So don't blame him.'

But there was a part of the story Rosemary never revealed to her daughter. When the baby was born, the clerk at the hospital said, 'We're filling out the birth certificate. The baby's name is Julia Nelson?'

Rosemary had started to say yes, and then she thought fiercely, *No! She's Harry Stanford's daughter. She's entitled to his name, and his support.*

'My daughter's name is Julia Stanford.'

She had written to Harry Stanford, telling him about Julia, but she had never had a reply.

Julia was fascinated by the idea that she had a family she had not known about, and also by the fact that they were famous enough to be written about in the press. She went to the public library and looked up

114

everything she could about Harry Stanford. There were dozens of articles about him. He was a billionaire, and he lived in another world, a world that Julia and her mother were totally excluded from.

One day, when one of Julia's classmates teased her about being poor, Julia said defiantly, 'I'm not poor! My father is one of the richest men in the world. We have a yacht and an airplane, and a dozen beautiful homes.'

Her teacher heard her. 'Julia, come up here.'

Julia approached the teacher's desk. 'You must not tell a lie like that.'

'It's not a lie,' Julia retorted. 'My father is a billionaire! He knows presidents and kings!'

The teacher looked at the young girl standing before her in her shabby cotton dress and said, 'Julia, that's not true.'

'It is!' Julia said stubbornly.

She was sent to the principal's office. She never mentioned her father at school again.

Julia learned that the reason she and her mother kept moving from city to city was because of the news media. Harry Stanford was constantly in the press, and the gossip newspapers and magazines kept digging up the old scandal. Investigative reporters would eventually discover who Rosemary Nelson was and where she lived, and she would have to take Julia and flee.

Julia read every newspaper story that appeared about Harry Stanford, and each time, she was tempted to telephone him. She wanted to believe that during all those years he had been desperately searching for her mother. *I'll call and say, 'This is your daughter. If you want to see us . . .'*

And he would come to them and fall in love all over again, and marry her mother, and they would all live happily together.

Julia Stanford grew into a beautiful young woman. She had lustrous dark hair, a laughing, generous mouth, the luminous gray eyes of her father, and a gently curved figure. But when she smiled, people forgot about everything else but that smile.

Because they were forced to move so often, Julia went to schools in five different states. During the summers she worked as a clerk in a department store, behind the counter in a drugstore, and as a receptionist. She was always fiercely independent.

They were living in Kansas City, Kansas, when Julia finished college on a scholarship. She was not sure what she wanted to do with her life. Friends, impressed by her beauty, suggested that she become a movie actress.

'You'd be a star overnight!'

Julia had dismissed the idea with a casual, 'Who wants to get up that early every morning?'

But the real reason she was not interested was

because she wanted, above all, her privacy. It seemed to Julia that all their lives, she and her mother had been hounded by the press because of what had happened so many years earlier.

Julia's dream of one day uniting her mother and father ended the day her mother died. Julia felt an overpowering sense of loss. *My father has to know*, Julia thought. *Mother was a part of his life.* She looked up the telephone number of his business headquarters in Boston. A receptionist answered.

'Good morning, Stanford Enterprises.'

Julia hesitated.

'Stanford Enterprises. Hello? May I help you?'

Slowly Julia replaced the receiver. *Mother wouldn't have wanted me to make that call.*

She was alone now. She had no one.

Julia buried her mother at Memorial Park Cemetery in Kansas City. There were no mourners. Julia stood at the graveside and thought, *It isn't fair, Mama. You made one mistake and paid for it the rest of your life. I wish I could have taken some of your pain away. I love you very much, Mama. I'll always love you.* All she had left of her mother's years on earth was a collection of old photographs and clippings.

With her mother gone, Julia's thoughts turned to the Stanford family. They were rich. She could go to them for help. *Never*, she decided. *Not after the way Harry Stanford treated my mother*.

But she had to earn a living. She was faced with a career decision. She thought wryly, *Maybe I'll become a brain surgeon*.

Or a painter?

Opera singer?

Physicist?

Astronaut?

She settled for a secretarial course at night school at Kansas City, Kansas, Community College.

The day after Julia finished the course, she visited an employment agency. There were a dozen applicants waiting to see the employment counselor. Sitting next to Julia was an attractive woman her age.

'Hi! I'm Sally Connors.'

'Julia Stanford.'

'I've got to get a job today,' Sally moaned. 'I've been kicked out of my apartment.'

Julia heard her name called.

'Good luck!' Sally said.

'Thanks.'

Julia walked into the office of the employment counselor.

'Sit down, please.'

'Thank you.'

'I see from your application that you have a college education and summer work experience. And you have a high recommendation from the secretarial school.'

She looked at the dossier on her desk. 'You take short-hand at ninety words per minute, and type at sixty words per minute?'

'Yes, ma'am.'

'I might have just the thing for you. There's a small firm of architects that's looking for a secretary. The salary isn't very large, I'm afraid.'

'That's okay,' Julia said quickly.

'Very well. I'm going to send you over there.' She handed Julia a slip of paper with a typed name and address on it. 'They'll interview you at noon tomorrow.'

Julia smiled happily. 'Thank you.' She was filled with a sense of excitement.

When Julia came out of the office, Sally's name was being called.

'I hope you get something,' Julia said.

'Thanks!'

On an impulse, Julia decided to stay and wait. Ten minutes later, when Sally came out of the inner office, she was grinning.

'I got an interview! She telephoned, and I'm going to the American Mutual Insurance Company tomorrow for a receptionist job. How did you do?'

'I'll know tomorrow, too.'

'I'm sure we'll make it. Why don't we have lunch together and celebrate?'

'Fine.'

* * *

At lunch they talked, and their friendship clicked instantly.

'I looked at an apartment in Overland Park,' Sally said. 'It's a two-bedroom and bath, with a kitchen and living room. It's really nice. I can't afford it alone, but if the two of us . . .'

Julia smiled. 'I'd like that.' She crossed her fingers. 'If I get the job.'

'You'll get it!' Sally assured her.

On the way to the offices of Peters, Eastman & Tolkin, Julia thought, *This could be my big opportunity. This could lead anywhere. I mean, this isn't just a job. I'll be working for architects. Dreamers who build and shape the city's skyline, who create beauty and magic out of stone. Maybe I'll study architecture myself, so that I can help them and be a part of that dream.*

The office was in a dingy old commercial building on Amour Boulevard. Julia took the elevator to the third floor, got off and stopped at a scarred door marked PETERS, EASTMAN & TOLKIN, ARCHITECTS. She took a deep breath to calm herself and entered.

Three men were waiting for her in the reception room, examining her as she walked in the door.

'You're here for the secretarial job?'

'Yes, sir.'

'I'm Al Peters.' The bald one.

'Bob Eastman.' The ponytail.

'Max Tolkin.' The potbelly.

They all appeared to be somewhere in their forties.

'We understand this is your first secretarial job,' Al Peters said.

'Yes, it is,' Julia replied. Then quickly she added, 'But I'm a fast learner. I'll work very hard.' She decided not to mention her idea about going to school to study architecture yet. She would wait until they got to know her better.

'All right, we'll try you out,' Bob Eastman said, 'and see how it goes.'

Julia felt a sense of exhilaration. 'Oh, thank you! You won't be –'

'About the salary,' Max Tolkin said. 'I'm afraid we can't pay very much at the beginning.'

'That's all right,' Julia said. 'I . . .'

'Three hundred a week,' Al Peters told her.

They were right. It was not much money. Julia made a quick decision. 'I'll take it.'

They looked at one another and exchanged smiles.

'Great!' Al Peters said. 'Let me show you around.'

The tour took only a few seconds. There was the little reception room and three small offices that looked as though they had been furnished by the Salvation Army. The lavatory was down the hall. They were all architects, but Al Peters was the businessman, Bob Eastman was the salesman, and Max Tolkin handled construction.

'You'll be working for all of us,' Peters told her.

'Fine.' Julia knew she was going to make herself indispensable to them.

Al Peters looked at his watch. 'It's twelve thirty. How about some lunch?'

Julia felt a little thrill. She was part of the team now. *They're inviting me to lunch.*

He turned to Julia. 'There's a delicatessen down the block. I'll have a corned beef sandwich on rye with mustard, potato salad, and a Danish.'

'Oh.' *So much for 'They're inviting me to lunch.'*

Tolkin said, 'I'll have a pastrami and some chicken soup.'

'Yes, sir.'

Bob Eastman spoke up. 'I'll have the pot roast platter and a soft drink.'

'Oh, make sure the corned beef is lean,' Al Peters told her.

'Lean corned beef.'

Max Tolkin said, 'Make sure that the soup is hot.'

'Right. Soup hot.'

Bob Eastman said, 'Make my soft drink a diet cola.'

'Diet cola.'

'Here's some money.' Al Peters handed her a twenty-dollar bill.

Ten minutes later, Julia was in the delicatessen, talking to the man behind the counter. 'I want one lean corned beef sandwich on rye with mustard, potato salad, and a Danish. A pastrami sandwich and very

122

hot chicken soup. And a pot roast platter and diet cola.'

The man nodded. 'You work for Peters, Eastman, & Tolkin, huh?'

Julia and Sally moved into the apartment in Overland Park the following week. The apartment consisted of two small bedrooms, a living room with furniture that had seen too many tenants, a kitchenette, dinette, and a bathroom. *They'll never confuse this place with the Ritz*, Julia thought.

'We'll take turns at cooking,' Sally suggested.

'Fine.'

Sally prepared the first meal, and it was delicious.

The next night was Julia's turn. Sally took one bite of the dish that Julia had made and said, 'Julia, I don't have a lot of life insurance. Why don't I do the cooking and you do the cleaning?'

The two roommates got along well. On weekends they would go to see movies at the Glenwood 4, and shop at the Bannister Mall. They bought their clothes at the Super Flea Discount House. One night a week they went out to an inexpensive restaurant for dinner – Stephenson's Old Apple Farm or the Café Max for Mediterranean specialties. When they could afford it, they would drop in at Charlie Charlies to hear jazz.

*　　*　　*

Julia enjoyed working for Peters, Eastman & Tolkin. To say that the firm was not doing well was an understatement. Clients were scarce. Julia felt that she wasn't doing much to help build the skyline of the city, but she enjoyed being around her three bosses. They were like a surrogate family, and each one confided his problems to Julia. She was capable and efficient, and she very quickly reorganized the office.

Julia decided to do something about the lack of clients. But what? She soon had the answer. There was an item in the *Kansas City Star* about a luncheon for a new executive secretary organization. The chairperson was Susan Bandy.

The following day, at noon, Julia said to Al Peters, 'I may be a little late coming back from lunch.'

He smiled. 'No problem, Julia.' He thought how lucky they were to have her.

Julia arrived at the Plaza Inn and went to the room where the luncheon was being given. The woman seated at the table near the door said, 'May I help you?'

'Yes. I'm here for the Executive Women's luncheon.'

'Your name?'

'Julia Stanford.'

The woman looked at the list in front of her. 'I'm afraid I don't see your –'

Julia smiled. 'Isn't that just like Susan? I'll have to

have a talk with her. I'm the executive secretary with Peters, Eastman, & Tolkin.'

The woman looked uncertain. 'Well . . .'

'Don't worry about it. I'll just go in and find Susan.'

In the banquet room was a group of well-dressed women chatting among themselves. Julia approached one of them. 'Which one is Susan Bandy?'

'She's over there.' She indicated a tall, striking-looking woman in her forties.

Julia went up to her. 'Hi. I'm Julia Stanford.'

'Hello.'

'I'm with Peters, Eastman, & Tolkin. I'm sure you've heard of them.'

'Well, I . . .'

'They're the fastest growing architectural firm in Kansas City.'

'I see.'

'I don't have a lot of time to spare, but I would like to contribute whatever I can to the organization.'

'Well, that's very kind of you, Miss . . . ?'

'Stanford.'

That was the beginning.

The Executive Women's organization represented most of the top firms in Kansas City, and in no time at all, Julia was networking with them. She had lunch with one or more of the individual members at least once a week.

'Our company is going to put up a new building in Olathe.'

And Julia would immediately report back to her bosses.

'Mr Hanley wants to build a summer home in Tonganoxie.'

And before anyone else found out about it, Peters, Eastman & Tolkin had the jobs.

Bob Eastman called Julia in one day and said, 'You deserve a raise, Julia. You're doing a great job. You're one hell of a secretary!'

'Would you do me a favor?' Julia asked.

'Sure.'

'Call me an executive secretary. It will help my credibility.'

From time to time, Julia would read newspaper articles about her father, or watch him being interviewed on television. She never mentioned him to Sally or to her employers.

When Julia was younger, one of her daydreams had been that, like Dorothy, she would one day be whisked away from Kansas to some beautiful, magical place. It would be a place filled with yachts and private planes and palaces. But now, with the news of her father's death, that dream was ended forever. *Well, I got the Kansas part right*, she thought wryly.

I have no family left. But I do, Julia corrected herself. *I have two half brothers and a half sister. They're family.*

126

Should I go visit them? Good idea? Bad idea? I wonder how we would feel about one another?

Her decision turned out to be a matter of life or death.

Chapter Twelve

It was the gathering of a clan of strangers. It had been years since they had seen or communicated with one another.

Judge Tyler Stanford arrived in Boston by plane.

Kendall Stanford Renaud flew in from Paris. Marc Renaud took the train from New York.

Woody Stanford and Peggy drove up from Hobe Sound.

The heirs had been notified that the funeral services would take place at King's Chapel. The street outside the church was barricaded, and there were policemen to hold back the crowd that had gathered to watch the dignitaries arrive. The vice president of the United States was there, as well as senators and ambassadors and statesmen from as far away as Turkey and Saudi Arabia. During his lifetime, Harry Stanford had cast a large shadow, and all seven hundred seats in the chapel would be occupied.

* * *

Tyler and Woody and Kendall, with their spouses, met inside the vestry. It was an awkward meeting. They were alien to one another, and the only thing they had in common was the body of the man in the hearse outside the church.

'This is my husband, Marc,' Kendall said.

'This is my wife, Peggy. Peggy, my sister, Kendall, and my brother, Tyler.'

There were polite exchanges of hellos. They stood there, uncomfortably studying one another, until an usher came up to the group.

'Excuse me,' he said in a hushed voice. 'The services are about to begin. Would you follow me, please?'

He led them to a reserved pew at the front of the chapel. They took their seats and waited, each preoccupied with his or her own thoughts.

To Tyler, it felt strange to be back in Boston. The only good memories he had of it were when his mother and Rosemary were alive. When he was eleven, Tyler had seen a print of the famous Goya painting *Saturn Devouring His Son*, and he had always identified it with his father.

And now, Tyler, looking over at his father's coffin as it was carried into the church by the pallbearers, thought, *Saturn is dead.*

'I know your dirty little secret.'

The minister stepped into the chapel's historic wine-glass shaped pulpit.

' "Jesus said unto her, I am the resurrection and the life: he that believeth in me, though he were dead, yet shall he live: and whosoever liveth and believeth in me shall never die." '

Woody was feeling exhilarated. He had taken a hit of heroin before coming to the church, and it had not worn off yet. He glanced over at his brother and sister. *Tyler has put on weight. He looks like a judge. Kendall has turned into a beauty, but she seems to be under a strain. I wonder if it's because Father died? No. She hated him as much as I did.* He looked at his wife, seated next to him. *I'm sorry I didn't get to show her off to the old man. He would have died of a heart attack.*

The minister was speaking.

' "Like as a father pitieth *his* children, *so* the Lord pitieth them that fear him. For he knoweth our frame; he remembereth that we are dust." '

Kendall was not listening to the service. She was thinking about the red dress. Her father had telephoned her in New York one afternoon.

'So you've become a big-shot designer, have you? Well, let's see how good you are. I'm taking my new girlfriend to a charity ball Saturday night. She's your size. I want you to design a dress for her.'

'Saturday? I can't, Father. I . . .'

'You'll do it.'

130

And she had designed the ugliest dress she could conceive of. It had a large black bow in front and yards of ribbons and lace. It was a monstrosity. She had sent it to her father, and he had telephoned her again.

'*I got the dress. By the way, my girlfriend can't make it Saturday, so you're going to be my date, and you're going to wear that dress.*'

'*No!*'

And then the terrible phrase: '*You don't want to disappoint me, do you?*'

And she had gone, not daring to change the dress, and had spent the most humiliating evening of her life.

' "For we brought nothing into this world, and it is certain we can carry nothing out. The Lord gave, and the Lord hath taken away; blessed be the name of the Lord!" '

Peggy Stanford was uncomfortable. She was awed by the splendor of the huge church and the elegant-looking people in it. She had never been to Boston before, and to her it meant the world of Stanfords, with all its pomp and glory. These people were so much better than she was. She took her husband's hand.

' "All flesh is grass, and all the goodliness thereof is as the flower of the field ... The grass withereth, the flower fadeth; but the word of our God shall stand forever." '

* * *

131

Marc was thinking about the blackmail letter that his wife had received. It had been worded very carefully, very cleverly. It would be impossible to find out who was behind it. He looked at Kendall, seated next to him, pale and tense. *How much more can she take?* he wondered. He moved closer to her.

' "Unto God's gracious mercy and protection we commit you. The Lord bless you and keep you. The Lord make his face to shine upon you and be gracious unto you. The Lord lift up the light of his countenance upon you and give you peace, now and forever. Amen." '

With the service finished, the minister announced, 'The burial services will be private – family members only.'

Tyler looked at the coffin and thought about the body inside. Last night, before the casket was secured, he had gone straight from Boston's Logan International Airport to the viewing at the funeral home.

He wanted to see his father dead.

Woody watched as the coffin was carried out of the church past the staring mourners, and he smiled: *Give the people what they want.*

The graveside ceremony at the old Mount Auburn Cemetery in Cambridge was brief. The family watched Harry Stanford's body being lowered to its final resting place, and as the dirt was being thrown onto the casket the minister said, 'There's no need for you to stay any longer if you don't wish to.'

Woody nodded. 'Right.' The effect of the heroin was beginning to wear off, and he was starting to feel jittery. 'Let's get the hell out of here.'

Marc said, 'Where are we going?'

Tyler turned to the group. 'We're staying at Rose Hill. It's all been arranged. We'll stay there until the estate is settled.'

A few minutes later, they were in limousines on their way to the house.

Boston had a strict social hierarchy. The nouveaux riches lived on Commonwealth Avenue, and the social climbers on Newbury Street. Less affluent old families lived on Marlborough Street. Back Bay was the city's newest and most prestigious address, but Beacon Hill was still the citadel for Boston's oldest and wealthiest families. It was a rich mixture of Victorian townhouses and brownstones, old churches and chic shopping areas.

Rose Hill, the Stanford estate, was a beautiful old Victorian house that stood amid three acres of land on Beacon Hill. The house that the Stanford children had grown up in was filled with unpleasant memories. When the limousines arrived in front of the house, the passengers got out and stared up at the old mansion.

'I can't believe Father isn't going to be inside, waiting for us,' Kendall said.

Woody grinned. 'He's too busy trying to run things in hell.'

Tyler took a deep breath. 'Let's go.'

As they approached the front door it opened, and Clark, the butler, stood there. He was in his seventies, a dignified, capable servant who had worked at Rose Hill for more than thirty years. He had watched the children grow up, and had lived through all the scandals.

Clark's face lit up as he saw the group. 'Good afternoon!'

Kendall gave him a warm hug. 'Clark, it's so good to see you again.'

'It's been a long time, Miss Kendall.'

'It's Mrs Renaud now. This is my husband, Marc.'

'How do you do, sir?'

'My wife has told me a great deal about you.'

'Nothing too terrible I hope, sir.'

'On the contrary. She has only fond memories of you.'

'Thank you, sir.' Clark turned to Tyler. 'Good afternoon, Judge Stanford.'

'Hello, Clark.'

'It's a pleasure to see you, sir.'

'Thank you. You're looking very well.'

'So are you, sir. I'm so sorry about what has happened.'

'Thank you. Are you set up here to take care of all of us?'

'Oh, yes. I think we can make everyone comfortable.'

'Am I in my old room?'

Clark smiled. 'That's right.' He turned to Woody. 'I'm pleased to see you, Mr Woodrow. I want to –'

Woody grabbed Peggy's arm. 'Come on,' he said curtly. 'I want to get freshened up.'

The others watched as Woody pushed past them and took Peggy upstairs.

The rest of the group walked into the huge drawing room. The room was dominated by a pair of massive Louis XIV armoires. Scattered around the room were a giltwood console table with a molded marble top, and an array of exquisite period chairs and couches. An ormolu chandelier hung from the high ceiling. On the walls were dark medieval paintings.

Clark turned to Tyler. 'Judge Stanford, I have a message for you. Mr Simon Fitzgerald would like you to telephone him to tell him when it would be convenient to arrange a meeting with the family.'

'Who is Simon Fitzgerald?' Marc asked.

Kendall replied. 'He's the family attorney. Father has been with him forever but we've never met him.'

'I presume he wants to discuss the disposition of the estate,' Tyler said. He turned to the others. 'If it's all right with all of you, I'll arrange for him to meet us here tomorrow morning.'

'That will be fine,' Kendall said.

'The chef is preparing dinner,' Clark told them. 'Will eight o'clock be satisfactory?'

'Yes,' Tyler said. 'Thank you.'

'Eva and Millie will show you to your rooms.'

Tyler turned to his sister and her husband. 'We'll meet down here at eight, shall we?'

As Woody and Peggy entered their bedroom upstairs, Peggy asked, 'Are you all right?'

'I'm fine,' Woody snapped. 'Leave me alone.'

She watched him go into the bathroom and slam the door shut. She stood there, waiting.

Ten minutes later, Woody came out. He was smiling. 'Hi, baby.'

'Hi.'

'Well, how do you like the old house?'

'It's . . . it's enormous.'

'It's a monstrosity.' He walked over to the bed and put his arms around Peggy. 'This is my old room. These walls were covered with sports posters – the Bruins, the Celtics, the Red Sox. I wanted to be an athlete. I had big dreams. In my senior year in boarding school, I was captain of the football team. I got offers of admission from half a dozen college coaches.'

'Which one did you take?'

He shook his head. 'None of them. My father said they were only interested in the Stanford name, that they just wanted money from him. He sent me to an engineering school where they didn't play football.'

He was silent for a moment. Then he mumbled, 'I could'a been a contenda . . .'

She looked at him puzzled. 'What?'

He looked up. 'Didn't you ever see *On the Waterfront*?'

'No.'

'It was a line that Marlon Brando said. It means we both got screwed.'

'Your father must have been tough.'

Woody gave a short, derisive laugh. 'That's the nicest thing anyone has ever said about him. I remember when I was just a kid, I fell off a horse. I wanted to get back on and ride again. My father wouldn't let me. "You'll never be a rider," he said. "You're too clumsy."' Woody looked up at her. 'That's why I became a nine-goal polo player.'

They came together at the dinner table, strangers to one another, seated in an uncomfortable silence, their only connection childhood traumas.

Kendall looked around the room. Terrible memories mingled with an appreciation for its beauty. The dining table was classical French, an early Louis XV, surrounded by Directoire walnut chairs. In one corner was a blue-and-cream painted French provincial corner armoire. On the walls were drawings by Watteau and Fragonard.

Kendall turned to Tyler. 'I read about your decision in the *Fiorello* case. He deserved what you gave him.'

'It must be exciting being a judge,' Peggy said.

'Sometimes it is.'

'What kind of cases do you handle?' Marc inquired.

'Criminal cases – rapes, drugs, murder.'

Kendall turned pale and started to say something, and Marc grabbed her hand and squeezed it as a warning.

Tyler said politely to Kendall, 'You've become a successful designer.'

Kendall was finding it hard to breathe. 'Yes.'

'She's fantastic,' Marc said.

'And Marc, what do you do?'

'I'm with a brokerage house.'

'Oh, you're one of those young Wall Street millionaires.'

'Well, not exactly, judge. I'm really just getting started.'

Tyler gave Marc a patronizing look. 'I guess it's lucky you have a successful wife.'

Kendall blushed and whispered in Marc's ear, 'Pay no attention. Remember I love you.'

Woody was beginning to feel the effect of the drug. He turned to look at his wife. 'Peggy could use some decent clothes,' he said. 'But she doesn't care how she looks. Do you, angel?'

Peggy sat there, embarrassed, not knowing what to say.

'Maybe a little waitress costume?' Woody suggested.

Peggy said, 'Excuse me.' She got up from the table and fled upstairs.

They were all staring at Woody.

He grinned. 'She's oversensitive. So, we're having a discussion about the will tomorrow, eh?'

'That's right,' Tyler said.

'I'll make you a bet the old man didn't leave us one dime.'

Marc said, 'But there's so much money in the estate . . .'

Woody snorted. 'You didn't know our father. He probably left us his old jackets and a box of cigars. He liked to use his money to control us. His favorite line was "*You don't want to disappoint me, do you?*" And we all behaved like good little children because, as you said, there was so much money. Well, I'll bet the old man found a way to take it with him.'

Tyler said, 'We'll know tomorrow, won't we?'

Early the following morning, Simon Fitzgerald and Steve Sloane arrived. Clark escorted them into the library. 'I'll inform the family that you're here,' he said.

'Thank you.' They watched him leave.

The library was huge and opened onto a garden through two large French doors. The room was paneled in dark-stained oak, and the walls were lined with bookcases filled with handsome leather-bound volumes. There was a scattering of comfortable chairs and Italian reading lamps. In one corner stood a customized beveled-glass and ormolu-mounted mahogany cabinet that displayed Harry Stanford's enviable gun collection. Special drawers had been designed beneath the display case to house the ammunition.

'It's going to be an interesting morning,' Steve said. 'I wonder how they're going to react.'

'We'll find out soon enough.'

Kendall and Marc came into the room first.

Simon Fitzgerald said, 'Good morning. I'm Simon Fitzgerald. This is my associate, Steve Sloane.'

'I'm Kendall Renaud, and this is my husband, Marc.' The men shook hands.

Woody and Peggy entered the room.

Kendall said, 'Woody, this is Mr Fitzgerald and Mr Sloane.'

Woody nodded. 'Hi. Did you bring the cash with you?'

'Well, we really . . .'

'I'm only kidding! This is my wife, Peggy.' Woody looked at Steve. 'Did the old man leave me anything or . . . ?'

Tyler entered the room. 'Good morning.'

'Judge Stanford?'

'Yes.'

'I'm Simon Fitzgerald, and this is Steve Sloane, my associate. It was Steve who arranged to have your father's body brought back from Corsica.'

Tyler turned to Steve. 'I appreciate that. We're not

sure what happened exactly. The press has had so many different versions of the story. Was there foul play involved?'

'No. It seems to have been an accident. Your father's yacht was caught in a terrible storm off the coast of Corsica. According to a deposition from Dmitri Kaminsky, his bodyguard, your father was standing on the outside veranda of his cabin and the wind blew some papers out of his hand. He reached for them, lost his balance, and fell overboard. By the time they recovered his body, it was too late.'

'What a horrible way to die.' Kendall shuddered.

'Did you talk to this Kaminsky person?' Tyler asked.

'Unfortunately, no. By the time I arrived in Corsica, he had left.'

Fitzgerald said, 'The captain of the yacht had advised your father not to sail into that storm, but for some reason, he was in a hurry to return here. He had arranged for a helicopter to bring him back. There was some kind of urgent problem.'

Tyler asked, 'Do you know what the problem was?'

'No. I cut short my vacation to meet him back here. I don't know what –'

Woody interrupted. 'That's all very interesting, but it's ancient history, isn't it? Let's talk about the will. Did he leave us anything or not?' His hands were twitching.

'Why don't we sit down?' Tyler suggested.

They took chairs. Simon Fitzgerald sat at the desk,

141

facing them. He opened a briefcase and started to take out some papers.

Woody was ready to explode. '*Well?* For God's sake, did he or didn't he?'

Kendall said, 'Woody . . .'

'I know the answer,' Woody said angrily. 'He didn't leave us a damn cent.'

Fitzgerald looked into the faces of the children of Harry Stanford. 'As a matter of fact,' he said, 'each of you will share equally in the estate.'

Steve could feel the sudden euphoria that swept through the room.

Woody was staring at Fitzgerald, openmouthed. '*What?* Are you serious?' He jumped to his feet. 'That's fantastic!' He turned to the others. 'Did you hear that? The old bastard finally came through!' He looked at Simon Fitzgerald. 'How much money are we talking about?'

'I don't have the exact figure. According to the latest issue of *Forbes* magazine, Stanford Enterprises is worth six billion dollars. Most of it is invested in various corporations, but there is roughly four hundred million dollars available in liquid assets.'

Kendall was listening, stunned. 'That's more than a hundred million dollars for each of us. I can't believe it!' *I'm free,* she thought. *I can pay them off and be rid of them forever.* She looked at Marc, her face shining, and squeezed his hand.

'Congratulations,' Marc said. He knew more than

142

the others what the money would mean.

Simon Fitzgerald spoke up. 'As you know, ninety-nine percent of the shares in Stanford Enterprises was held by your father. So those shares will be divided equally among you. Also, now that his father is deceased, Judge Stanford owns outright that other one percent that had been held in trust. Of course, there will be certain formalities. Furthermore, I should inform you that there is a possibility of another heir being involved.'

'Another heir?' Tyler asked.

'Your father's will specifically provides that the estate is to be divided equally among his issue.'

Peggy looked puzzled. 'What . . . what do you mean by *issue*?'

Tyler spoke up. 'Natural-born descendants and legally adopted descendants.'

Fitzgerald nodded. 'That is correct. Any descendant born out of wedlock is deemed a descendant of the mother and the father, whose protection is established under the law of the jurisdiction.'

'What are you saying?' Woody asked impatiently.

'I'm saying that there may be another claimant.'

Kendall looked at him. 'Who?'

Simon Fitzgerald hesitated. There was no way to be tactful. 'I'm sure that you are all aware of the fact that a number of years ago, your father sired a child by a governess who worked here.'

'Rosemary Nelson,' Tyler said.

143

'Yes. Her daughter was born at St Joseph's Hospital in Milwaukee. She named her Julia.'

The room was thick with silence.

'Hey!' Woody exclaimed. 'That was twenty-five years ago.'

'Twenty-six, to be exact.'

Kendall asked, 'Does anyone know where she is?'

Simon Fitzgerald could hear Harry Stanford's voice: *She wrote to tell me that it was a girl. Well, if she thinks she's going to get a dime out of me, she can go to hell.*

'No,' Fitzgerald said slowly. 'No one knows where she is.'

'Then what the hell are we talking about?' Woody demanded.

'I just wanted all of you to be aware that if she does appear, she will be entitled to an equal share of the estate.'

'I don't think we have anything to worry about,' Woody said confidently. 'She probably never even knew who her father was.'

Tyler turned to Simon Fitzgerald. 'You say you don't know the exact amount of the estate. May I ask why not?'

'Because our firm handles only your father's personal affairs. His corporate affairs are represented by two other law firms. I've been in touch with them and have asked them to prepare financial statements as soon as possible.'

'What kind of timeframe are we talking about?'

144

Kendall asked anxiously. *We will need $100,000 immediately to cover our expenses.*

'Probably two to three months.'

Marc saw the consternation on his wife's face. He turned to Fitzgerald. 'Isn't there some way to hurry things along?'

Steve Sloane answered. 'I'm afraid not. The will has to go through probate court, and their calendar is rather heavy right now.'

'What is a probate court?' Peggy asked.

'*Probate* is from the past participle of *probare* – to prove. It's the act of –'

'She didn't ask you for a damned English lesson!' Woody exploded. 'Why can't we just wrap things up now?'

Tyler turned to his brother. 'The law doesn't work that way. When there's a death, the will has to be filed in the probate court. There has to be an appraisal of all assets – real estate, closely held corporations, cash, jewelry – then an inventory has to be prepared and filed in the court. Taxes have to be taken care of, and specific bequests paid. After that, a petition is filed for permission to distribute the balance of the estate to the beneficiaries.'

Woody grinned, 'What the hell. I've waited almost forty years to be a millionaire. I guess I can wait another month or two.'

Simon Fitzgerald stood up. 'Aside from your father's bequests to you, there are some minor gifts, but they don't affect the bulk of the estate.' Fitzgerald looked around the room. 'Well, if there's nothing else . . .'

Tyler rose. 'I think not. Thank you, Mr Fitzgerald, Mr Sloane. If there are any problems, we'll be in touch.'

Fitzgerald nodded to the group. 'Ladies and gentlemen.' He turned and went toward the door, Steve Sloane following him.

Outside, in the driveway, Simon Fitzgerald turned to Steve. 'Well, now you've met the family. What do you think?'

'It was more like a celebration than a mourning. I'm puzzled by something, Simon. If their father hated them as much as they seem to hate him, why did he leave them all that money?'

Simon Fitzgerald shrugged. 'That's something we'll never know. Maybe that's why he was coming to see me, to leave the money to someone else.'

None of the group was able to sleep that night, each lost in his or her own thoughts.

Tyler was thinking, *It's happened. It's really happened! I can afford to give Lee the world. Anything! Everything!*

Kendall was thinking, *As soon as I get the money, I'll find a way to buy them off permanently, and I'll make sure they never bother me again.*

Woody was thinking, *I'm going to have the best string*

146

of polo ponies in the world. No more borrowing other people's ponies. I'm going to be ten goals! He glanced over at Peggy, sleeping at his side. *The first thing I'll do is get rid of this stupid bitch.* Then he thought, *No, I can't do that* . . . He got out of bed and went into the bathroom. When he came out, he was feeling wonderful.

The atmosphere at breakfast the next morning was exuberant.

'Well,' Woody said happily, 'I suppose all of you have been making plans.'

Marc shrugged. 'How does one plan for something like this? It is an unbelievable amount of money.'

Tyler looked up. 'It's certainly going to change all our lives.'

Woody nodded. 'The bastard should have given it to us while he was alive, so we could have enjoyed it then. If it's not impolite to hate the dead, I have to tell you something . . .'

Kendall said reproachfully, 'Woody . . .'

'Well, let's not be hypocrites. We all despised him, and he deserved it. Just look what he tried to –'

Clark came into the room. He stood there, apologetically. 'Excuse me,' he said. 'There is a Miss Julia Stanford at the door.'

NOON

Chapter Thirteen

'Julia Stanford?'

They stared at one another, frozen.

'The hell she is!' Woody exploded.

Tyler said quickly, 'I suggest we adjourn to the library.' He turned to Clark. 'Would you send the young lady in there, please?'

'Yes, sir.'

She stood in the doorway, looking at each of them, obviously ill at ease. 'I . . . I probably shouldn't have come,' she said.

'You're damn right!' Woody said. 'Who the hell are you?'

'I'm Julia Stanford.' She was almost stammering in her nervousness.

'No. I mean who are you *really*?'

She started to say something, then shook her head. 'I . . . My mother was Rosemary Nelson. Harry Stanford was my father.'

The group looked at one another.

'Do you have any proof of that?' Tyler asked.

She swallowed. 'I don't think I have any *real* proof.'

'Of course you don't,' Woody snapped. 'How do you have the nerve to – ?'

Kendall interrupted. 'This is rather a shock to all of us, as you can imagine. If what you're saying is true, then you're . . . you're our half sister.'

Julia nodded. 'You're Kendall.' She turned to Tyler. 'You're Tyler.' She turned to Woody. 'And you're Woodrow. They call you Woody.'

'As *People* Magazine could have told you,' Woody said sarcastically.

Tyler spoke up. 'I'm sure you can understand our position, Miss . . . er . . . Without some positive proof, there's no way we could possibly accept . . .'

'I understand.' She looked around nervously. 'I don't know why I came here.'

'Oh, I think you do,' Woody said. 'It's called money.'

'I'm not interested in the money,' she said indignantly. 'The truth is that I . . . I came here hoping to meet my family.'

Kendall was studying her. 'Where is your mother?'

'She passed away. When I read that our father died . . .'

'You decided to look us up,' Woody said mockingly.

Tyler spoke. 'You say you have no legal proof of who you are.'

'Legal? I . . . I suppose not. I didn't even think about

152

that. But there are things I couldn't possibly know about unless I had heard them from my mother.'

'For example?' Marc said.

She stopped to think. 'I remember my mother used to talk about a greenhouse in the back. She loved plants and flowers, and she would spend hours there.'

Woody spoke up. 'Photographs of that greenhouse were in a lot of magazines.'

'What else did your mother tell you?' Tyler asked.

'Oh, there were so many things! She loved to talk about all of you and the good times you used to have.' She thought for a moment. 'There was the day she took you on the swan boats when you were very young. One of you almost fell overboard. I don't remember which one.'

Woody and Kendall looked over at Tyler.

'I was the one,' he said.

'She took you shopping at Filene's. One of you got lost, and everyone was in a panic.'

Kendall said slowly, 'I got lost that day.'

'Yes? What else?' Tyler asked.

'She took you to the Union Oyster House and you tasted your first oyster and got sick.'

'I remember that.'

They stared at each other, silent.

She looked at Woody. 'You and Mother went to the Charlestown Navy Yard to see the USS *Constitution*, and you wouldn't leave. She had to drag you away.' She turned to Kendall. 'And in the Public

Garden one day, you picked some flowers and were almost arrested.'

Kendall swallowed. 'That's right.'

They were all listening to her intently now, fascinated.

'One day, Mother took all of you to the Natural History museum, and you were terrified of the mastodon and sea serpent skeleton.'

Kendall said slowly, 'None of us slept that night.'

Julia turned to Woody. 'One Christmas, she took you skating. You fell down and broke a tooth. When you were seven years old, you fell out of a tree and had to have your leg stitched up. You had a scar.'

Woody said reluctantly, 'I still do.'

She turned to the others. 'One of you was bitten by a dog. I forgot which one. My mother rushed you to the emergency room at Massachusetts General.'

Tyler nodded. 'I had to have shots against rabies.'

Her words were coming out in a torrent now. 'Woody, when you were eight years old, you ran away. You were going to Hollywood to become an actor. Your father was furious with you. He made you go to your room without dinner. Mother sneaked some food up to your room.'

Woody nodded, silent.

'I ... I don't know what else I can tell you. I ...' She suddenly remembered something. 'I have a photograph in my purse.' She opened her purse and took it out. She handed the picture to Kendall.

They all gathered around to look at it. It was a picture of the three of them when they were children, standing next to an attractive young woman in a governess's uniform.

'Mother gave me that.'

Tyler asked, 'Did she leave you anything else?'

She shook her head. 'No. I'm sorry. She didn't want anything around that reminded her of Harry Stanford.'

'Except you, of course,' Woody said.

She turned to him, defiantly. 'I don't care whether you believe me or not. You don't understand . . . I . . . I was so hoping –' She broke off.

Tyler spoke. 'As my sister said, your sudden appearance is rather a shock for us. I mean . . . someone appearing out of nowhere and claiming to be a member of the family . . . you can see our problem. I think we need a little time to discuss this.'

'Of course, I understand.'

'Where are you staying?'

'At the Tremont House.'

'Why don't you go back there? We'll have a car take you. And we'll be in touch shortly.'

She nodded. 'All right.' She looked at each of them for a moment, and then said softly, 'No matter what you think – you're my family.'

'I'll walk you to the door,' Kendall said.

She smiled. 'That's all right. I can find my own way. I feel as if I know every inch of this house.'

They watched her turn and walk out of the room.

Kendall said, 'Well! It . . . it looks as though we have a sister.'

'I don't believe it,' Woody retorted.

'It seems to me . . . ,' Marc began.

They were all talking at once. Tyler raised a hand. 'This isn't getting us anywhere. Let's look at this logically. In a sense, this person is on trial here and we're her jurors. It's up to us to determine her innocence or guilt. In a jury trial, the decision must be unanimous. We must all agree.'

Woody nodded. 'Right.'

Tyler said, 'Then I would like to cast the first vote. I think the lady is a fraud.'

'A fraud? How can she be?' Kendall demanded. 'She couldn't possibly know all those intimate details about us if she weren't real.'

Tyler turned to her. 'Kendall, how many servants worked in this house when we were children?'

Kendall looked at him, puzzled. 'Why?'

'Dozens, right? And some of them would have known everything this young lady told us. Over the years, there have been maids, chauffeurs, butlers, chefs. Any one of them could have given her that photograph as well.'

'You mean . . . she could be in league with someone?'

'One or more,' Tyler said. 'Let's not forget that there's an enormous amount of money involved.'

156

'She says she doesn't want the money.' Marc reminded them.

Woody nodded. 'Sure, that's what she *says*.' He looked at Tyler. 'But how do we prove she's a fake? There's no way that –'

'There *is* a way,' Tyler said thoughtfully.

They all turned to him.

'How?' Marc asked.

'I'll have the answer for you tomorrow.'

Simon Fitzgerald said slowly, 'Are you saying that Julia Stanford has appeared after all these years?'

'A woman who *claims* she's Julia Stanford has appeared.' Tyler corrected him.

'And you don't believe her?' Steve asked.

'Absolutely not. The only so-called proof of her identity that she offered were some incidents from our childhood that at least a dozen former employees could have been aware of and an old photograph that really doesn't prove a thing. She could be in league with any one of them. I intend to prove she's a fraud.'

Steve frowned. 'How do you propose to do that?'

'It's very simple. I want a DNA test done.'

Steve Sloane was surprised. 'That would mean exhuming your father's body.'

'Yes.' Tyler turned to Simon Fitzgerald. 'Will that be a problem?'

'Under the circumstances, I could probably obtain an exhumation order. Has she agreed to this test?'

'I haven't asked her yet. If she refuses, it's an affirm-
ation that she's afraid of the results.' He hesitated. 'I
have to confess that I don't like doing this. But I think
it's the only way we can determine the truth.'

Fitzgerald was thoughtful for a moment. 'Very well.'
He turned to Steve. 'Will you handle this?'

'Of course.' He looked at Tyler. 'You're probably
familiar with the procedure. The next of kin – in this
case, any of the deceased's children – has to apply to
the coroner's office for an exhumation permit. You'll
have to tell them the reason for the request. If it's
approved, the coroner's office will contact the funeral
home and give them permission to go ahead. Someone
from the coroner's office has to be present at the
exhumation.'

'How long will this take?' Tyler asked.

'I'd say three or four days to get an approval. Today
is Wednesday. We should be able to exhume the body
on Monday.'

'Good.' Tyler hesitated. 'We're going to need a
DNA expert, someone who will be convincing in a
courtroom, if it ever goes that far. I was hoping you
might know someone.'

Steve said, 'I know just the man. His name is Perry
Winger. He's here in Boston. He's given expert testimony in trials all over the country. I'll call him.'

'I'd appreciate it. The sooner we get this over with,
the better it will be for all of us.'

*　　*　　*

158

At ten o'clock the following morning, Tyler walked into the Rose Hill library, where Woody, Peggy, Kendall and Marc were waiting. At Tyler's side was a stranger.

'I want you to meet Perry Winger,' Tyler said.

'Who is he?' Woody asked.

'He's our DNA expert.'

Kendall looked at Tyler. 'What in the world do we need a DNA expert for?'

Tyler said, 'To prove that this stranger, who so conveniently appeared out of nowhere, is an impostor. I have no intention of letting her get away with this.'

'You're going to dig the old man up?' Woody asked.

'That's right. I have our attorneys working on the exhumation order now. If the woman is our half sister, the DNA will prove it. If she's not – it will prove that, too.'

Marc said, 'I'm afraid I don't understand about this DNA.'

Perry Winger cleared his throat. 'Simply put, deoxyribonucleic acid – or DNA – is the molecule of heredity. It contains each individual's unique genetic code. It can be extracted from traces of blood, semen, saliva, hair roots, and even bone. Traces of it can last in a corpse for more than fifty years.'

'I see. So it is really quite simple,' Marc said.

Perry Winger frowned. 'Believe me, it is not. There are two types of DNA testing. A PCR test, which takes three days to get results, and the more complex RFLP test, which takes six to eight weeks. For our purposes, the simpler test will be sufficient.'

'How do you do the test?' Kendall asked.

'There are several steps. First, the sample is collected and the DNA is cut into fragments. The fragments are sorted by length by placing them on a bed of gel and applying an electric current. The DNA, which is negatively charged, moves toward the positive and, several hours later, the fragments have arranged themselves by length.' He was just getting warmed up. 'Alkaline chemicals are used to split the DNA fragments apart, then the fragments are transferred to a nylon sheet, which is immersed in a bath, and radioactive probes –'

The eyes of his listeners were beginning to glaze over.

'How accurate is this test?' Woody interrupted.

'It's one hundred percent accurate in determining if the man is *not* the father. If the test is positive, it's ninety-nine point nine percent accurate.'

Woody turned to his brother. 'Tyler, you're a judge. Let's say for the sake of argument that she really is Harry Stanford's child. Her mother and our father were never married. Why should she be entitled to anything?'

'Under the law,' Tyler explained, 'if our father's paternity is established, she would be entitled to an equal share with the rest of us.'

'Then I say let's go ahead with the damned DNA test and expose her!'

*   *   *

Tyler, Woody, Kendall, Marc and Julia were seated at a table in the dining-room restaurant at the Tremont House.

Peggy remained behind at Rose Hill. 'All this talk about digging up a body gives me the creeps,' she said.

Now the group was facing the woman claiming to be Julia Stanford.

'I don't understand what you're asking me to do.'

'It's really very simple,' Tyler informed her. 'A doctor will take a skin sample from you to compare with our father's. If the DNA molecules match, it's positive proof that you're really his daughter. On the other hand, if you're not willing to take the test . . .'

'I . . . I don't like it.'

Woody closed in. 'Why not?'

'I don't know.' She shuddered. 'The idea of digging up my father's body to . . . to . . .'

'To prove who you are.'

She looked into each of their faces. 'I wish all of you would –'

'Yes?'

'There's no way I can convince you, is there?'

'Yes,' Tyler said. 'Agree to take this test.'

There was a long silence.

'All right. I'll do it.'

The exhumation order had been more difficult to obtain than anyone had anticipated. Simon Fitzgerald had spoken to the coroner personally.

'No! For God's sake, Simon! I can't do that! Do you know what a stink that would cause? I mean, we aren't dealing with John Doe here; we're dealing with Harry Stanford. If this ever leaked out, the media would have a field day!'

'Marvin, this is important. Billions of dollars are at stake here. So you make sure it doesn't leak out.'

'Isn't there some other way you can . . . ?'

'I'm afraid not. The woman is very convincing.'

'But the family is not convinced.'

'No.'

'Do you think she's a fraud, Simon?'

'Frankly, I don't know. But my opinion doesn't matter. In fact, none of our opinions matters. A court will demand proof, and the DNA test will provide that.'

The coroner shook his head. 'I knew old Harry Stanford. He would have hated this. I really shouldn't let . . .'

'But you will.'

The coroner sighed. 'I suppose so. Would you do me a favor?'

'Of course.'

'Keep this quiet. Let's not have a media circus.'

'You have my word. Top secret. I'll have just the family there.'

'When do you want to do this?'

'We would like to do it on Monday.'

The coroner sighed again. 'All right. I'll call the funeral home. You owe me one, Simon.'

'I won't forget this.'

At nine o'clock Monday morning, the entrance to the section of Mount Auburn Cemetery where Harry Stanford's body was buried was temporarily closed off 'for maintenance repairs'. No strangers were allowed into the grounds. Woody, Peggy, Tyler, Kendall, Marc, Julia, Simon Fitzgerald, Steve Sloane, and Dr Collins, a representative from the coroner's office, stood at the site of Harry Stanford's grave, watching four employees of the cemetery raise his coffin. Perry Winger waited off to the side.

When the coffin reached ground level, the foreman turned to the group. 'What do you want us to do now?'

'Open it, please,' Fitzgerald said. He turned to Perry Winger. 'How long will this take?'

'No more than a minute. I'll just get a quick skin sample.'

'All right,' Fitzgerald said. He nodded to the foreman. 'Go ahead.'

The foreman and his assistants began to unseal the coffin.

'I don't want to see this,' Kendall said. 'Do we have to?'

'Yes!' Woody told her. 'We really do.'

They all watched, fascinated, as the lid of the coffin

was slowly removed and pushed to one side. They stood there, staring down.

'Oh, my God!' Kendall exclaimed.

The coffin was empty.

Chapter Fourteen

Back at Rose Hill, Tyler had just gotten off the phone. 'Fitzgerald says there won't be any media leaks. The cemetery certainly doesn't want that kind of bad publicity. The coroner has ordered Dr Collins to keep his mouth shut, and Perry Winger can be trusted not to talk.'

Woody wasn't paying any attention. 'I don't know how the bitch did it!' he said. 'But she isn't going to get away with it!' He glared at the others. 'I suppose you don't think she arranged it?'

Tyler said slowly, 'I'm afraid I have to agree with you, Woody. No one else possibly could have had a reason for doing this. The woman is clever and resourceful, and she's obviously not working alone. I'm not sure exactly what we're up against.'

'What are we going to do now?' Kendall asked.

Tyler shrugged. 'Frankly, I don't know. I wish I did. I'm sure she plans to go to court to contest the will.'

'Does she have a chance of winning?' Peggy asked timidly.

'I'm afraid she does. She's very persuasive. She had some of us convinced.'

'There must be *something* we can do,' Marc exclaimed. 'What about bringing the police in on this?'

'Fitzgerald says they're already looking into the disappearance of the body, and they've come to a dead end. No pun intended,' Tyler said. 'What's more, the police want this kept quiet, or they'll have every weirdo in town turning up a body.'

'We can ask them to investigate this phony!'

Tyler shook his head. 'This is not a police matter. It's a private –' He stopped for a moment, then said thoughtfully, 'You know . . .'

'What?'

'We *could* hire a private investigator to try to expose her.'

'That's not a bad idea. Do you know one?'

'No, not locally. But we could ask Fitzgerald to find someone. Or . . .' He hesitated. 'I've never met him, but I've heard about a private detective the district attorney in Chicago uses a great deal. He has an excellent reputation.'

Marc spoke up. 'Why don't we find out if we can hire him?'

Tyler looked around. 'That's up to the rest of you.'

'What can we lose?' Kendall asked.

'He could be expensive,' Tyler warned.

Woody snorted. 'Expensive? We're talking about billions of dollars.'

166

Tyler nodded. 'Of course. You're right.'

'What's his name?'

Tyler frowned. 'I can't remember. Simpson . . . Simmons . . . No, that's not it. It sounds something like that. I can call the district attorney's office in Chicago.'

The group watched as Tyler picked up the telephone on the console and dialed a number. Two minutes later, he was speaking to an assistant district attorney. 'This is Judge Tyler Stanford. I understand that your office retains a private detective from time to time who does excellent work for you. His name is something like Simmons or –'

The voice on the other end said, 'Oh, you must mean Frank Timmons.'

'Timmons! Yes, that's it.' Tyler looked at the others and smiled. 'I wonder if you could give me his telephone number so I can contact him directly?'

After he wrote down the telephone number, Tyler replaced the receiver.

He turned to the group, and said, 'Well, then, if we all agree, I'll try to reach him.'

Everyone nodded.

The following afternoon, Clark came into the drawing room, where the group was waiting. 'Mr Timmons is here.'

He was a man in his forties, with a pale complexion and the solid build of a boxer. He had a broken nose and bright, inquisitive eyes. He looked from Tyler to

Marc and Woody, questioningly. 'Judge Stanford?'

Tyler nodded. 'I'm Judge Stanford.'

'Frank Timmons,' he said.

'Please have a seat, Mr Timmons.'

'Thank you.' He sat down. 'You're the one who telephoned, right?'

'Yes.'

'To be honest, I don't know what I can do for you. I don't have any official connections here.'

'This is purely unofficial,' Tyler assured him. 'We merely want to trace the background of a young woman.'

'You told me on the phone she claims to be your half sister, and there's no way of running a DNA test.'

'That's right,' Woody said.

He looked at the group. 'And you don't believe she's your half sister?'

There was a moment's hesitation.

'We don't,' Tyler told him. 'On the other hand, it's just possible that she is telling the truth. What we want to hire you to do is provide irrefutable evidence that she is either genuine or a fraud.'

'Fair enough. It will cost you a thousand dollars a day and expenses.'

Tyler said, 'A *thousand* . . . ?'

'We'll pay it.' Woody cut in.

'I'll need all the information you have on this woman.'

Kendall said, 'There doesn't seem to be very much.'

Tyler spoke up. 'She has no proof of any kind. She came in with a lot of stories that she says her mother told her about our childhood, and –'

He held up a hand. 'Hold it. Who was her mother?'

'Her *purported* mother was a governess we had as children named Rosemary Nelson.'

'What happened to her?'

They looked at one another uncomfortably.

Woody spoke up. 'She had an affair with our father and got pregnant. She ran away and had a baby girl.' He shrugged. 'She disappeared.'

'I see. And this woman claims to be her child?'

'That's right.'

'That's not a lot to go on.' He sat there, thinking. Finally he looked up. 'All right. I'll see what I can do.'

'That's all we ask,' Tyler said.

The first move he made was to go to the Boston Public Library and read all the micro-*fiche* about the twenty-six-year-old scandal involving Harry Stanford, the governess, and Mrs Stanford's suicide. There was enough material for a novel.

His next step was to visit Simon Fitzgerald.

'My name is Frank Timmons. I'm –'

'I know who you are, Mr Timmons. Judge Stanford asked me to cooperate with you. What can I do for you?'

'I want to trace Harry Stanford's illegitimate daughter. She'd be about twenty-eight, right?'

'Yes. She was born August ninth, 1969, at St Joseph's Hospital in Milwaukee, Wisconsin. Her mother named her Julia.' He shrugged. 'They disappeared. I'm afraid that's all the information we have.'

'It's a beginning,' he said. 'It's a beginning.'

Mrs Dougherty, the superintendent at St Joseph's Hospital in Milwaukee, was a gray-haired woman in her sixties.

'Yes, of course, I remember,' she said. 'How could I ever forget it? There was a terrible scandal. There were stories in all the newspapers. The reporters here found out who she was, and they wouldn't leave the poor girl alone.'

'Where did she go when she and the baby left here?'

'I don't know. She left no forwarding address.'

'Did she pay her bill in full before she left, Mrs Dougherty?'

'As a matter of fact . . . she didn't.'

'How do you happen to remember that?'

'Because it was so sad. I remember she sat in that very chair you're sitting in, and she told me that she could pay only part of her bill, but she promised to send me the money for the rest of it. Well, that was against hospital rules, of course, but I felt so sorry for her, she was so ill when she left here, and I said yes.'

'And did she send you the rest of the money?'

'She certainly did. About two months later. Now

I recall she had gotten a job at some secretarial service.'

'You wouldn't happen to remember where that was, would you?'

'No. Goodness, that was about twenty-five years ago, Mr Timmons.'

'Mrs Dougherty, do you keep all your patients' records on file?'

'Of course.' She looked up at him. 'Do you want me to go through the records?'

He smiled pleasantly. 'If you wouldn't mind.'

'Will it help Rosemary?'

'It could mean a great deal to her.'

'If you'll excuse me.' Mrs Dougherty left the office.

She returned fifteen minutes later, holding a paper in her hand. 'Here it is. Rosemary Nelson. The return address is, The Elite Typing Service. Omaha, Nebraska.'

The Elite Typing Service was run by a Mr Otto Broderick, a man in his sixties.

'We hire so many temporary employees,' he protested. 'How do you expect me to remember someone who worked here that long ago?'

'This was a rather special case. She was a single woman in her late twenties, in poor health. She had just had a baby and –'

'Rosemary!'

'That's right. Why do you remember her?'

'Well, I like to associate things, Mr Timmons. Do you know what mnemonics is?'

'Yes.'

'Well, that's what I use. I associate words. There was a movie out called *Rosemary's Baby*. So when Rosemary came in and told me she had a baby, I put the two things together and . . .'

'How long was Rosemary Nelson with you?'

'Oh, about a year, I guess. Then the press found out who she was, somehow, and they wouldn't leave her alone. She left town in the middle of the night to get away from them.'

'Mr Broderick, do you have any idea where Rosemary Nelson went when she left here?'

'Florida, I think. She wanted a warmer climate. I recommended her to an agency I knew there.'

'May I have the name of that agency?'

'Certainly. It's the Gale Agency. I can remember it because I associated it with the big storms they have down in Florida every year.'

Ten days after his meeting with the Stanford family, he returned to Boston. He had telephoned ahead, and the family was waiting for him. They were seated in a semi-circle, facing him as he entered the drawing room at Rose Hill.

'You said you had some news for us, Mr Timmons,' Tyler said.

'That's right.' He opened a briefcase and pulled out

172

some papers. 'This has been a most interesting case,' he said. 'When I began –'

'Cut to the chase,' Woody said impatiently. 'Is she a fraud or not?'

He looked up. 'If you don't mind, Mr Stanford, I would like to present this in my own way.'

Tyler gave Woody a warning look. 'That's fair enough. Please go ahead.'

They watched him consult his notes. 'The Stanford governess, Rosemary Nelson, had a female child sired by Harry Stanford. She and the child went to Omaha, Nebraska, where she went to work for The Elite Typing Service. Her employer told me that she had difficulty with the weather.

'Next, I traced her and her daughter to Florida, where she worked for the Gale Agency. They moved around a great deal. I followed the trail to San Francisco, where they were living up to ten years ago. That was the end of the trail. After that, they disappeared.' He looked up.

'That's *it*, Timmons?' Woody demanded. 'You lost the trail ten years ago?'

'No, that is *not* it.' He reached into his briefcase and took out another paper. 'The daughter, Julia, applied for a driver's license when she was seventeen.'

'What good is that?' Marc asked.

'In the state of California drivers are required to have their fingerprints taken.' He held up a card. 'These are the real Julia Stanford's fingerprints.'

173

Tyler said, excitedly, 'I see! If they match –'

'Then she would really be our sister.' Woody interrupted.

He nodded. 'That's right. I brought a portable fingerprint kit with me, in case you want to check her out now. Is she here?'

Tyler said, 'She's at a local hotel. I've been talking to her every morning, trying to persuade her to stay here until we get this resolved.'

'We've got her!' Woody said. 'Let's get over there!'

Half an hour later, the group was entering a hotel room at the Tremont House. As they walked in, she was packing a suitcase.

'Where are you going?' Kendall asked.

She turned to face them. 'Home. It was a mistake for me to come here in the first place.'

Tyler said, 'You can't blame us for . . . ?'

She turned on him, furious. 'Ever since I arrived, I've been met with nothing but suspicion. You think I came here to take some money away from you. Well, I didn't. I came because I wanted to find my family. I . . . never mind.' She returned to her packing.

Tyler said, 'This is Frank Timmons. He's a private detective.'

She looked up. 'Now what? Am I being arrested?'

'No, ma'am. Julia Stanford obtained a driver's license in San Francisco when she was seventeen years old.'

174

She stopped. 'That's right. Is that against the law?'

'No, ma'am. The point is –'

'The point is' – Tyler interrupted – 'that Julia Stanford's fingerprints are on that license.'

She looked at them. 'I don't understand. What . . . ?'

Woody spoke up. 'We want to check them against your fingerprints.'

Her lips tightened. 'No! I won't allow it!'

'Are you saying that you won't let us take your fingerprints?'

'That's right.'

'Why not?' Marc asked.

Her body was rigid. 'Because all of you make me feel like I'm some kind of criminal. Well, I've had enough! I want you to leave me alone.'

Kendall said gently, 'This is your chance to prove who you really are. We've been as upset by all this as you have. We would like to settle it.'

She stood there, looking into their faces, one by one. Finally she said wearily, 'All right. Let's get this over with.'

'Good.'

'Mr Timmons . . . ,' Tyler said.

'Right.' He took out a small fingerprint kit and set it up on the table. He opened the ink pad. 'Now, if you'll just step over here, please.'

The others watched as she walked over to the table. He picked up her hand and, one by one, pressed her fingertips onto the pad. Next, he pressed them onto a piece of white paper. 'There. That wasn't so bad, was it?' He placed the driver's license next to the fresh fingerprints.

The group walked over to the table and looked down at the two sets of prints.

They were identical.

Woody was the first to speak.

'They're . . . the . . . same.'

Kendall was looking at her with a mixture of feelings. 'You really are our sister, aren't you?'

She was smiling through her tears. 'That's what I've been trying to tell you.'

Everybody was suddenly talking at once.

'It's incredible . . . !'

'After all these years . . .'

'Why didn't your mother ever come back . . . ?'

'I'm sorry we gave you such a bad time.'

Her smile lit up the room. 'It's all right. Everything's all right now.'

Woody picked up the fingerprint card and looked at it in awe. 'My God! This is a billion-dollar card.' He put the card in his pocket. 'I'm going to have it bronzed.'

Tyler turned to the group. 'This calls for a real celebration! I suggest we all go back to Rose Hill.' He turned to her and smiled. 'We'll give you a welcome home party. Let's get you checked out of here.'

She looked around at them, and her eyes were

shining. 'It's like a dream come true. I finally have a family!'

Half an hour later they were back at Rose Hill, and she was settling into her new room. The others were downstairs, talking excitedly.

'She must feel as though she's just been through the Inquisition,' Tyler mused.

'She has,' Peggy replied. 'I don't know how she stood it.'

Kendall said, 'I wonder how she's going to adjust to her new life.'

'The same way we're all going to adjust,' Woody said dryly. 'With a lot of champagne and caviar.'

Tyler rose. 'I, for one, am glad it's finally settled. Let me go up and see if she needs any help.'

He went upstairs and walked along the corridor to her room. He knocked at her door and called loudly, 'Julia?'

'It's open. Come in.'

He stood in the doorway, and they stared silently at each other. And then Tyler carefully closed the door, held out his hands, and broke into a slow grin.

When he spoke, he said, 'We did it, Margo! We did it!'

NIGHT

Chapter Fifteen

He had plotted it with the ineffable skill of a chess master. Only this had been the most lucrative chess game in history, with stakes of billions of dollars – and he had won! He was filled with a sense of invincible power. *Is this how you felt when you closed a big deal, Father? Well, this is a bigger deal than you ever made. I've planned the crime of the century, and I've gotten away with it.*

In a sense, it had all started with Lee. *Beautiful, wonderful Lee.* The person he loved most in the world. They had met in the Berlin, the gay bar on West Belmont Avenue. Lee was tall and muscular and blond, and he was the most beautiful man Tyler had ever seen.

Their meeting had started with, 'May I buy you a drink?'

Lee had looked him over and nodded. 'That would be nice.'

After the second drink, Tyler had said, 'Why don't we have a drink over at my place?'

Lee had smiled. 'I'm expensive.'

'How expensive?'

'Five hundred dollars for the night.'

Tyler had not hesitated. 'Let's go.'

They spent the night at Tyler's home.

Lee was warm and sensitive and caring, and Tyler felt a closeness to him that he had never had with any other human being. He was flooded with emotions he had not known existed. By morning, Tyler was madly in love.

In the past, he had picked up young men at the Cairo and the Bijou Theater and several other gay hangouts in Chicago, but now he knew that all that was going to change. From now on, he wanted only Lee.

In the morning, while Tyler was preparing breakfast, he said, 'What would you like to do tonight?'

Lee looked at him in surprise. 'Sorry. I have a date tonight.'

Tyler felt as though he had been hit in the stomach.

'But, Lee, I thought that you and I . . .'

'Tyler, dear, I'm a very valuable piece of merchandise. I go to the highest bidder. I like you, but I'm afraid you really can't afford me.'

'I can give you anything you want,' Tyler said.

Lee smiled lazily. 'Really? Well, what I want is a trip to St Tropez on a beautiful white yacht. Can you afford that?'

'Lee, I'm richer than all your friends put together.'

'Oh? I thought you said you are a judge.'

'Well, I am, yes, but I'm *going* to be rich. I mean . . . very rich.'

Lee put his arm around him. 'Don't fret, Tyler. I'm free a week from Thursday. Those eggs look delicious.'

That was the beginning. Money had been important to Tyler before, but now it became an obsession. He needed it for Lee. He could not get him out of his mind. The thought of him making love with other men was unbearable. *I've got to have him for my own.*

From the age of twelve, Tyler had known that he was homosexual. One day, his father had caught him fondling and kissing a boy from his school, and Tyler had borne the full brunt of his father's fury. 'I can't believe I have a son who's a faggot! Now that I know your dirty little secret, I'm going to keep a close eye on you, sister.'

Tyler's marriage was a cosmic joke, perpetrated by a god with a macabre sense of humor.

'There's someone I want you to meet,' Harry Stanford said.

It was Christmas and Tyler was at Rose Hill for the holidays. Kendall and Woody had already made their departures and Tyler was planning his when the bombshell dropped.

'You're going to get married.'

'Married? That's out of the question! I don't . . .'

'Listen to me, sister. People are beginning to talk about you, and I can't have that. It's bad for my reputation. If you get married, that will shut them up.'

Tyler was defiant. 'I don't care what people say. This is my life.'

'And I want it to be a rich life for you, Tyler. I'm getting older. Pretty soon . . .' He shrugged.

The carrot and the stick.

Naomi Schuyler was a plain-looking woman, from a middle-class family, whose flaming desire in life was to 'better' herself. She was so impressed by Harry Stanford's name that she would probably have married his son if he were pumping gas instead of being a judge.

Harry Stanford had taken Naomi to bed once. When someone asked him why, Stanford replied, 'Because she was there.'

She quickly bored him, and he decided she would be perfect for Tyler.

What Harry Stanford wanted, Harry Stanford got.

The wedding took place two months later. It was a small wedding – one hundred and fifty people – and the bride and groom went to Jamaica for their honeymoon. It was a fiasco.

On their wedding night Naomi said, 'What kind of man have I married, for God's sake? What have you got a dick for?'

Tyler tried to reason with her. 'We don't need sex. We can live separate lives. We'll stay together, but we'll each have our own . . . friends.'

'You're damned right, we will!'

Naomi took out her vengeance on him by becoming a black-belt shopper. She bought everything at the most expensive stores in the city, and took shopping trips to New York.

'I can't afford your extravagances on my income,' Tyler protested.

'Then get a raise. I'm your wife. I'm entitled to be supported.'

Tyler went to his father and explained the situation.

Harry Stanford grinned. 'Women can be damned expensive, can't they? You'll just have to handle it.'

'But, Father, I need some –'

'Someday you'll have all the money in the world.'

Tyler tried to explain it to Naomi, but she had no intentions of waiting until 'someday'. She sensed that that 'someday' might never come. When Naomi had squeezed what she could out of Tyler, she sued for divorce, settled for what was left of his bank account, and disappeared.

When Harry Stanford heard the news, he said, 'Once a faggot, always a faggot.'

And that was the end of that.

His father went out of his way to demean Tyler. One day, when Tyler was on the bench, in the middle of a trial, his bailiff came up to him and whispered, 'Excuse me, Your Honor . . .'

Tyler had turned to him, impatiently. 'Yes?'

'There's a telephone call for you.'

'*What?* What's the matter with you? I'm in the middle of –'

'It's your father, Your Honor. He says it's very urgent and he must talk to you immediately.'

Tyler was furious. His father had no right to interrupt him. He was tempted to ignore the call. But on the other hand, if it was that urgent . . .

Tyler stood up. 'Court is recessed for fifteen minutes.'

Tyler hurried into his chambers and picked up the telephone. 'Father?'

'I hope I'm not disturbing you, Tyler.' There was malice in his voice.

'As a matter of fact, you are. I'm in the middle of a trial and –'

'Well, give him a traffic ticket and forget it.'

'Father . . .'

'I need your help with a serious problem.'

'What kind of problem?'

'My chef is stealing from me.'

Tyler could not believe what he was hearing. He was so angry he could hardly speak. 'You called me off the bench because . . . ?'

'You're the law, aren't you? Well, he's breaking the law. I want you to come back to Boston and check out my whole staff. They're robbing me blind!'

It was all Tyler could do to keep from exploding. 'Father . . .'

'You just can't trust those damn employment agencies.'

'I'm in the middle of a trial. I can't possibly go to Boston now.'

There was a moment of ominous silence. 'What did you say?'

'I said . . .'

'You aren't going to disappoint me again, are you, Tyler? Maybe I should talk to Fitzgerald about some changes in my will.'

And there was the carrot again. The money. His share of the billions of dollars waiting for him when his father died.

Tyler cleared his throat. 'If you could send your plane for me . . .'

'Hell, no! If you play your cards right, judge, that plane will belong to you one day. Just think about that. Meanwhile, fly commercial like everyone else. But I want you to get your ass back here!' The line went dead.

Tyler sat there, filled with humiliation. *My father has done this to me all my life. To hell with him! I won't go. I won't go.*

Tyler flew to Boston that evening.

* * *

Harry Stanford employed a staff of twenty-two. There was a phalanx of secretaries, butlers, housekeepers, maids, chefs, chauffeurs, gardeners, and a bodyguard.

'Thieves, every damned one of them,' Harry Stanford complained to Tyler.

'If you're so worried, why don't you hire a private detective or go to the police?'

'Because I have you,' Harry Stanford said. 'You're a judge, right? Well, you judge them for me.'

It was pure malevolence.

Tyler looked around the huge house with its exquisite furniture and paintings, and he thought of the dreary little house he lived in. *This is what I deserve to have,* he thought. *And one day, I'll have it.*

Tyler talked to the butler, Clark, and other senior members of the staff. He interviewed the servants, one by one, and checked their résumés. Most of the employees were fairly new because Harry Stanford was an impossible man to work for. The staff turnover at the house was extraordinary. Some of them lasted only a day or two. A few new employees were guilty of petty pilfering, and one was an alcoholic, but other than that, Tyler could see no problem.

Except for Dmitri Kaminsky.

Dmitri Kaminsky had been hired by his father as a bodyguard and masseur. Sitting on the bench had made Tyler a good judge of character, and there was something about Dmitri that Tyler instantly mistrusted. He was the most recent employee. Harry Stanford's former bodyguard had quit – Tyler could imagine why – and he had recommended Kaminsky.

The man was huge, with a barrel chest and large, muscular arms. He spoke English with a thick Russian accent. 'You want to see me?'

'Yes.' Tyler gestured to a chair. 'Sit down.' He had looked at the man's employment record, and it had told him very little, except that Dmitri had come from Russia recently. 'You were born in Russia?'

'Yes.' He was watching Tyler warily.

'What part?'

'Smolensk.'

'Why did you leave Russia to come to America?'

Kaminsky shrugged. 'There is more opportunity here.'

Opportunity for what? Tyler wondered. There was something evasive about the man's manner. They spoke for twenty minutes, and at the end of that time Tyler was convinced that Dmitri Kaminsky was concealing something.

Tyler telephoned Fred Masterson, an acquaintance of his with the FBI.

'Fred, I want you to do me a favor.'

'Sure. If I'm ever in Chicago, will you fix my traffic tickets?'

'I'm serious.'

'Shoot.'

'I want you to check on a Russian who came over here six months ago.'

'Wait a minute. You're talking CIA, aren't you?'

'Maybe, but I don't know anyone at CIA.'

'Neither do I.'

'Fred, if you could do this for me, I would really be grateful.'

Tyler heard a sigh.

'Okay. What's his name?'

'Dmitri Kaminsky.'

'I'll tell you what I'll do. I know someone at the Russian Embassy in DC. I'll see if he has any information on Kaminsky. If not, I'm afraid I can't help you.'

'I'd appreciate it.'

That evening, Tyler had dinner with his father. Subconsciously, Tyler had hoped that his father would have aged, would have become more fragile, more vulnerable with time. Instead, Harry Stanford looked hale and hearty, in his prime. *He's going to live forever*. Tyler thought despairingly. *He'll outlive all of us*.

The conversation at dinner was completely one-sided.

'I just closed a deal to buy the power company in Hawaii . . .

'I'm flying over to Amsterdam next week to straighten out some GATT complication . . .

'The secretary of state has invited me to accompany him to China . . .'

Tyler scarcely got in a word. At the end of the meal, his father rose. 'How are you coming along with the servant problem?'

'I'm still checking them out, Father.'

'Well, don't take forever,' his father growled, and walked out of the room.

The following morning, Tyler received a call from Fred Masterson at the FBI.

'Tyler?'

'Yes.'

'You picked a real beauty.'

'Oh?'

'Dmitri Kaminsky was a hit man for *polgoprudnenskaya*.'

'What the hell is that?'

'I'll explain. There are eight criminal groups that have taken over in Moscow. They all fight among themselves, but the two most powerful groups are the *chechens* and the *polgoprudnenskaya*. Your friend Kaminsky worked for the second group. Three months ago, they handed him a contract on one of the leaders of the *chechens*. Instead of carrying out the contract, Kaminsky went to him to make a better deal. The *polgoprudnenskaya* found out about it and put out a contract on Kaminsky. Gangs have a quaint custom over there. First they chop off your fingers, then they let you bleed for a while, and then they shoot you.'

'My God!'

'Kaminsky got himself smuggled out of Russia, but they're still looking for him. And looking hard.'

'That's incredible,' Tyler said.

'That's not all. He's also wanted by the state police for a few murders. If you know where he is, they'd love to have that information.'

Tyler was thoughtful for a moment. He could not afford to get involved in this. *It could mean giving testimony and wasting a lot of time.*

'I have no idea. I was just checking him out for a Russian friend. Thanks, Fred.'

Tyler found Dmitri Kaminsky in his room, reading a hardcore porno magazine. Dmitri rose as Tyler walked into the room.

'I want you to pack your things and get out of here.'

Dmitri stared at him. 'What's the matter?'

'I'm giving you a choice. You're either out of here by this afternoon, or I'll tell the Russian police where you are.'

Dmitri's face turned pale.

'Do you understand?'

'*Da.* I understand.'

Tyler went to see his father. *He's going to be pleased,* he thought. *I've done him a real favor.* He found him in the study.

'I checked on all the staff,' Tyler said, 'and . . .'

'I'm impressed. Did you find any little boys to take to bed with you?'

Tyler's face turned red. 'Father . . .'

'You're a queer, Tyler, and you'll always be a queer. I don't know how the hell anything like you came from my loins. Go on back to Chicago with your gutter friends.'

Tyler stood there, fighting to control himself. 'Right,' he said stiffly. He started to leave.

'Is there anything about the staff you found out that I should know?'

Tyler turned and studied his father a moment. 'No,' he said slowly. 'Nothing.'

When Tyler went to Kaminsky's room, he was packing.

'I'm going,' Kaminsky said sullenly.

'Don't. I've changed my mind.'

Dmitri looked up, puzzled. 'What?'

'I don't want you to leave. I want you to stay on as my father's bodyguard.'

'What about . . . you know, the other thing?'

'We're going to forget about that.'

Dmitri was watching him, warily. 'Why? What do you want me to do?'

'I'd like you to be my eyes and ears here. I need someone to keep an eye on my father, and let me know what goes on.'

'Why should I?'

'Because if you do as I say, I'm not going to turn you over to the Russians. And because I'm going to make you a rich man.'

Dmitri Kaminsky studied him a moment. A slow grin lit his face. 'I'll stay.'

It was the opening gambit. The first pawn had been moved.

That had been two years earlier. From time to time, Dmitri had passed on information to Tyler. It was mostly unimportant gossip about Harry Stanford's latest romance or bits of business that Dmitri had overheard. Tyler had begun to think he had made a mistake, that he should have turned Dmitri in to the police. And then the fateful telephone call had come from Sardinia, and the gamble had paid off.

'I'm with your father on his yacht. He just called his attorney. He's meeting him in Boston Monday to change his will.'

Tyler thought of all the humiliations his father had heaped on him through the years, and he was filled with a terrible rage. *If he changes his will, I've taken all those years of abuse for nothing. I'm not going to let him get away with this! There is only one way to stop him.*

'Dmitri, I want you to call me again on Saturday.'

'Right.'

Tyler replaced the receiver and sat there, thinking. It was time to bring in the knight.

Chapter Sixteen

In the Circuit Court of Cook County, there was a constant ebb and flow of defendants accused of arson, rape, drug dealing, murder, and a variety of other illegal and unsavory activities. In the course of a month, Judge Tyler Stanford dealt with at least half a dozen murder cases. The majority never went to trial since the attorneys for the defendant would offer to plea bargain, and because the court calendars and prisons were so overcrowded, the State would usually agree. The two sides would then strike a deal and go to Judge Stanford for his approval.

The case of Hal Baker was an exception.

Hal Baker was a man with good intentions and bad luck. When he was fifteen, his older brother had talked him into helping him rob a grocery store. Hal had tried to dissuade him, and when he couldn't, he went along with him. Hal was caught, and his brother escaped. Two years later, when Hal Baker got out of reform school, he was determined never to get in trouble with the law again. One month later, he accompanied a friend to a jewelry store.

'I want to pick out a ring for my girlfriend.'

Once inside the store, his friend pulled out a gun and yelled, 'This is a holdup!'

In the ensuing excitement, a clerk was shot to death. Hal Baker was caught and arrested for armed robbery. His friend escaped.

While Baker was in prison, Helen Gowan, a social worker who had read about his case and felt sorry for him, went to visit him. It was love at first sight, and when Baker was released from prison, he and Helen were married. Over the next eight years, they had four lovely children.

Hal Baker adored his family. Because of his prison record, he had a difficult time finding jobs, and to support his family he reluctantly went to work for his brother, carrying out various acts of arson, robbery and assault. Unfortunately for Baker, he was caught flagrante delicto in the commission of a burglary. He was arrested, held in jail, and tried in Judge Tyler Stanford's court.

It was time for sentencing. Baker was a second offender with a bad juvenile record, and it was such a clear-cut case that the assistant district attorneys were making bets on how many years Judge Stanford would give Baker. 'He'll throw the book at him!' one of them said. 'I'll bet he gives him twenty years. Stanford's not called the Hanging Judge for nothing.'

Hal Baker, who felt deep in his heart that he was innocent, was acting as his own attorney. He stood before the bench, dressed in his best suit, and said, 'Your Honor, I know I made a mistake, but we're all human, aren't we? I have a wonderful wife and four children. I wish you could meet them, Your Honor – they're great. What I did, I did for them.'

Tyler Stanford sat on the bench, listening, his face impassive. He was waiting for Hal Baker to finish so he could pass sentence. *Does this fool really think he's going to get off with that stupid sob story?*

Hal Baker was finishing, '. . . and so you see, Your Honor, even though I did the wrong thing, I did it for the right reason: family. I don't have to tell you how important that is. If I go to prison, my wife and children will starve. I know I made a mistake, but I'm willing to make up for it. I'll do anything you want me to do, Your Honor . . .'

And that was the phrase that caught Tyler Stanford's attention. He looked at the defendant before him with a new interest. *'Anything you want me to do.'* Tyler suddenly had the same instinct he had had about Dmitri Kaminsky. Here was a man who might be very useful one day.

To the prosecutor's utter astonishment, Tyler said, 'Mr Baker, there are extenuating circumstances in this case. Because of them and because of your family, I

197

am going to put you on probation for five years. I will expect you to perform six hundred hours of public service. Come into my chambers, and we will discuss it.'

In the privacy of his chambers, Tyler said, 'You know, I could still send you to prison for a long, long time.'

Hal Baker turned pale. 'But, Your Honor! You said . . .'

Tyler leaned forward. 'Do you know the most impressive thing about you?'

Hal Baker sat there, trying to think what was impressive about himself. 'No, Your Honor.'

'Your feelings about your family,' Tyler said piously. 'I really admire that.'

Hal Baker brightened. 'Thank you, sir. They're the most important thing in the world to me. I –'

'Then you wouldn't want to lose them, would you? If I sent you to prison, your children would grow up without you; your wife would probably find another man. Do you see what I'm getting at?'

Hal Baker was baffled. 'N . . . no, Your Honor. Not exactly.'

'I'm saving your family for you, Baker. I would think you'd be grateful.'

Hal Baker said fervently, 'Oh, I *am*, Your Honor! I can't tell you how grateful I am.'

'Perhaps you can prove it to me in the future. I may be calling on you to do some little errands for me.'

'*Anything!*'

'Good. I'm placing you on probation, and if I should find anything in your behavior that displeases me . . .'

'You just tell me what you want,' Baker begged.

'I'll let you know when the time comes. Meanwhile, this will be strictly confidential between the two of us.'

Hal Baker put his hand over his heart. 'I would die before I'd tell anyone.'

'You're right,' Tyler assured him.

It was a short time after that when Tyler received the phone call from Dmitri Kaminsky. '*Your father just called his attorney. He's meeting him in Boston on Monday to change his will.*'

Tyler knew that he had to see that will. It was time to call Hal Baker.

'. . . the name of the firm is Renquist, Renquist, & Fitzgerald. Make a copy of the will and bring it to me.'

'No problem. I'll take care of it, Your Honor.'

Twelve hours later, Tyler had a copy of the will in his hands. He read it and was filled with a sense of elation. He and Woody and Kendall were the sole heirs. *And on Monday Father is planning to change the will. The bastard is going to take it away from us!* Tyler thought bitterly. *After all we've gone through . . . those billions belong to us. He's made us earn them!* There was only one way to stop him.

*   *   *

When Dmitri's second telephone call came, Tyler said, 'I want you to kill him. Tonight.'

There was a long silence. 'But if I'm caught . . .'

'Don't get caught. You'll be at sea. A lot of things can happen there.'

'All right. When it's over . . . ?'

'The money and a plane ticket to Australia will be waiting for you.'

And then later, the last wonderful phone call.

'I did it. It was easy.'

'No! No! No! I want to hear the details. Tell me everything. Don't leave anything out . . .'

And as Tyler listened, he could visualize the scene unfolding before his eyes.

'We were in a bad storm on our way to Corsica. He called and asked me to come to his cabin and give him a massage . . .'

Tyler found himself gripping the phone. 'Yes. Go on . . .'

Dmitri had fought to keep his balance against the wild pitching of the yacht as he headed for Harry Stanford's stateroom. He knocked at the cabin door and, after a moment, he heard Stanford's voice.

'Come in!' Stanford yelled. He was stretched out on the massage table. 'It's my lower back.'

'I'll take care of it. Just relax, Mr Stanford.'

Dmitri went over to the massage table and spread oil on Stanford's back. His strong fingers went to work, skillfully kneading the tight muscles. He could feel Stanford begin to relax.

'That feels good.' Stanford sighed.

'Thank you.'

The massage lasted an hour, and when Dmitri was through, Stanford was almost asleep.

'I'm going to run a warm bath for you,' Dmitri said. He went into the bathroom, stumbling with the motion of the ship. He turned on the warm seawater tap in the black onyx tub and returned to the bedroom. Stanford was still lying on the table, his eyes closed.

'Mr Stanford . . .'

Stanford opened his eyes.

'Your bath is ready.'

'I don't think I need . . .'

'It will really make sure you get a good night's sleep.' He helped Stanford off the table and steered him toward the bathroom.

Dmitri watched Harry Stanford lower himself into the tub.

Stanford looked up into Dmitri's cold eyes, and in that instant, his instinct told him what was about to happen. 'No!' he cried. He started to get up.

Dmitri put his huge hands on top of Harry Stanford's head and pushed him under the water. Stanford struggled violently, trying to come up for air, but he was no match for the giant. Dmitri held him under while the seawater got into his victim's lungs, and finally all movement stopped. He stood there, breathing hard, then staggered into the other room.

Dmitri went over to the desk, fighting the rolling motion of the ship, picked up some papers and slid open the glass door to the outside veranda, letting in the howling wind. He scattered some of the papers on the veranda and threw some overboard.

Satisfied, he returned to the bathroom once more and pulled Stanford's body out of the tub. He dressed him in his pajamas, robe and slippers, and carried the body out onto the veranda. Dmitri stood at the railing a moment, then heaved the body overboard. He counted to five seconds, then picked up the telephone and shouted, 'Man overboard!'

Listening to Dmitri recount the story of the murder, Tyler felt a sexual thrill. He could taste the seawater filling his father's lungs and feel the gasping for breath, the terror. And then nothingness.

It's over, Tyler thought. Then he corrected himself. *No. The game is just beginning. It's time to play the queen.*

Chapter Seventeen

The last chess piece fell into place by accident.

Tyler had been thinking about his father's will, and he felt outraged that Woody and Kendall were getting an equal share of the estate with him. *They don't deserve it. If it had not been for me, they both would have been cut out of the will completely. They would have had nothing. It's not fair, but what can I do about it?*

He had the one share of stock that his mother had given him long ago, and he remembered his father's words: *'What do you think he's going to do with that share? Take over the company?'*

Together, Tyler thought, *Woody and Kendall have two-thirds of Father's Stanford Enterprises stock. How can I get control with only my one extra share?* And then the answer came to him, and it was so ingenious that it stunned him.

'I should inform you that there is a possibility of another heir being involved ... Your father's will specifically provides that the estate is to be divided equally among

his issue. Your father sired a child by a governess who worked here . . .'

If Julia showed up, there would be four of us, Tyler thought. *And if I could control her share, I would then have fifty percent of Father's stock plus the one percent I already own. I could take over Stanford Enterprises. I could sit in my father's chair.* His next thought was, *Rosemary is dead, and she probably never told her daughter who her father was. Why does it have to be the real Julia Stanford?*

The answer was Margo Posner.

He had first encountered her two months earlier, as court was called into session. The bailiff had turned to the spectators in the courtroom. 'Oyez, oyez. The Circuit Court of Cook County is now in session, the Honorable Judge Tyler Stanford presiding. All rise.'

Tyler walked in from his chambers and sat down at the bench. He looked down at the docket. The first case was *State of Illinois* v. *Margo Posner*. The charges were assault and attempted murder.

The prosecuting attorney rose. 'Your Honor, the defendant is a dangerous person who should be kept off the streets of Chicago. The State will prove that the defendant has a long criminal history. She has been convicted of shoplifting, larceny, and is a known prostitute. She was one of a stable of women working for a notorious pimp named Rafael. In January of this year, they got into an altercation and the defendant willfully and cold-bloodedly shot him and his companion.'

'Did either victim die?' Tyler asked.

'No, Your Honor. They were hospitalized with serious injuries. The gun in Margo Posner's possession was an illegal weapon.'

Tyler turned to look at the defendant, and he felt a sense of surprise. She did not fit the image of what he had just heard about her. She was a well-dressed, attractive young woman in her late twenties, and there was a quiet elegance about her that completely belied the charges against her. *That just goes to prove,* Tyler thought wryly, *you never know*.

He listened to the arguments from both sides, but his eyes were drawn to the defendant. There was something about her that reminded him of his sister.

When the summations were finished the case went to the jury, and in less than four hours they returned with a verdict of guilty on all counts.

Tyler looked down at the defendant and said, 'The court cannot find any extenuating circumstances in this case. You are herewith sentenced to five years at Dwight Correctional Center. Next case.'

And it was not until Margo Posner was being led away that Tyler realized what it was about her that reminded him so much of Kendall. She had the same dark gray eyes. The Stanford eyes.

*　　*　　*

Tyler did not think about Margo Posner again until the telephone call from Dmitri.

The beginning chess game had been successfully completed. Tyler had planned each move carefully in his mind. He'd used the classical queen's gambit: Decline opening, moving the queen pawn two squares. It was time to move into the middle game.

Tyler went to visit Margo Posner at the women's prison.

'Do you remember me?' Tyler asked.

She stared at him. 'How could I forget you? You're the one who sent me to this place.'

'How are you getting along?' Tyler asked.

She grimaced. 'You must be kidding! It's a hellhole here.'

'How would you like to get out?'

'How would I . . . ? Are you serious?'

'I'm very serious. I can arrange it.'

'Well, that . . . that's great! Thanks. But what do I have to do for it?'

'Well, there *is* something I want you to do for me.'

She looked at him, flirtatiously. 'Sure. That's no problem.'

'That's not what I had in mind.'

She said, warily, 'What *did* you have in mind, judge?'

'I want you to help me play a little joke on someone.'

'What kind of joke?'

'I want you to impersonate someone.'

'Impersonate someone? I wouldn't know how to –'

'There's twenty-five thousand dollars in it for you.'

Her expression changed. 'Sure,' she said quickly. 'I can impersonate anyone. Who did you have in mind?'

Tyler leaned forward and began to talk.

Tyler had Margo Posner released into his custody.

As he explained to Keith Percy, the chief judge, 'I learned that she's a very talented artist, and she's eager to live a normal, decent life. I think it's important that we rehabilitate that type of person whenever we can, don't you?'

Keith was impressed and surprised. 'Absolutely, Tyler. That's a wonderful thing you're doing.'

Tyler moved Margo into his home and spent five full days briefing her on the Stanford family.

'What are the names of your brothers?'

'Tyler and Woodruff.'

'Woodrow.'

'That's right – Woodrow.'

'What do we call him?'

'Woody.'

'Do you have a sister?'

'Yes. Kendall. She's a designer.'

'Is she married?'

'She's married to a Frenchman. His name is . . . Marc Renoir.'

'Renaud.'

'Renaud.'

'What was your mother's name?'

'Rosemary Nelson. She was a governess to the Stanford children.'

'Why did she leave?'

'She got knocked up by . . .'

'Margo!' Tyler admonished her.

'I mean, she became pregnant by Harry Stanford.'

'What happened to Mrs Stanford?'

'She committed suicide.'

'What did your mother tell you about the Stanford children?'

Margo stopped to think for a minute.

'Well?'

'There was the time you fell out of the swan boat.'

'I didn't fall out!' Tyler said. 'I *almost* fell out.'

'Right. Woody almost got arrested for picking flowers in the Public Garden.'

'That was Kendall . . .'

He was ruthless. They went over the scenario again and again, late into the nights, until Margo was exhausted.

'Kendall was bitten by a dog.'

'*I* was bitten by the dog.'

She rubbed her eyes. 'I can't think straight anymore. I'm so tired. I need some sleep.'

'You can sleep later!'

'How long is this going to go on?' she asked defiantly.

'Until I think you're ready. Now let's go through it again.'

And on it went, over and over, until Margo became letter perfect. When the day finally arrived that she knew the answer to every question Tyler asked, he was satisfied.

'You're ready,' he said. He handed her some legal documents.

'What's this?'

'It's just a technicality,' Tyler said casually.

What he had her sign was a paper giving her share of the Stanford estate to a corporation controlled by a second corporation, which in turn was controlled by an offshore subsidiary of which Tyler Stanford was the sole owner. There was no way they could trace the transaction back to Tyler.

Tyler handed Margo five thousand dollars in cash. 'You'll get the balance when the job is done,' he told her. '*If* you convince them that you're Julia Stanford.'

From the moment Margo had appeared at Rose Hill, Tyler had played the devil's advocate. It was the classic antipositional chess move.

'*I'm sure you can understand our position, Miss . . . er . . . Without some positive proof, there's no way . . .*

'*. . . I think the lady is a fraud . . .*

'*How many servants worked in this house when we were children? . . . Dozens, right? And some of them would have known everything this young lady told us . . .*

Any one of them could have given her that photograph . . . Let's not forget that there's an enormous amount of money involved.'

His crowning move had been when he had demanded a DNA test. He had called Hal Baker and given him his new instructions: *'Dig up Harry Stanford's body and dispose of it.'*

And then his inspiration of calling in a private detective. With the family present, he had telephoned the district attorney's office in Chicago.

'This is Judge Tyler Stanford. I understand that your office retains a private detective from time to time who does excellent work for you. His name is something like Simmons or –'

'Oh, you must mean Frank Timmons.'

'Timmons! Yes, that's it. I wonder if you could give me his telephone number so I can contact him directly?'

Instead, he had summoned Hal Baker and introduced him as Frank Timmons.

At first Tyler had planned for Hal Baker merely to pretend to go through the motions of checking on Julia Stanford, but then he decided it would make a more impressive report if Baker really pursued it. The family had accepted Baker's findings without question.

Tyler's plan had gone off without a hitch. Margo Posner had played her part perfectly, and the fingerprints had been the crowning touch. Everyone was convinced that she was the real Julia Stanford.

210

'I, for one, am glad it's finally settled. Let me go up and see if she needs any help.'

He went upstairs and walked along the corridor to Julia's room. He knocked at her door and called loudly, 'Julia?'

'It's open. Come in.'

He stood in the doorway and they stared silently at each other. And then Tyler carefully closed the door, held out his hands, and broke into a slow grin.

When he spoke, he said, 'We did it, Margo! We did it!'

Chapter Eighteen

In the offices of Renquist, Renquist & Fitzgerald, Steve Sloane and Simon Fitzgerald were having coffee.

'As the great bard once said, "Something is rotten in the state of Denmark."'

'What's bothering you?' Fitzgerald asked.

Steve sighed. 'I'm not sure. It's the Stanford family. They puzzle me.'

Simon Fitzgerald snorted. 'Join the club.'

'I keep coming back to the same question, Simon, but I can't find the answer to it.'

'What's the question?'

'The family was anxious to exhume Harry Stanford's body so they could check his DNA against the woman's. So I think we have to assume that the only possible motive for getting rid of the body would be to ensure that the woman's DNA could *not* be checked against Harry Stanford's. The only one who could have anything to gain from that would be the woman herself, if she were a fraud.'

'Yes.'

'And yet this private detective, Frank Timmons – I

checked with the district attorney's office in Chicago, and he has a great reputation – came up with fingerprints that prove she *is* the real Julia Stanford. My question is, who the hell dug up Harry Stanford's body and why?'

'That's a billion-dollar question. If . . .'

The intercom buzzed. A secretary's voice came over the box. 'Mr Sloane, there's a call for you on two.'

Steve Sloane picked up the telephone on the desk. 'Hello . . .'

The voice on the other end of the line said, 'Mr Sloane, this is Judge Stanford. I would appreciate it if you could drop by Rose Hill this morning.'

Steve Sloane glanced at Fitzgerald. 'Right. In about an hour?'

'That will be fine. Thank you.'

Steve replaced the receiver. 'My presence is requested at the Stanford house.'

'I wonder what they want.'

'Ten to one they want to speed up the probate so they can get their hands on all that beautiful money.'

'Lee? It's Tyler. How are you?'

'Fine, thanks.'

'I really miss you.'

There was a slight pause. 'I miss you too, Tyler.'

The words thrilled him. 'Lee, I have some really exciting news. I can't discuss it over the phone, but it's

213

something that's going to make you very happy. When you and I –'

'Tyler, I have to go. Someone's waiting for me.'

'But . . .'

The line went dead.

Tyler sat there a moment. Then he thought, *He wouldn't have said he missed me if he didn't mean it.*

With the exception of Woody and Peggy, the family was gathered in the drawing room at Rose Hill. Steve studied their faces.

Judge Stanford seemed very relaxed.

Steve glanced at Kendall. She seemed unnaturally tense. Her husband had come up from New York the day before for the meeting. Steve looked over at Marc. The Frenchman was good-looking, a few years younger than his wife.

And then there was Julia. She seemed to be taking her acceptance into the family very calmly. *I would have expected someone who had just inherited a billion dollars or so to be a little more excited*, Steve thought.

He glanced at their faces again, wondering if one of them was responsible for having Harry Stanford's body stolen, and if so, which one? And why?

Tyler was speaking. 'Mr Sloane, I'm familiar with the probate laws in Illinois, but I don't know how much they differ from the laws in Massachusetts. We were wondering whether there wasn't some way to expedite the procedure.'

Steve smiled to himself. *I should have made Simon take that bet*. He turned to Tyler. 'We're already working on it, Judge Stanford.'

Tyler said pointedly, 'The Stanford name might be useful in speeding things up.'

He's right about that, Steve thought. He nodded. 'I'll do everything I can. If it's at all possible to –'

There were voices from the staircase.

'Just shut up, you stupid bitch! I don't want to hear another word. Do you understand?'

Woody and Peggy came down the stairs and into the room. Peggy's face was badly swollen, and she had a black eye. Woody was grinning, and his eyes were bright.

'Hello, everybody. I hope the party's not over.'

The group was looking at Peggy in shock.

Kendall rose. 'What happened to you?'

'Nothing. I . . . I bumped into a door.'

Woody took a seat. Peggy sat next to him. Woody patted her hand and asked solicitously, 'Are you all right, my dear?'

Peggy nodded, not trusting herself to speak.

'Good.' Woody turned to the others. 'Now, what did I miss?'

Tyler looked at him disapprovingly. 'I just asked Mr Sloane if he could expedite the probating of the will.'

Woody grinned. 'That would be nice.' He turned to

215

Peggy. 'You'd like some new clothes, wouldn't you, darling?'

'I don't need any new clothes,' she said timidly.

'That's right. You don't go anywhere, do you?' He turned to the others. 'Peggy is very shy. She doesn't have anything to talk about, do you?'

Peggy got up and ran out of the room.

'I'll see if she's all right,' Kendall said. She rose and hurried after her.

My God! Steve thought. *If Woody behaves like this in front of others, what must it be like when he and his wife are alone?*

Woody turned to Steve. 'How long have you been with Fitzgerald's law firm?'

'Five years.'

'How they could stand working for my father, I'll never know.'

Steve said carefully, 'I understand your father was . . . could be difficult.'

Woody snorted. 'Difficult? He was a two-legged monster. Did you know he had nicknames for all of us? Mine was Charlie. He named me after Charlie McCarthy, a dummy that a ventriloquist named Edgar Bergen had. He called my sister Pony, because he said she had a face like a horse. Tyler was called . . .'

Steve said, uncomfortably, 'I really don't think you should –'

Woody grinned. 'It's all right. A billion dollars heals a lot of wounds.'

Steve rose. 'Well, if there's nothing else, I think I had better be going.' He could not wait to get outside, into the fresh air.

Kendall found Peggy in the bathroom, putting a cold cloth to her swollen cheek.

'Peggy? Are you all right?'

Peggy turned. 'I'm fine. Thank you. I . . . I'm sorry about what happened down there.'

'You're apologizing? You should be furious. How long has he been beating you?'

'He doesn't beat me,' Peggy said obstinately. 'I bumped into a door.'

Kendall moved closer to her. 'Peggy, why do you put up with this? You don't have to, you know.'

There was a pause. 'Yes, I do.'

Kendall looked at her, puzzled. 'Why?'

She turned. 'Because I love him.' She went on, the words pouring out. 'He loves me, too. Believe me, he doesn't always act like this. The thing is, he – sometimes he's not himself.'

'You mean, when he's on drugs.'

'No!'

'Peggy . . .'

'No!'

'Peggy . . .'

Peggy hesitated. 'I suppose so.'

'When did it start?'

'Right . . . right after we got married.' Peggy's voice

217

was ragged. 'It started because of a polo game. Woody fell off his pony and was badly hurt. While he was in the hospital, they gave him drugs to help with the pain. *They* got him started.' She looked at Kendall, pleadingly. 'So you see, it wasn't his fault, was it? After Woody got out of the hospital, he . . . he kept on using drugs. Whenever I tried to get him to quit, he would . . . beat me.'

'Peggy, for God's sake! He needs help! Don't you see that? You can't do this alone. He's a drug addict. What does he take? Cocaine?'

'No.' There was a small silence. 'Heroin.'

'My God! Can't you make him get some help?'

'I've tried.' Her voice was a whisper. 'You don't know how I've tried! He's gone to three rehabilitation hospitals.' She shook her head. 'He's all right for a while, and then . . . he starts again. He . . . he can't help it.'

Kendall put her arms around Peggy. 'I'm so sorry,' she said.

Peggy forced a smile. 'I'm sure Woody will be all right. He's trying hard. He really is.' Her face lit up. 'When we were first married, he was so much fun to be with. We used to laugh all the time. He would bring me little presents and –' Her eyes filled with tears. 'I love him so much!'

'If there's anything I can do . . .'

'Thank you,' Peggy whispered. 'I appreciate that.'

Kendall squeezed her hand. 'We'll talk again.'

218

Kendall started down the stairs to join the others. She was thinking, *When we were children, before Mother died, we made such wonderful plans. 'You're going to be a famous designer, Sis, and I'm going to be the world's greatest athlete!' And the sad part of it,* Kendall thought, *is that he could have been. And now this.*

Kendall was not sure if she felt more sorry for Woody or for Peggy.

As Kendall reached the bottom of the stairs, Clark approached her, carrying a tray with a letter on it. 'Excuse me, Miss Kendall. A messenger just delivered this for you.' He handed her the envelope.

Kendall looked at it in surprise. 'Who . . . ?' She nodded. 'Thank you, Clark.'

Kendall opened the envelope, and as she began to read the letter, she turned pale. 'No!' she said, under her breath. Her heart was pounding, and she felt a wave of dizziness. She stood there, bracing herself against a table, trying to catch her breath.

After a moment, she turned and walked into the drawing room, her face pale. The meeting was breaking up.

'Marc . . .' Kendall forced herself to appear calm. 'May I see you for a moment?'

He looked at her, concerned. 'Yes, certainly.'

Tyler asked Kendall, 'Are you all right?'

She forced a smile. 'I'm fine, thank you.'

She took Marc's hand and led him upstairs. When

219

they entered the bedroom, Kendall closed the door.

Marc said, 'What is it?'

Kendall handed him the envelope. The letter read:

> *Dear Mrs Renaud,*
>
> *Congratulations! Our Wild Animal Protection Association was delighted to read of your good fortune. We know how interested you are in the work we are doing, and we are counting on your further support. Therefore, we would appreciate it if you would deposit 1 million US dollars in our numbered bank account in Zurich within the next ten days. We look forward to hearing from you shortly.*

As in the other letters, all the Es were broken.

'The bastards!' Marc exploded.

'How did they know I was here?' Kendall asked.

Marc said bitterly, 'All they had to do was pick up a newspaper.' He read the letter again and shook his head. 'They aren't going to quit. We *have* to go to the police.'

'No!' Kendall cried. 'We can't! It's too late! Don't you see? It would be the end of everything. *Everything!*'

Marc took her in his arms and held her tightly. 'All right. We'll find a way.'

But Kendall knew that there was no way.

*   *   *

220

It had happened a few months earlier, on what had started out to be a glorious spring day. Kendall had gone to a friend's birthday party in Ridgefield, Connecticut. It had been a wonderful party, and Kendall had chatted with old friends. She had had a glass of champagne. In the middle of a conversation, she had suddenly looked at her watch. 'Oh, no! I had no idea it was so late. Marc is waiting for me.'

There were hasty good-byes, and Kendall had gotten into her car and driven off. Driving back to New York, she had decided to take a winding country road over to I684. She was traveling at almost fifty miles per hour as she rounded a sharp curve and spotted a car parked on the right side of the road. Kendall automatically swerved to the left. At that moment, a woman carrying a handful of freshly picked flowers started to cross the narrow road. Kendall tried frantically to avoid her, but it was too late. Everything seemed to happen in a blur. She heard a sickening thud as she hit the woman with her left front fender. Kendall brought the car to a screeching stop, her whole body trembling violently. She ran back to where the woman was lying in the road, covered with blood.

Kendall stood there, frozen. Finally she bent down and turned the woman over, and looked into her sightless eyes. 'Oh, my God!' Kendall whispered. She felt the bile rising in her throat. She looked up, desperate, not knowing what to do. She swung around in a panic. There were no cars in sight. *She's dead,* Kendall thought. *I can't help her. This was not my fault, but they'll accuse me of reckless drunk driving. My blood will show alcohol. I'll go to prison!*

She took one last look at the body of the woman, then hurried back to her car. The left front fender was dented, and there were blood spots on it. *I've got to put the car away in a garage,* Kendall thought. *The police will be searching for it.* She got into the car and drove off.

For the rest of the drive into New York, she kept looking into the rearview mirror, expecting to see flashing red lights and to hear the sound of a siren. She drove into the garage on Ninety-sixth Street where she kept her car. Sam, the owner of the garage, was talking to Red, his mechanic. Kendall got out of the car.

'Evenin', Mrs Renaud,' Sam said.

'Go . . . Good evening.' She was fighting to keep her teeth from chattering.

'Put it away for the night?'

'Yes . . . yes, please.'

Red was looking at the fender. 'You got a bad dent here, Mrs Renaud. Looks like there's blood on it.'

The two men were looking at her.

Kendall took a deep breath. 'Yes. I . . . I hit a deer on the highway.'

'You're lucky it didn't do more damage,' Sam said. 'A friend of mine hit a deer and it ruined his car.' He grinned. 'Didn't do much for the deer either.'

'If you'll just put it away,' Kendall said tightly.
'Sure.'

Kendall walked over to the garage door, then looked back. The two men were staring at the fender.

When Kendall got home and told Marc about the terrible thing that had happened, he took her in his arms and said, 'Oh, my God! Darling, how could . . . ?'

Kendall was sobbing. 'I . . . I couldn't help it. She started across the road right in front of me. She . . . she had been picking flowers and –'

'Ssh! I'm sure it wasn't your fault. It was an accident. We've got to report this to the police.'

'I know. You're right. I . . . I should have stayed there and waited for them to come. I just . . . panicked, Marc. Now it's a hit-and-run. But there wasn't anything I could do for her. She was dead. You should have seen her face. It was awful.'

He held her for a long time, until she quieted down.

When Kendall spoke, she said tentatively, 'Marc . . . do we have to go to the police?'

He frowned. 'What do you mean?'

She was fighting hysteria. 'Well, it's over, isn't it? Nothing can bring her back. What good would it do for them to punish me? I didn't mean to do it. Why couldn't we just pretend it never happened?'

'Kendall, if they ever traced –'

'How can they? There was no one around.'

'What about your car? Was it damaged?'

223

'There's a dent. I told the garage attendant I hit a deer.' She was fighting for control. 'Marc, no one saw the accident. Do you know what would happen to me if they arrested me and sent me to prison? I'd lose my business, everything I've built up all these years, and for what? For something that's already done! It's over!' She began to sob again.

He held her close. 'Ssh! We'll see. We'll see.'

The morning papers gave the story a big play. What gave it added drama was the fact that the dead woman had been on her way to Manhattan to be married. The *New York Times* covered it as a straight news story, but the *Daily News* and *Newsday* played it up as a heart-tugging drama.

Kendall bought a copy of each newspaper, and she became more and more horrified at what she had done. Her mind was filled with all the terrible ifs.

If I hadn't gone to Connecticut for my friend's birthday . . .

If I had stayed home that day . . .

If I hadn't had anything to drink . . .

If the woman had picked the flowers a few seconds earlier or a few seconds later . . .

I'm responsible for murdering another human being!

Kendall thought of the terrible grief she had caused the woman's family, and her fiancé's family, and she felt sick to her stomach again.

According to the newspapers, the police were asking

for information from anyone who might have a clue about the hit-and-run.

They have no way of finding me, Kendall thought. *All I have to do is act as if nothing happened.*

When Kendall went to the garage to pick up her car the next morning, Red was there.

'I wiped the blood off the car,' he said. 'Do you want me to fix the dent?'

Of course! She should have thought of it sooner. 'Yes, please.'

Red was looking at her strangely. Or was it her imagination?

'Sam and I talked about it last night,' he said. 'It's funny, you know. A deer should have done a lot more damage.'

Kendall's heart began to beat wildly. Her mouth was suddenly so dry she could hardly speak. 'It was . . . a small deer.'

Red nodded laconically. 'Must have been real small.'

Kendall could feel his eyes on her as she drove out of the garage.

When Kendall walked into her office her secretary, Nadine, took one look at her and said, 'What happened to you?'

Kendall froze. 'What . . . what do you mean?'

'You look shaky. Let me get you some coffee.'

'Thanks.'

225

Kendall walked over to the mirror. Her face looked pale and drawn. *They're going to know just by looking at me!*

Nadine came into the office with a cup of hot coffee. 'Here. This will make you feel better.' She looked at Kendall curiously. 'Is everything all right?'

'I . . . I had a little accident yesterday,' Kendall said.

'Oh? Was anyone hurt?'

In her mind, she could see the face of the dead woman. 'No. I . . . I hit a deer.'

'What about your car?'

'It's being repaired.'

'I'll call your insurance company.'

'Oh, no, Nadine, please don't.'

Kendall saw the surprised look in Nadine's eyes.

It was two days later that the first letter came:

> *Dear Mrs Renaud,*
>
> *I'm the chairman of the Wild Animal Protection Association, which is in desperate need. I'm sure that you would like to help us out. The organization needs money to preserve wild animals. We are especially interested in deer. You can wire $50,000 to account number 804072-A at the Crédit Suisse bank in Zurich. I would strongly suggest that the money be there within the next five days.*

It was unsigned. All the Es in the letter were broken. Enclosed in the envelope was a newspaper clipping about the accident.

Kendall read the letter twice. The threat was unmistakable. She agonized over what to do. *Marc was right,* she thought. *I should have gone to the police.* But now everything was worse. She was a fugitive. If they found her now, it would mean prison and disgrace, as well as the end of her business.

At lunchtime, she went to her bank. 'I want to wire fifty thousand dollars to Switzerland.'

When Kendall got home that evening, she showed the letter to Marc.

He was stunned. 'My God!' he said. 'Who could have sent this?'

'Nobody . . . nobody knows.' She was trembling.

'Kendall, *someone* knows.'

Her body was twitching. 'There was no one around, Marc! I –'

'Wait a minute. Let's try to figure this out. Exactly what happened when you returned to town?'

'Nothing. I . . . I put the car in the garage, and –' She stopped. '*You got a bad dent here, Mrs Renaud. Looks like there's blood on it.*'

Marc saw the expression on her face. 'What?'

She said slowly, 'The owner of the garage and his mechanic were there. They saw the blood on the fender. I told them I hit a deer, and they said there should have been a lot more damage.' She remembered something else. 'Marc . . .'

'Yes?'

'Nadine, my secretary. I told her the same thing. I could see that she didn't believe me either. So it had to be one of the three of them.'

'No,' Marc said slowly.

She stared at him. 'What do you mean?'

'Sit down, Kendall, and listen to me. If any of them was suspicious of you, they could have told your story to a dozen people. The report of the accident has been in all the newspapers. Someone has put two and two together. I think the letter was a bluff, testing you. It was a terrible mistake to send that money.'

'But why?'

'Because now they *know* you're guilty, don't you see? You've given them the proof they needed.'

'Oh, God! What should I do?' Kendall asked.

Marc Renaud was thoughtful for a moment. 'I have an idea how we can find out who these bastards are.'

At ten o'clock the following morning, Kendall and Marc were seated in the office of Russell Gibbons, vice president of the Manhattan First Security Bank.

'And what can I do for you, today?' Mr Gibbons asked.

Marc said, 'We would like to check on a numbered bank account in Zurich.'

'Yes?'

'We want to know whose account it is.'

Gibbons rubbed his hands across his chin. 'Is there a crime involved?'

Marc said quickly, 'No! Why do you ask?'

'Well, unless there's some kind of criminal activity, such as laundering money or breaking the laws of Switzerland or the United States, Switzerland will not violate the secrecy of its numbered bank accounts. Their reputation is built on confidentiality.'

'Surely, there's some way to . . . ?'

'I'm sorry. I'm afraid not.'

Kendall and Marc looked at each other. Kendall's face was filled with despair.

Marc rose. 'Thank you for your time.'

'I'm sorry I couldn't help you.' He ushered them out of his office.

When Kendall drove into the garage that evening, neither Sam nor Red was around. Kendall parked her car, and as she passed the little office, through the window she saw a typewriter on a stand. She stopped, staring at it, wondering if it had a broken letter E. *I have to find out*, she thought.

She walked over to the office, hesitated a moment, then opened the door and stepped inside. As she moved toward the typewriter, Sam suddenly appeared out of nowhere.

'Evenin', Mrs Renaud,' he said. 'Can I help you?'

She spun around, startled. 'No. I . . . I just left my

car. Good night.' She hurried toward the door.

'Good night, Mrs Renaud.'

In the morning, when Kendall passed the garage office, the typewriter was gone. In its place was a personal computer.

Sam saw her staring at it. 'Nice, huh? I decided to bring this place into the twentieth century.'

Now that he could afford it?

When Kendall told Marc about it that evening, he said thoughtfully, 'It's a possibility, but we need proof.'

Monday morning, when Kendall went to her office, Nadine was waiting for her.

'Are you feeling better, Mrs Renaud?'

'Yes. Thank you.'

'Yesterday was my birthday. Look what my husband got me!' She walked over to a closet and pulled out a luxurious mink coat. 'Isn't it beautiful?'

Chapter Nineteen

Julia Stanford enjoyed having Sally as a roommate. She was always upbeat and fun and cheerful. She had had a bad marriage and had sworn never to get involved with a man again. Julia wasn't sure what Sally's definition of *never* was, because she seemed to be out with a different man every week.

'Married men are the best,' Sally philosophized. 'They feel guilty, so they're always buying you presents. With a single man, you have to ask yourself, why is he still single?'

She said to Julia, 'You aren't dating anyone, are you?'

'No.' Julia thought of the men who had wanted to take her out. 'I don't want to go out just for the sake of going out, Sally. I have to be with someone I really care about.'

'Well, have I got a man for you!' Sally said. 'You're going to love him! His name is Tony Vinetti. I told him all about you, and he's dying to meet you.'

'I really don't think –'

'He'll pick you up tomorrow night at eight o'clock.'

* * *

Tony Vinetti was tall, very tall, in an appealing, ungainly way. His hair was thick and dark, and his smile exploded disarmingly as he looked at Julia.

'Sally wasn't exaggerating. You're a knockout!'

'Thank you,' Julia said. She felt a little shiver of pleasure.

'Have you ever been to Houston's?'

It was one of the finest restaurants in Kansas City.

'No.' The truth was that she could not afford to eat at Houston's. Not even with the raise she had been given.

'Well, that's where we have a reservation.'

At dinner, Tony talked mostly about himself, but Julia did not mind. He was entertaining and charming. '*He's drop-dead gorgeous*,' Sally had said. And he was.

The dinner was delicious. For dessert, Julia had ordered chocolate soufflé and Tony had ice cream. As they were lingering over coffee, Julia thought, *Is he going to ask me to his apartment, and if he does, will I go? No. I can't do that. Not on the first date. He'll think I'm cheap. When we go out the next time . . .*

The check arrived. Tony scanned it and said, 'It looks right.' He ticked off the items on the check. 'You had the pâté and the lobster . . .'

'Yes.'

'And you had the French fries and salad, and the soufflé, right?'

She looked at him, puzzled. 'That's right . . .'

232

'Okay.' He did some quick addition. 'Your share of the bill is fifty dollars and forty cents.'

Julia sat there in shock. 'I beg your pardon?'

Tony grinned. 'I know how independent you women are today. You won't let guys do anything for you, will you? There,' he said magnanimously, 'I'll take care of your share of the tip.'

'I'm sorry it didn't work out,' Sally apologized. 'He's really a honey. Are you going to see him again?'

'I can't afford him,' Julia said bitterly.

'Well, I have someone else for you. You'll love –'

'No. Sally, I really don't want . . .'

'Trust me.'

Ted Riddle was a man in his late thirties and, Julia had to admit, quite attractive. He took her to Jennie's Restaurant on Historic Strawberry Hill, famous for its authentic Croatian food.

'Sally really did me a favor,' Riddle said. 'You're very lovely.'

'Thank you.'

'Did Sally tell you I have an advertising agency?'

'No. She didn't.'

'Oh, yes. I have one of the biggest firms in Kansas City. Everybody knows me.'

'That's nice. I –'

'We handle some of the biggest clients in the country.'

233

'You do? I'm not –'

'Oh, yes. We handle celebrities, banks, big businesses, chain stores . . .'

'Well, I –'

'. . . supermarkets. You name it, we represent them all.'

'That's –'

'Let me tell you how I got started.'

He never stopped talking during dinner, and the only subject was Ted Riddle.

'He was probably just nervous,' Sally apologized.

'Well, I can tell you, he made *me* nervous. If there's anything you want to know about the life of Ted Riddle since the day he was born, just ask me!'

'Jerry McKinley.'

'What?'

'Jerry McKinley. I just remembered. He used to date a girlfriend of mine. She was absolutely crazy about him.'

'Thanks, Sally, but no.'

'I'm going to call him.'

The following night, Jerry McKinley appeared. He was nice-looking, and he had a sweet and engaging personality. When he walked in the door and looked at Julia he said, 'I know blind dates are always difficult. I'm rather shy myself, so I know how you must feel, Julia.'

She liked him immediately.

They went to the Evergreen Chinese Restaurant on State Avenue for dinner.

'You work for an architectural firm. That must be exciting. I don't think people realize how important architects are.'

He's sensitive, Julia thought happily. She smiled. 'I couldn't agree with you more.'

The evening was delightful, and the more they talked, the more Julia liked him. She decided to be bold.

'Would you like to come back to the apartment for a nightcap?' she asked.

'No. Let's go back to my place.'

'Your place?'

He leaned forward and squeezed her hand. 'That's where I keep the whips and chains.'

Henry Wesson owned an accounting firm in the building where Peters, Eastman & Tolkin was quartered. Two or three mornings a week, Julia would find herself in the elevator with him. He seemed a pleasant enough man. He was in his thirties, quietly intelligent-looking, sandy-haired, and he wore black-rimmed glasses.

The acquaintance began with polite nods, then, 'Good morning,' then, 'You're looking very well today,' and after a few months, 'I wonder if you'd like to have dinner with me some evening?' He was watching her eagerly, waiting for an answer.

Julia smiled. 'All right.'

It was instant love on Henry's part. On their first date, he took Julia to EBT, one of the top restaurants in Kansas City. He was obviously thrilled to be out with her.

He told her a little about himself. 'I was born right here in good old KC. My father was born here, too. The acorn doesn't fall far from the oak. You know what I mean?'

Julia knew what he meant.

'I always knew I wanted to be an accountant. When I got out of school, I went to work for the Bigelow & Benson Financial Corporation. Now I have my own firm.'

'That's nice,' Julia said.

'That's about all there is to tell about me. Tell me about you.'

Julia was silent for a moment. *I'm the illegitimate daughter of one of the richest men in the world. You've probably heard of him. He just drowned. I'm an heiress to his estate.* She looked around the elegant room. *I could buy this restaurant, if I wanted to. I could probably buy this whole town, if I wanted to.*

Henry was staring at her. 'Julia?'

'Oh! I . . . I'm sorry. I was born in Milwaukee. My . . . my father died when I was young. My mother and I traveled around the country a great deal. When she passed away, I decided to stay here and get a job.' *I hope my nose isn't growing.*

Henry Wesson put a hand over hers. 'So you've never had a man to take care of you.' He leaned forward and said earnestly, 'I would like to take care of you for the rest of your life.'

Julia looked at him in surprise. 'I don't mean to sound like Doris Day, but we hardly know each other.'

'I want to change that.'

When Julia got home, Sally was waiting for her. 'Well?' she asked. 'How did your date go?'

Julia said, thoughtfully, 'He's very sweet, and . . .'

'He's crazy about you!'

Julia smiled. 'I think he proposed.'

Sally's eyes widened. 'You *think* he proposed? My God! Don't you know if the man proposed or not?'

'Well, he said he wanted to take care of me for the rest of my life.'

'That's a proposal!' Sally exclaimed. 'That's a proposal! Marry him! Quick! Marry him before he changes his mind!'

Julia laughed. 'What's the hurry?'

'Listen to me. Invite him over here for dinner. I'll cook it, and you tell him you made it.'

Julia laughed. 'Thank you. No. When I find the man I want to marry, we may be eating Chinese food out of cartons, but believe me, the dinner table will be beautifully set with flowers and candlelight.'

On their next date, Henry said, 'You know, Kansas City is a great place to bring up kids.'

'Yes, it is.' Julia's only problem was that she wasn't sure that she wanted to bring up *his* children. He was reliable, sober, decent, but . . .

She discussed it with Sally.

'He keeps asking me to marry him,' Julia said.

'What's he like?'

She thought for a moment, trying to think of the most romantic and exciting things she could say about Henry Wesson. 'He's reliable, sober, decent . . .'

Sally looked at her a moment. 'In other words, he's dull.'

Julia said defensively, 'He isn't exactly dull.'

Sally nodded, knowingly. 'He's dull. Marry him.'

'What?'

'Marry him. Good dull husbands are hard to find.'

Getting from one payday to the next was a financial minefield. There were paycheck deductions, and rent, and automobile expenses, and groceries, and clothes to buy. Julia owned a Toyota Tercel, and it seemed to her that she spent more on it than she did on herself. She was constantly borrowing money from Sally.

* * *

One evening, when Julia was getting dressed, Sally said, 'It's another big Henry night, huh? Where's he taking you tonight?'

'We're going to Symphony Hall. Cleo Laine is performing.'

'Has old Henry proposed again?'

Julia hesitated. The truth was that Henry proposed every time they were together. She felt pressured, but she could not bring herself to say yes.

'Don't lose him,' Sally warned.

Sally is probably right, Julia thought. *Henry Wesson would make a good husband. He's . . .* She hesitated. *He's sober, reliable, decent . . . Is that enough?*

As Julia was going out the door, Sally called, 'Can I borrow your black shoes?'

'Sure.' And Julia was gone.

Sally went into Julia's bedroom and opened the closet door. The pair of shoes she wanted was on the top shelf. As she reached for them, a cardboard box that was sitting precariously on the shelf fell down, and its contents spilled out all over the floor.

'Damn!' Sally bent down to gather up the papers. They consisted of dozens of newspaper clippings, photographs, and articles, and they were all about the Harry Stanford family. There seemed to be hundreds of them.

Suddenly, Julia came hurrying back into the room. 'I forgot my –' She stopped as she saw the papers on the floor. 'What are you doing?'

'I'm sorry,' Sally apologized. 'The box fell down.'

Blushing, Julia bent down and started putting the papers back in the box.

'I had no idea you were so interested in the rich and famous,' Sally said.

Silently, Julia kept shoving the papers into the box. As she gathered a handful of photographs, she came across a small gold heart-shaped locket that her mother had given her before she died. Julia put the locket aside.

Sally was studying her, puzzled. 'Julia?'

'Yes.'

'Why are you so interested in Harry Stanford?'

'I'm not. I . . . This was my mother's.'

Sally shrugged. 'Okay.' She reached for a paper. It was from a scandal magazine, and the headline caught her eye: TYCOON GETS CHILDREN'S GOVERNESS PREGNANT — BABY BORN OUT-OF-WEDLOCK — MOTHER AND BABY DISAPPEAR!

Sally was staring at Julia, openmouthed. 'My God! You're Harry Stanford's daughter!'

Julia's mouth tightened. She shook her head and continued putting the papers back.

'Aren't you?'

Julia stopped. 'Please, I'd rather not talk about it, if you don't mind.'

Sally jumped to her feet. '*You'd rather not talk about it? You're the daughter of one of the richest men in the world, and you'd rather not talk about it? Are you insane?*'

'Sally . . .'

'Do you know how much he was worth? Billions.'

'That has nothing to do with me.'

'If you're his daughter, it has *everything* to do with you. You're an heiress! All you have to do is tell the family who you are, and –'

'No.'

'No . . . what?'

'You don't understand.' Julia rose and then sank down on the bed. 'Harry Stanford was an awful man. He abandoned my mother. She hated him, and I hate him.'

'You don't *hate* anyone with that much money. You *understand* them.'

Julia shook her head. 'I don't want any part of them.'

'Julia, heiresses don't live in crummy apartments and buy clothes at flea markets, and borrow to pay the rent. Your family would *hate* knowing you live like this. They'd be humiliated.'

'They don't even know I'm alive.'

'Then you've got to tell them.'

'Sally . . .'

'Yes?'

'Drop the subject.'

Sally looked at her for a long time. 'Sure. By the way, you couldn't loan me a million or two till payday, could you?'

Chapter Twenty

Tyler was becoming frantic. For the past twenty-four hours he had been dialing Lee's home number, and there had been no answer. *Who is he with?* Tyler agonized. *What is he doing?*

He picked up the telephone and dialed once again. The phone rang for a long time, and just as Tyler was about to hang up, he heard Lee's voice. 'Hello.'

'Lee! How are you?'

'Who the hell is this?'

'It's Tyler.'

'Tyler?' There was a pause. 'Oh, yes.'

Tyler felt a twinge of disappointment. 'How are you?'

'Fine,' Lee said.

'I told you I was going to have a wonderful surprise for you.'

'Yes?' He sounded bored.

'Do you remember what you said to me about going to St Tropez on a beautiful white yacht?'

'What about it?'

'How would you like to leave next month?'

'Are you serious?'

'You bet I am.'

'Well, I don't know. You've got a friend with a yacht?'

'I'm about to *buy* a yacht.'

'You're not on something, are you, judge?'

'On . . . ? No, no! I've just come into some money. A lot of money.'

'St Tropez, huh? Yeah, that sounds great. Sure, I'd love to go with you.'

Tyler felt a deep sense of relief. 'Wonderful! Meanwhile, don't . . .' He couldn't bring himself even to think about it. 'I'll be in touch with you, Lee.' He replaced the receiver and sat on the edge of his bed. '*I'd love to go with you.*' He could visualize the two of them on a beautiful yacht, cruising around the world together. *Together.*

Tyler picked up the telephone book and turned to the yellow pages.

The offices of John Alden Yachts Inc. are located on Boston's Commercial Wharf. The sales manager came up to Tyler as he entered.

'What can I do for you today, sir?'

Tyler looked at him and said casually, 'I'd like to buy a yacht.' The words rolled off his tongue.

His father's yacht would probably be part of the estate, but Tyler had no intention of sharing a ship with his brother and sister.

'Motor or sail?'

'I ... er ... I'm not sure. I want to be able to go around the world in it.'

'We're probably talking motor.'

'It must be white.'

The sales manager looked at him strangely. 'Yes, of course. How large a boat did you have in mind?'

Blue Skies *is one hundred and eighty feet.*

'Two hundred feet.'

The sales manager blinked. 'Ah. I see. Of course, a yacht like that would be very expensive, Mr – . . .'

'Judge Stanford. My father was Harry Stanford.'

The man's face lit up.

'Money is no object,' Tyler said.

'Certainly not! Well, Judge Stanford, we're going to find you a yacht that everyone will envy. White, of course. Meanwhile, here is a portfolio of some available yachts. Call me when you decide which ones you're interested in.'

Woody Stanford was thinking about polo ponies. All his life he had had to ride his friends' ponies, but now he could afford to buy the finest string in the world.

He was on the telephone, talking to Mimi Carson. 'I want to buy your ponies,' Woody said. His voice was filled with excitement. He listened a moment. 'That's right, the whole stable. I'm very serious. Right.'

The conversation lasted half an hour, and when

Woody replaced the receiver, he was grinning. He went to find Peggy.

She was seated alone on the veranda. Woody could still see the bruises on her face where he had hit her.

'Peggy . . .'

She looked up, warily. 'Yes?'

'I have to talk to you. I . . . I don't know where to begin.'

She sat there, waiting.

He took a deep breath. 'I know I've been a rotten husband. Some of the things I've done are inexcusable. But, darling, all that is going to change now. Don't you see? We're rich. Really rich. I want to make everything up to you.' He took her hand. 'I'm going to get off drugs this time. I really am. We're going to have a whole different life.'

She looked into his eyes, and said tonelessly, 'Are we, Woody?'

'Yes. I promise. I know I've said it before, but this time it's really going to work. I've made up my mind. I'm going to a clinic somewhere where they can cure me. I want to get out of this hell I've been in. Peggy . . .' There was desperation in his voice. 'I can't do it without you. You know I can't.'

She looked at him a long time, then cradled him in her arms. 'Poor baby. I know,' she whispered. 'I know. I'll help you . . .'

* * *

245

It was time for Margo Posner to leave.

Tyler found her in the study. He closed the door. 'I just wanted to thank you again, Margo.'

She smiled. 'It's been fun. I really had a good time.' She looked up at him archly. 'Maybe I should become an actress.'

He smiled. 'You'd be good at it. You certainly fooled this audience.'

'I did, didn't I?'

'Here's the rest of your money.' He took an envelope out of his pocket. 'And your plane ticket back to Chicago.'

'Thank you.'

He looked at his watch. 'You'd better get going.'

'Right. I just want you to know that I appreciate everything. I mean, your getting me out of prison and all.'

He smiled. 'That's all right. Have a good trip.'

'Thanks.'

He watched her go upstairs to pack. The game was over.

Check and check mate.

Margo Posner was in her bedroom finishing packing when Kendall walked in.

'Hi, Julia. I just wanted to –' She stopped. 'What are you doing?'

'I'm going home.'

Kendall looked at her in surprise. 'So soon? Why? I

was hoping we might spend some time together and get acquainted. We have so many years to catch up on.'

'Sure. Well, some other time.'

Kendall sat on the edge of the bed. 'It's like a miracle, isn't it? Finding each other after all these years?'

Margo went on with her packing. 'Yeah. It's a miracle, all right.'

'You must feel like Cinderella. I mean, one minute you're living a perfectly average life and the next minute someone hands you a billion dollars.'

Margo stopped her packing. 'What?'

'I said . . .'

'A *billion* dollars?'

'Yes. According to Father's will, that's what we each inherit.'

Margo was looking at Kendall, stunned. 'We each get a billion dollars?'

'Didn't they tell you?'

'No,' Margo said slowly. 'They didn't tell me.' There was a thoughtful expression on her face. 'You know, Kendall, you're right. Maybe we should get better acquainted.'

Tyler was in the solarium, looking at photographs of yachts, when Clark approached him.

'Excuse me, Judge Stanford. There's a telephone call for you.'

'I'll take it in here.'

It was Keith Percy in Chicago.

'Tyler?'

'Yes.'

'I have some really great news for you!'

'Oh?'

'Now that I'm retiring, how would you like to be appointed chief judge?'

It was all Tyler could do to keep from giggling. 'That would be wonderful, Keith.'

'Well, it's yours!'

'I . . . I don't know what to say.' *What should I say? 'Billionaires don't sit on the bench in a dirty little courtroom in Chicago, handing out sentences to the misfits of the world?' Or 'I'll be too busy sailing around the world on my yacht?'*

'How soon can you get back to Chicago?'

'It will be a while,' Tyler said. 'I have a lot to do here.'

'Well, we'll all be waiting for you.'

Don't hold your breath. 'Good-bye.' He replaced the receiver and glanced at his watch. It was time for Margo to be leaving for the airport. Tyler went upstairs to see if she was ready.

When he walked into Margo's bedroom, she was unpacking her suitcase.

He looked at her in surprise. 'You're not ready.'

She looked up at him and smiled. 'No. I'm unpacking. I've been thinking. I like it here. Maybe I should stay awhile.'

248

He frowned. 'What are you talking about? You're catching a plane to Chicago.'

'There'll be another plane along, judge.' She grinned. 'Maybe I'll even buy my own.'

'What are you saying?'

'You told me you wanted me to help you play a little joke on someone.'

'Yes?'

'Well, the joke seems to be on me. I'm worth a billion dollars.'

Tyler's expression hardened. 'I want you to get out of here. Now.'

'Do you? I think I'll go when I'm ready,' Margo said. 'And I'm not ready.'

Tyler stood there, studying her. 'What . . . what is it you want?'

She nodded. 'That's better. The billion dollars I'm supposed to get. You were planning to keep it for yourself, right? I figured you were pulling a little scam to pick up some extra money, but a billion dollars! That's a different ball game. I think I deserve a share of that.'

There was a knock at the bedroom door.

'Excuse me,' Clark said. 'Luncheon is served.'

Margo turned to Tyler. 'You go along. I won't be joining you. I have some important errands to run.'

Later that afternoon, packages began to arrive at Rose Hill. There were boxes of dresses from Armani,

249

sportswear from Scaasi Boutique, lingerie from Jordan Marsh, a sable coat from Neiman Marcus, and a diamond bracelet from Cartier. All the packages were addressed to Miss Julia Stanford.

When Margo walked in the door at four thirty, Tyler was waiting to confront her, furious.

'What do you think you're doing?' he demanded.

She smiled. 'I needed a few things. After all, your sister has to be well dressed, doesn't she? It's amazing how much credit a store will give you when you're a Stanford. You will take care of the bills, won't you?'

'Julia . . .'

'Margo.' She reminded him. 'By the way, I saw the pictures of yachts on the table. Are you planning to buy one?'

'That's none of your business.'

'Don't be too sure. Maybe you and I will take a cruise. We'll name the yacht *Margo*. Or should we name it *Julia*? We can go around the world together. I don't like being alone.'

Tyler took a deep breath. 'It seems that I underestimated you. You're a very clever young woman.'

'Coming from you, that's a big compliment.'

'I hope that you're also a reasonable young woman.'

'That depends. What do you call reasonable?'

'One million dollars. Cash.'

Her heart began to beat faster. 'And I can keep the things I bought today?'

'All of them.'

She took a deep breath. 'You have a deal.'

'Good. I'll get the money to you as quickly as I can. I'll be going back to Chicago in the next few days.' He took a key from his pocket and handed it to her. 'Here's the key to my house. I want you to stay there and wait for me. And don't talk to anyone.'

'All right.' She tried to hide her excitement. *Maybe I should have asked for more,* she thought.

'I'll book you on the next plane out of here.'

'What about the things I bought . . . ?'

'I'll have them sent on to you.'

'Good. Hey, we both came out of this great, didn't we?'

He nodded. 'Yes. We did.'

Tyler took Margo to Logan International Airport to see her off.

At the airport she said, 'What are you going to tell the others? About my leaving, I mean.'

'I'll tell them that you had to go visit a very good friend who became ill, a friend in South America.'

She looked at him wistfully. 'Do you want to know something, judge? That yachting trip would have been fun.'

Over the loudspeaker, her flight was being called.

'That's me, I guess.'

'Have a nice flight.'

'Thanks. I'll see you in Chicago.'

Tyler watched her go into the departures terminal

and stood there, waiting until the plane took off. Then he went back to the limousine and said to the driver, 'Rose Hill.'

When Tyler arrived back at the house, he went directly to his room and telephoned Chief Judge Keith Percy.

'We're all waiting for you, Tyler. When are you coming back? We're planning a little celebration in your honor.'

'Very soon, Keith,' Tyler said. 'Meanwhile, I could use your help with a problem I've run into.'

'Certainly. What can I do for you?'

'It's about a felon I tried to help. Margo Posner. I believe I told you about her.'

'I remember. What's the problem?'

'The poor woman has deluded herself into believing she's my sister. She followed me to Boston and tried to murder me.'

'My God! That's terrible!'

'She's on her way back to Chicago now, Keith. She stole the key to my house, and I don't know what she plans to do next. The woman is a dangerous lunatic. She's threatened to kill my whole family. I want her committed to the Reed Mental Health Facility. If you'll fax me the commitment papers, I'll sign them. I'll arrange for her psychiatric examinations myself.'

'Of course. I'll take care of it immediately, Tyler.'

'I'd appreciate it. She's on United Airlines Flight 307. It arrives at eight fifteen tonight. I suggest that you have people there at the airport to pick her up. Tell them to be careful. She should be put in maximum security at Reed, and not allowed any visitors.'

'I'll see to it. I'm sorry you had to go through this, Tyler.'

There was a shrug in Tyler's voice. 'You know what they say, Keith: "No good deed, no matter how small, goes unpunished."'

At dinner that evening Kendall asked, 'Isn't Julia joining us tonight?'

Tyler said regretfully, 'Unfortunately, no. She asked me to say good-bye to all of you. She's gone to take care of a friend in South America who's had a stroke. It was rather sudden.'

'But the will has not been ...'

'Julia has given me her power of attorney and wants me to arrange for her share to go into a trust fund.'

A servant placed a bowl of Boston clam chowder in front of Tyler.

'Ah,' he said. 'That looks delicious! I'm hungry tonight.'

United Airlines Flight 307 was making its final approach to O'Hare International Airport on schedule. A metallic voice came over the loudspeaker. 'Ladies and gentlemen, would you fasten your seat belts, please?'

Margo Posner had enjoyed the flight tremendously.

She had spent most of the time dreaming about what she was going to do with the million dollars and all the clothes and jewelry she had bought. *And all because I was busted! Isn't that a kick!*

When the plane landed, Margo gathered the things she had carried on board and started to walk down the ramp. A flight attendant stayed directly behind her. Near the plane was an ambulance, flanked by two paramedics in white jackets, and a doctor. The flight attendant saw them and pointed to Margo.

As Margo stepped off the ramp, one of the men approached her. 'Excuse me,' he said.

Margo looked up at him. 'Yes?'

'Are you Margo Posner?'

'Why, yes. What's . . . ?'

'I'm Dr Zimmerman.' He took her arm. 'We'd like you to come with us, please.' He started leading her toward the ambulance.

Margo tried to jerk away. 'Wait a minute! What are you doing?' she demanded.

The other two men had moved to either side of her to hold her arms.

'Just come along quietly, Miss Posner,' the doctor said.

'Help!' Margo screamed. 'Help me!'

The other passengers were standing there, gaping.

'What's the matter with all of you?' Margo yelled. 'Are you blind? I'm being kidnapped! I'm Julia Stanford! I'm Harry Stanford's daughter!'

'Of course, you are,' Dr Zimmerman said soothingly. 'Just calm down.'

The observers watched in astonishment as Margo was carried into the back of the ambulance, kicking and screaming.

Inside the ambulance, the doctor took out a syringe and pressed the needle into Margo's arm. 'Relax,' he said. 'Everything is going to be all right.'

'You must be crazy!' Margo said. 'You must be . . .' Her eyes began to droop.

The ambulance doors closed, and the ambulance sped away.

When Tyler got the report, he laughed out loud. He could visualize the greedy bitch being carried off. He would arrange for her to be kept in a mental health facility for the rest of her life.

Now the game is really over, he thought. *I've done it! The old man would turn over in his grave – if he still had one – if he knew that I was getting control of Stanford Enterprises. I'll give Lee everything he's ever dreamed of.*

Perfect. Everything was perfect.

The events of the day had filled Tyler with a sexual excitement. *I need some relief.* He opened his suitcase and from the back of it took out a copy of *Damron's Guide.* There were several gay bars listed in Boston. He chose the Quest on Boylston Street. *I'll skip dinner.*

I'll go straight to the club. And then he thought, *What an oxymoron!*

Julia and Sally were getting dressed to go to work. Sally asked, 'How was your date with Henry last night?'

'The same.'

'That bad, huh? Have the marriage banns been posted yet?'

'God forbid!' Julia said. 'Henry is sweet, but . . .' She sighed. 'He isn't for me.'

'*He* might not be,' Sally said, 'but *these* are for you.' She handed Julia five envelopes.

They were all bills. Julia opened them. Three of them were marked OVERDUE and another was marked THIRD NOTICE. Julia studied them a moment.

'Sally, I wonder if you could lend me . . . ?'

Sally looked at her in amazement. 'I don't understand you.'

'What do you mean?'

'You're working like a galley slave, you can't pay your bills, and all you have to do is lift your little finger and you could come up with a few million dollars, give or take some change.'

'It's not my money.'

'Of course, it's your money!' Sally snapped. 'Harry Stanford was your father, wasn't he? Ergo, you're entitled to a share of his estate. And I don't use the word *ergo* very often.'

256

'Forget it. I told you how he treated my mother. He wouldn't have left me a dime.'

Sally sighed. 'Damn! And I was looking forward to living with a millionaire!'

They walked down to the parking lot where they kept their cars. Julia's space was empty. She stared at it in shock. 'It's gone!'

'Are you sure you parked your car here last night?' Sally asked.

'Yes.'

'Someone stole it!'

Julia shook her head. 'No,' she said slowly.

'What do you mean?'

She turned to look at Sally. 'They must have repossessed it. I'm three payments behind.'

'Wonderful,' Sally said tonelessly. 'That's just wonderful.'

Sally was unable to get her roommate's situation out of her mind. *It's like a fairy tale,* Sally thought. *A princess who doesn't know she's a princess. Only in this case, she knows it, but she's too proud to do anything about it. It's not fair! The family has all that money, and she has nothing. Well, if she won't do something about it, I damn well will. She'll thank me for it.*

That evening, after Julia went out, Sally examined the box of clippings again. She took out a recent newspaper article mentioning that the Stanford heirs had gone back to Rose Hill for the funeral services.

If the princess won't go to them, Sally thought, *they're going to come to the princess.*

She sat down and began to write a letter. It was addressed to Judge Tyler Stanford.

Chapter Twenty-one

Tyler Stanford signed the commitment papers putting Margo Posner in Reed Mental Health Facility. Three psychiatrists were required to agree to the commitment, but Tyler knew that that would be easy for him to handle.

He reviewed everything he had done from the very beginning, and decided that there had been no flaws in his game plan. Dmitri had disappeared in Australia, and Margo Posner had been disposed of. That left Hal Baker, but he would be no problem. Everyone had an Achilles' heel, and his was his stupid family. *No, Baker will never talk because he couldn't bear the thought of spending his life in prison, away from his dear ones.*

Everything was perfect.

The minute the will is probated, I'll return to Chicago and pick up Lee. Maybe we'll even buy a house in St Tropez. He began to get aroused at the thought. *We'll sail around the world in my yacht. I've always wanted to see Venice . . . and Positano . . . and Capri . . . We'll go on safari in Kenya, and see the Taj Mahal*

*together in the moonlight. And who do I owe all this to?
To Daddy. Dear old Daddy. 'You're a queer, Tyler, and
you'll always be a queer. I don't know how the hell
anything like you came from my loins.'*

Well, who has the last laugh now, Father?

Tyler went downstairs to join his brother and sister
for lunch. He was hungry again.

'It's really a pity that Julia had to leave so quickly,'
Kendall said. 'I would have liked to have gotten to
know her better.'

'I'm sure she plans to return as soon as she can,'
Marc said.

That's certainly true, Tyler thought. He would make
sure she never got out.

The talk turned to the future.

Peggy said, shyly, 'Woody is going to buy a group
of polo ponies.'

'It's not a group!' Woody snapped. 'It's a string. A
string of polo ponies.'

'I'm sorry, darling. I just –'

'Forget it!'

Tyler said to Kendall, 'What are your plans?'

'*. . . We are counting on your further support . . . We
would appreciate it if you would deposit 1 million US
dollars . . . within the next ten days.*'

'Kendall?'

'Oh. I'm going to . . . to expand the business. I'll
open shops in London and in Paris.'

'That sounds exciting,' Peggy said.

'I have a show in New York in two weeks. I have to run down there and get it ready.'

Kendall looked over at Tyler. 'What are you going to do with your share of the estate?'

Tyler said piously, 'Charity, mostly. There are so many worthy organizations that need help.'

He was only half listening to the conversation at the table. He looked around the table at his brother and sister. *If it weren't for me, you'd be getting nothing. Nothing!*

He turned to look at Woody. His brother had become a dope addict, throwing his life away. *Money won't help him,* Tyler thought. *It will only buy him more dope.* He wondered where Woody was getting the stuff.

Tyler turned to his sister. Kendall was bright and successful, and she had made the most of her talents.

Marc was seated next to her, telling an amusing anecdote to Peggy. *He's attractive and charming. Too bad he's married.*

And then there was Peggy. He thought of her as Poorpeggy. Why she put up with Woody was beyond him. *She must love him very much. She certainly hasn't gotten anything out of her marriage.*

He wondered what the expressions on their faces would be if he stood up and said, '*I control Stanford Enterprises. I had our father murdered, his body dug up, and I hired someone to impersonate our half sister.*' He smiled at the thought. It was difficult holding a secret as delicious as the one he had.

After lunch, Tyler went to his room to telephone Lee again. There was no answer. *He's out with someone,* Tyler thought, despairingly. *He doesn't believe me about the yacht. Well, I'll prove it to him! When is that damn will going to be probated? I'll have to call Fitzgerald, or that young lawyer, Steve Sloane.*

There was a knock at the door. Clark stood there. 'Excuse me, Judge Stanford. A letter arrived for you.'

Probably from Keith Percy, congratulating me. 'Thank you, Clark.' He took the envelope. It had a Kansas City return address. He stared at it a moment, puzzled, then opened it and began to read the letter.

> *Dear Judge Stanford,*
> *I think you should know that you have a half sister named Julia. She is the daughter of Rosemary Nelson and your father. She lives here in Kansas City. Her address is 1425 Metcalf Avenue, Apartment 3B, Kansas City, Kansas.*
> *I'm sure Julia would be most happy to hear from you.*
> *Sincerely,*
> *A Friend*

Tyler stared at the letter disbelievingly, and he felt a cold chill. 'No!' he cried aloud. 'No!' *I won't have it!*

Not now! Maybe she's a fake. But he had a terrible feeling that this Julia was genuine. *And now the bitch is coming forward to claim her share of the estate! My share*, Tyler corrected himself. *It doesn't belong to her. I can't let her come here. It would ruin everything. I would have to explain the other Julia, and. . .* He shuddered. 'No!' *I have to have her taken care of. Fast.*

He reached for the telephone and dialed Hal Baker's number.

Chapter Twenty-two

The dermatologist shook his head. 'I've seen cases similar to yours, but never one this bad.'

Hal Baker scratched his hand and nodded.

'You see, Mr Baker, we were confronted with three possibilities. Your itching could have been caused by a fungus, an allergy, or it could be neurodermatitis. The skin scraping I took from your hand and put under the microscope showed me that it wasn't a fungus. And you said you didn't handle chemicals on the job . . .'

'That's right.'

'So, we've narrowed it down. What you have is lichen simplex chronicus or localized neurodermatitis.'

'That sounds awful. Is there something you can do about it?'

'Fortunately, there is.' The doctor took a tube from a cabinet in a corner of the office and opened it. 'Is your hand itching now?'

Hal Baker scratched again. 'Yes. It feels like it's on fire.'

'I want you to rub some of this cream on your hand.'

Hal Baker squeezed out some of the cream and began to rub it into his hand. It was like a miracle.

'The itching has stopped!' Baker said.

'Good. Use that, and you won't have any more problem.'

'Thank you, doctor. I can't tell you what a relief this is.'

'I'll give you a prescription. You can take the tube with you.'

'Thank you.'

Driving home, Hal Baker was singing aloud. It was the first time since he had met Judge Tyler Stanford that his hand had not itched. It was a wonderful feeling of freedom. Still whistling, he pulled into the garage, and walked into the kitchen. Helen was waiting for him.

'You had a telephone call,' she said. 'A Mr Jones. He said it was urgent.'

His hand began itching.

He had hurt some people, but he had done it for the love of his kids. He had committed some crimes, but it was for the family. Hal Baker did not believe he really had been at fault. This was different. This was a cold-blooded murder.

When he had returned the phone call, he had protested. 'I can't do that, judge. You'll have to find someone else.'

There had been a silence. And then, 'How's the family?'

The flight to Kansas City was uneventful. Judge Stanford had given him detailed instructions. *'Her name is Julia Stanford. You have her address and apartment number. She won't be expecting you. All you have to do is go there and handle her.'*

He took a taxi from the Kansas City Downtown Airport to downtown Kansas City.

'Beautiful day,' the taxi driver said.

'Yep.'

'Where did you come in from?'

'New York. I live here.'

'Nice place to live.'

'Sure is. I have a little repair work to do around the house. Would you drop me off at a hardware store?'

'Right.'

Five minutes later, Hal Baker was saying to a clerk in the store, 'I need a hunting knife.'

'We have just the thing, sir. Would you come this way, please?'

The knife was a thing of beauty, about six inches long, with a sharp pointed end and serrated edges.

'Will this do?'

'I'm sure it will,' Hal Baker said.

'Will that be cash or charge?'

'Cash.'

His next stop was at a stationery store.

Hal Baker studied the apartment building at 1425 Metcalf Avenue for five minutes, examining exits and entrances. He left and returned at 8 P.M., when it began to get dark. He wanted to make sure that if Julia Stanford had a job, she would be home from work. He had noted that the apartment building had no doorman. There was an elevator, but he took the stairs. It was not smart to be in small enclosed places. They were traps. He reached the third floor. Apartment 3B was down the hall on the left. The knife was taped to the inside pocket of his jacket. He rang the doorbell. A moment later, the door opened, and he found himself facing an attractive woman.

'Hello.' She had a nice smile. 'Can I help you?'

She was younger than he had expected, and he wondered fleetingly why Judge Stanford wanted her killed. *Well, that's none of my business*. He took out a card and handed it to her.

'I'm with the A. C. Nielsen Company,' he said smoothly. 'We don't have any of the Nielsen family in this area, and we're looking for people who might be interested.'

She shook her head. 'No, thanks.' She started to close the door.

'We pay one hundred dollars a week.'

The door stayed half open.

267

'A hundred dollars a week?'

'Yes, ma'am.'

The door was wide open now.

'All you have to do is record the names of the programs you watch. We'll give you a contract for one year.'

Five thousand dollars! 'Come in,' she said.

He walked into the apartment.

'Sit down, Mr –'

'Allen. Jim Allen.'

'Mr Allen. How did you happen to select me?'

'Our company does random checking. We have to make sure that none of the people is involved in television in any way, so we can keep our survey accurate. You don't have any connection with any television production programs or networks, do you?'

She laughed. 'Gosh, no. What would I have to do exactly?'

'It's really very simple. We'll give you a chart with all the television programs listed on it, and all you have to do is make a check mark every time you watch a program. That way our computer can figure out how many viewers each program has. The Nielsen family is scattered around the United States, so we get a clear picture of which shows are popular in which areas and with whom. Would you be interested?'

'Oh, yes.'

He took out some printed forms and a pen. 'How many hours a day do you watch television?'

'Not very many. I work all day.'

'But you do watch some television?'

'Oh, certainly. I watch the news at night, and sometimes an old movie. I like Larry King.'

He made a note. 'Do you watch much educational television?'

'I watch PBS on Sundays.'

'By the way, do you live alone here?'

'I have a roommate, but she's not here.'

So they were alone.

His hand began to itch. He started to reach into his inside pocket to untape the knife. He heard footsteps in the hall outside. He stopped.

'Did you say I get five thousand dollars a year just for doing this?'

'That's right. Oh, I forgot to mention. We also give you a new color TV set.'

'That's fantastic!'

The footsteps were gone. He reached inside his pocket again, and felt the handle of the knife. 'Could I have a glass of water, please? It's been a long day.'

'Certainly.' He watched her get up and go over to the small bar in the corner. He slipped the knife out of its sheath and moved up behind her.

She was saying, 'My roommate watches PBS more than I do.'

He lifted the knife, ready to strike.

'But Julia's more intellectual than I am.'

Baker's hand froze in midair. 'Julia?'

'My roommate. Or she was. She's gone. I found a note when I got home saying she had left and didn't know when she'd be –' She turned around, holding the glass of water, and saw the upraised knife in his hand. 'What . . . ?'

She screamed.

Hal Baker turned and fled.

Hal Baker telephoned Tyler Stanford. 'I'm in Kansas City, but the girl is gone.'

'What do you mean, gone?'

'Her roommate says she left.'

He was silent for a moment. 'I have a feeling she's headed for Boston. I want you to get up here right away.'

'Yes, sir.'

Tyler Stanford slammed down the receiver and began to pace. *Everything had been going so perfectly!* The girl had to be found and disposed of. She was a loose cannon. Even after he received control of the estate, Tyler knew he would not rest easy as long as she was alive. *I've got to find her,* Tyler thought. *I've got to! But where?*

Clark came into the room. 'Excuse me, Judge Stanford. There is a Miss Julia Stanford here to see you.'

Chapter Twenty-three

It was because of Kendall that Julia decided to go to Boston. Returning from lunch one day, Julia passed an exclusive dress shop, and in the window was an original design by Kendall. Julia looked at it for a long time. *That's my sister,* Julia thought. *I can't blame her for what happened to my mother. And I can't blame my brothers.* And suddenly she was filled with an overpowering desire to see them, to meet them, to talk to them, to have a family at last.

When Julia returned to the office, she told Max Tolkin that she would be gone for a few days. Embarrassed, she said, 'I wonder if I could have an advance on my salary?'

Tolkin smiled. 'Sure. You have a vacation coming. Here. Have a good time.'

Will I have a good time? Julia wondered. *Or am I making a terrible mistake?*

When Julia returned home, Sally had not arrived yet. *I can't wait for her,* Julia decided. *If I don't go now, I'll never go*. She packed her suitcase and left a note.

On the way to the bus terminal, Julia had second thoughts. *What am I doing? Why did I make this sudden decision?* Then she thought wryly, *Sudden? It's taken me fourteen years!* She was filled with an enormous sense of excitement. What was her family going to be like? She knew that one of her brothers was a judge, the other was a famous polo player, and her sister was a famous designer. *It's a family of achievers,* Julia thought, *and who am I? I hope they don't look down on me.* Merely thinking about what lay ahead made Julia's heart skip a beat. She boarded a Greyhound bus and was on her way.

When the bus arrived at South Station in Boston, Julia found a taxi.

'Where to, lady?' the driver asked.

And Julia completely lost her nerve. She had intended to say, 'Rose Hill.' Instead, she said, 'I don't know.'

The taxi driver turned around to look at her. 'Gee, I don't know, either.'

'Could you just drive around? I've never been to Boston before.'

He nodded. 'Sure.'

They drove west along Summer Street until they reached the Boston Common.

The driver said, 'This is the oldest public park in the United States. They used to use it for hangings.'

And Julia could hear her mother's voice. *'I used to take the children to the Common in the winter to ice-skate. Woody was a natural athlete. I wish you could have met him, Julia. He was such a handsome boy. I always thought he was going to be the successful one in the family.'* It was as though her mother were with her, sharing this moment.

They had reached Charles Street, the entrance to the Public Garden. The driver said, 'See those bronze ducklings? Believe it or not, they've all got names.'

'We used to have picnics in the Public Garden. There are cute bronze ducklings at the entrance. They're named Jack, Kack, Lack, Mack, Nack, Ouack, Pack, and Quack.' Julia had thought that was so funny that she had made her mother repeat the names over and over again.

Julia looked at the meter. The drive was getting expensive. 'Could you recommend an inexpensive hotel?'

'Sure. How about the Copley Square Hotel?'

'Would you take me there, please?'

'Right.'

Five minutes later, they pulled up in front of the hotel.

'Enjoy Boston, lady.'

'Thank you.' *Am I going to enjoy it, or will it be a disaster?* Julia paid the driver and went into the hotel. She approached the young clerk behind the desk.

273

'Hello,' he said. 'May I help you?'

'I'd like a room, please.'

'Single?'

'Yes.'

'How long will you be staying?'

She hesitated. *An hour? Ten years?* 'I don't know.'

'Right.' He checked the key rack. 'I have a nice single for you on the fourth floor.'

'Thank you.' She signed the register in a neat hand. *Julia Stanford.*

The clerk handed her a key. 'There you are. Enjoy your stay.'

The room was small, but neat and clean. As soon as Julia unpacked, she telephoned Sally.

'Julia? My God! Where are you?'

'I'm in Boston.'

'Are you all right?' She sounded hysterical.

'Yes. Why?'

'Someone came to the apartment, looking for you, and I think he wanted to kill you!'

'What are you talking about?'

'He had a knife and . . . you should have seen the look on his face . . .' She was gasping for breath. 'When he found out I wasn't you, he ran!'

'I don't believe it!'

'He said he was with A. C. Nielsen, but I called their office, and they never heard of him! Do you know anyone who would want to harm you?'

'Of course not, Sally! Don't be ridiculous! Did you call the police?'

'I did. But there wasn't much they could do except tell me to be more careful.'

'Well, I'm just fine, so don't worry.'

She heard Sally take a deep breath. 'All right. As long as you're okay. Julia?'

'Yes.'

'Be careful, will you?'

'Of course.' *Sally and her imagination! Who in the world would want to kill me?*

'Do you know when you're coming back?'

The same kind of question the clerk had asked her. 'No.'

'You're there to see your family, aren't you?'

'Yes.'

'Good luck.'

'Thanks, Sally.'

'Keep in touch.'

'I will.'

Julia replaced the receiver. She stood there, wondering what to do next. *If I had any brains, I would get back on the bus and go home. I've been stalling. Did I come to Boston to see the sights? No. I came here to meet my family. Am I going to meet them? No . . . Yes . . .*

She sat on the edge of the bed, her mind in a turmoil. *What if they hate me? I must not think that. They're going to love me, and I'm going to love them.* She looked at the telephone and thought, *Maybe it would be better if I called them. No. Then they might not want to see me.* She went to the closet and selected her best dress. *If I don't do it now, I'll never do it,* Julia decided.

Thirty minutes later, she was in a taxi on her way to Rose Hill to meet her family.

Chapter Twenty-four

Tyler was staring at Clark in disbelief. 'Julia Stanford
. . . is here?'

'Yes, sir.' There was a puzzled tone in the butler's
voice. 'But it isn't the same Miss Stanford who was
here earlier.'

Tyler forced a smile. 'Of course not. I'm afraid it's
an impostor.'

'An impostor, sir?'

'Yes. They'll be coming out of the woodwork, Clark,
all claiming a right to the family fortune.'

'That's terrible, sir. Shall I call the police?'

'No,' Tyler said quickly. That was the last thing he
wanted. 'I'll handle it. Send her into the library.'

'Yes, sir.'

Tyler's mind was racing. So the real Julia Stanford
had finally showed up. It was fortunate that none of
the other members of the family was home at the
moment. He would have to get rid of her immediately.

Tyler walked into the library. Julia was standing in
the middle of the room, looking at a portrait of Harry
Stanford. Tyler stood there a moment, studying

the woman. She was beautiful. It was too bad that . . .

Julia turned around and saw him. 'Hello.'

'Hello.'

'You're Tyler.'

'That's right. Who are you?'

Her smile faded. 'Didn't . . . ? I'm Julia Stanford.'

'Really? You'll forgive my asking, but do you have any proof of that?'

'Proof? Well, yes . . . I . . . that is . . . no *proof*. I just assumed –'

He moved closer to her. 'How did you happen to come here?'

'I decided that it was time to meet my family.'

'After twenty-six years?'

'Yes.'

Looking at her, listening to her speak, there was no question in Tyler's mind. She was genuine, dangerous, and would have to be disposed of quickly.

Tyler forced a smile. 'Well, you can imagine what a shock this is to me. I mean, for you to appear here out of the blue and . . .'

'I know. I'm sorry. I probably should have called first.'

Tyler asked casually, 'You came to Boston alone?'

'Yes.'

His mind was racing. 'Does anyone else know you're here?'

'No. Well, my roommate, Sally, in Kansas City.'

'Where are you staying?'

'At the Copley Square Hotel.'

'That's a nice hotel. What room are you in?'

'Four nineteen.'

'All right. Why don't you go back to your hotel and wait there for us? I want to prepare Woody and Kendall for this. They're going to be as surprised as I was.'

'I'm sorry. I should have –'

'No problem. Now that we've met, I know that everything is going to be just fine.'

'Thank you, Tyler.'

'You're welcome' – he almost choked on the word. 'Julia. Let me call a taxi for you.'

Five minutes later, she was gone.

Hal Baker had just returned to his hotel room in downtown Boston when the telephone call came. He picked it up.

'Hal?'

'I'm sorry. I have no news yet, judge. I've combed this whole town. I went to the airport and –'

'She's here, stupid!'

'What?'

'She's here in Boston. She's staying at the Copley Square Hotel, room four nineteen. I want her taken care of tonight. And I don't want any more bungling, do you understand?'

'What happened was not my –'

'Do you understand?'

'Yes, sir.'

'Then do it!' Tyler slammed down the receiver. He went to find Clark.

'Clark, about that young woman who was here pretending she was my sister?'

'Yes, sir?'

'I wouldn't say anything about it to the other members of the family. It would just upset them.'

'I understand, sir. You're very thoughtful.'

Julia walked over to the Ritz-Carlton for dinner. The hotel was beautiful, just as her mother had described it. *On Sunday, I used to take the children there for brunch.* Julia sat in the dining room and visualized her mother there at a table with young Tyler, Woody and Kendall. *I wish I could have grown up with them,* Julia thought. *But at least I'm going to meet them now.* She wondered whether her mother would have approved of what she was doing. Julia had been taken aback by Tyler's reception. He had seemed . . . cold. *But that's only natural,* Julia thought. *A stranger walks in and says, 'I'm your sister.' Of course he would be suspicious. But I'm sure I can convince them.*

When the check came, Julia stared at it in shock. *I have to be careful,* she thought. *I have to have enough money left to take the bus back to Kansas.*

As she stepped outside the Ritz-Carlton, a tour bus was getting ready to leave. On an impulse, she boarded it. She wanted to see as much of her mother's city as she could.

Hal Baker strode into the lobby of the Copley Square Hotel as though he belonged there and took the stairs to the fourth floor. This time there would be no mistake. Room 419 was in the middle of the corridor. Hal Baker scanned the hallway to make sure no one was around, and knocked on the door. There was no answer. He knocked again. 'Miss Stanford?' Still no answer.

He took a small case from his pocket and selected a pick. It took him only seconds to open the door. Hal Baker stepped inside, closing the door behind him. The room was empty.

'Miss Stanford?'

He walked into the bathroom. Empty. He went back into the bedroom. He took a knife out of his pocket, moved a chair in back of the door, and sat in the dark, waiting. It was one hour later when he heard someone approaching.

Hal Baker rose quickly and stood behind the door, the knife in his hands. He heard the key turn in the lock, and the door started to swing open. He raised the knife high over his head, ready to strike. Julia Stanford stepped in and pressed the light switch on. He heard her say, 'Very well. Come in.'

A crowd of reporters poured into the room.

Chapter Twenty-five

It was Gordon Wellman, the night manager at the Copley Square Hotel, who inadvertently saved Julia's life. He had come on duty at six o'clock that evening, and had automatically checked the hotel register. When he came across the name of Julia Stanford, he stared at it in surprise. Ever since Harry Stanford had died, the newspapers had been full of stories about the Stanford family. They had dredged up the ancient scandal of Stanford's affair with the children's governess and the suicide of Stanford's wife. Harry Stanford had an illegitimate daughter named Julia. There were rumors that she had come to Boston in secret. Shortly after going on a shopping spree, she had reportedly left for South America. Now, it seemed that she was back. *And she's staying at my hotel!* Gordon Wellman thought excitedly.

He turned to the front-desk clerk. 'Do you know how much publicity this could mean for the hotel?'

A minute later, he was on the telephone to the press.

* * *

When Julia arrived back at the hotel after her sightseeing tour, the lobby was filled with reporters, eagerly awaiting her. As soon as she walked into the lobby, they pounced.

'Miss Stanford! I'm from the *Boston Globe*. We've been looking for you, but we heard that you had left town. Could you tell us . . . ?'

A television camera was pointed at her. 'Miss Stanford, I'm with WCVB-TV. We'd like to get a statement from you . . .'

'Miss Stanford, I'm from the *Boston Phoenix*. We want to know your reaction to . . .'

'Look this way, Miss Stanford! Smile! Thank you.' Flashes were popping.

Julia stood there, filled with confusion. *Oh, my God,* she thought. *The family is going to think that I'm some kind of publicity hound.* She turned to the reporters. 'I'm sorry. I have nothing to say.'

She fled into the elevator. They piled in after her.

'*People* magazine wants to do a story on your life, and what it feels like to be estranged from your family for over twenty-five years.'

'We heard you had gone to South America.'

'Are you planning to live in Boston . . . ?'

'Why aren't you staying at Rose Hill . . . ?'

She got out of the elevator at the fourth floor and hurried down the corridor. They were at her heels. There was no way to escape them.

Julia took out her key and opened the door to her

room. She stepped inside and turned on the light. 'Very well. Come in.'

Hidden behind the door, Hal Baker was caught by surprise, the knife in his raised hand. As the reporters shoved past him, he quickly put the knife back in his pocket and mingled with the group.

Julia turned to the reporters. 'All right. One question at a time, please.'

Frustrated, Baker backed toward the door and slipped out. Judge Stanford was not going to be pleased.

For the next thirty minutes, Julia answered questions as best she could. Finally, they were gone.

Julia locked the door and went to bed.

In the morning, the television stations and newspapers featured stories about Julia Stanford.

Tyler read the papers and was furious. Woody and Kendall joined him at the breakfast table.

'What's all this nonsense about some woman calling herself Julia Stanford?' Woody asked.

'She's a phony,' Tyler said glibly. 'She came to the door yesterday, demanding money, and I sent her away. I didn't expect her to pull a cheap publicity stunt like this. Don't worry. I'll take care of her.'

He put in a call to Simon Fitzgerald. 'Have you seen the morning papers?'

'Yes.'

'This con artist is going around town claiming that she's our sister.'

Fitzgerald said, 'Do you want me to have her arrested?'

'No! That would only create more publicity. I want you to get her out of town.'

'All right. I'll take care of it, Judge Stanford.'

'Thank you.'

Simon Fitzgerald sent for Steve Sloane.

'There's a problem,' he said.

Steve nodded. 'I know. I've heard the morning news and seen the papers. Who is she?'

'Obviously someone who thinks she can horn in on the family fortune. Judge Stanford suggested we get her out of town. Will you handle her?'

'My pleasure,' Steve said grimly.

One hour later, Steve was knocking on Julia's hotel room door.

When Julia opened the door and saw him standing there she said, 'I'm sorry. I'm not talking to any more reporters. I . . .'

'I'm not a reporter. May I come in?'

'Who are you?'

'My name is Steve Sloane. I'm with the law firm representing the Harry Stanford estate.'

'Oh. I see. Yes. Come in.'

Steve walked into the room.

285

'Did you tell the press that you are Julia Stanford?'

'I'm afraid I was caught off guard. I didn't expect them, you see, and . . .'

'But you *did* claim to be Harry Stanford's daughter?'

'Yes. I am his daughter.'

He looked at her and said cynically, 'Of course, you have proof of that.'

'Well, no,' Julia said slowly. 'I don't.'

'Come on,' Steve insisted. 'You must have *some* proof.' He intended to nail her with her own lies.

'I have nothing,' she said.

He studied her, surprised. She was not what he had expected. There was a disarming frankness about her. *She seems intelligent. How could she have been stupid enough to come here claiming to be Harry Stanford's daughter without any proof?*

'That's too bad,' Steve said. 'Judge Stanford wants you to get out of town.'

Julia's eyes widened. 'What?'

'That's right.'

'But . . . I don't understand. I haven't even met my other brother or sister.'

So she's determined to keep up the bluff, Steve thought. 'Look, I don't know who you are, or what your game is, but you could go to jail for this. We're giving you a break. What you're doing is against the law. You have a choice. Either you can get out of town and stop bothering the family, or we can have you arrested.'

286

Julia stood there in shock. 'Arrested? I . . . I don't know what to say.'

'It's your decision.'

'They don't even want to see me?' Julia asked numbly.

'That's putting it mildly.'

She took a deep breath. 'All right. If that's what they want, I'll go back to Kansas. I promise you, they'll never hear from me again.'

Kansas. You came a long way to pull your little scam. 'That's very wise.' He stood there a moment, watching her, puzzled. 'Well, good-bye.'

She did not reply.

Steve was in Simon Fitzgerald's office.

'Did you see the woman, Steve?'

'Yes. She's going back home.' He seemed distracted.

'Good. I'll tell Judge Stanford. He'll be pleased.'

'Do you know what's bugging me, Simon?'

'What?'

'The dog didn't bark.'

'I beg your pardon?'

'The Sherlock Holmes story. The clue was in what *didn't* happen.'

'Steve, what does that have to do with –'

'She came here without any *proof.*'

Fitzgerald looked at him, puzzled. 'I don't understand. That should have *convinced* you.'

'On the contrary. Why would she come here, all the

287

way from Kansas, claiming to be Harry Stanford's daughter, and not have a single thing to back it up?'

'There are a lot of weirdos out there, Steve.'

'She's not a weirdo. You should have seen her. And there are a couple of other things that bother me, Simon.'

'Yes?'

'Harry Stanford's body disappeared. When I went to talk to Dmitri Kaminsky, the only witness to Stanford's accident, *he* had disappeared ... And no one seems to know where the first Julia Stanford suddenly disappeared to.'

Simon Fitzgerald was frowning. 'What are you saying?'

Steve said, slowly, 'There's something going on that needs to be explained. I'm going to have another talk with the lady.'

Steve Sloane walked into the lobby of the Copley Square Hotel and approached the desk clerk. 'Would you ring Miss Julia Stanford, please?'

The clerk looked up. 'Oh, I'm sorry. Miss Stanford has checked out.'

'Did she leave a forwarding address?'

'No, sir. I'm afraid not.'

Steve stood there, frustrated. There was nothing more he could do. *Well, maybe I was wrong,* he thought philosophically. *Maybe she really is an impostor. Now we'll never know.* He turned and went out into the street. The doorman was ushering a couple into a taxi.

'Excuse me,' Steve said.

The doorman turned. 'Taxi, sir?'

'No. I want to ask you a question. Did you see Miss Stanford come out of the hotel this morning?'

'I certainly did. Everybody was staring at her. She's quite a celebrity. I got a taxi for her.'

'I don't suppose you know where she went?' He found that he was holding his breath.

'Sure. I told the cab driver where to take her.'

'And where was that?' Steve asked impatiently.

'To the Greyhound bus terminal at South Station. I thought it was strange that someone as rich as that would . . .'

'I do want a taxi.'

Steve walked into the crowded Greyhound bus terminal and looked around. Julia was nowhere to be seen. *She's gone*, Steve thought despairingly. A voice on a loudspeaker was calling out the departing buses. He heard the voice say, '. . . and Kansas City,' and Steve hurried out to the loading platform.

Julia was just starting to get on the bus.

'Hold it!' he called.

She turned, startled.

Steve hurried up to her. 'I want to talk to you.'

She looked at him, angry. 'I have nothing more to say to you.' She turned to go.

He grabbed her arm. 'Wait a minute! We really have to talk.'

'My bus is leaving.'

'There'll be another one.'

'My suitcase is on it.'

Steve turned to a porter. 'This woman is about to have a baby. Get her suitcase out of there. Quick!'

The porter looked at Julia in surprise. 'Right.' He hurriedly opened the luggage compartment. 'Which is yours, lady?'

Julia turned to Steve, puzzled. 'Do you know what you're doing?'

'No,' Steve said.

She studied him a moment, then made a decision. She pointed to her suitcase. 'That one.'

The porter pulled it out. 'Do you want me to get you an ambulance or anything?'

'Thank you. I'll be fine.'

Steve picked up the suitcase, and they headed for the exit. 'Have you had breakfast?'

'I'm not hungry,' she said coldly.

'You'd better have something. You're eating for two now, you know.'

They had breakfast at Julien. Julia sat across from Steve, her body rigid with anger.

When they had ordered, Steve said, 'I'm curious about something. What made you think you could claim part of the Stanford estate without any proof at all of your identity?'

She looked at him indignantly. 'I didn't go there to claim part of the Stanford estate. My father wouldn't have left anything to me. I wanted to meet my family. Obviously they didn't want to meet me.'

'Do you have *any* documents . . . any kind of proof at all of who you are?'

She thought of all the clippings piled up in her apartment and shook her head. 'No. Nothing.'

'There's someone I want you to talk to.'

'This is Simon Fitzgerald.' Steve hesitated. 'Er . . .'

'Julia Stanford.'

Fitzgerald said skeptically, 'Sit down, miss.'

Julia sat on the edge of a chair, ready to get up and walk out.

Fitzgerald was studying her. She had the Stanford deep gray eyes, but so did lots of other people. 'You claim you're Rosemary Nelson's daughter.'

'I don't claim anything. I *am* Rosemary Nelson's daughter.'

'And where is your mother?'

'She died a number of years ago.'

'Oh, I'm sorry to hear that. Could you tell us about her?'

'No,' Julia said. 'I really would rather not.' She stood up. 'I want to get out of here.'

'Look, we're trying to help you,' Steve said.

She turned on him. 'Are you? My family doesn't want to see me. You want to turn me over to the police. I don't need that kind of help.' She started toward the door.

Steve said, 'Wait! If you are who you say you are, you must have *something* that will prove you're Harry Stanford's daughter.'

'I told you, I don't,' Julia said. 'My mother and I shut Harry Stanford out of our lives.'

'What did your mother look like?' Simon Fitzgerald asked.

'She was beautiful,' Julia said. Her voice softened. 'She was the loveliest . . .' She remembered something. 'I have a picture of her.' She took a small gold heart-shaped locket from around her neck and handed it to Fitzgerald.

He looked at her a moment, then opened the locket. On one side was a picture of Harry Stanford, and on the other side a picture of Rosemary Nelson. The inscription read TO R. N. WITH LOVE, H. S. The date was 1969.

Simon Fitzgerald stared at the locket for a long time. When he looked up, his voice was husky.

'We owe you an apology, my dear.' He turned to Steve. 'This is Julia Stanford.'

Chapter Twenty-six

~~~~~~~

Kendall had been unable to get the conversation with Peggy out of her mind. Peggy seemed incapable of coping with the situation by herself. *'Woody's trying hard. He really is . . . Oh, I love him so much!'*

He needs a lot of help, Kendall thought. *I have to do something. He's my brother. I must talk to him.*

Kendall went to find Clark.

'Is Mr Woodrow at home?'

'Yes, ma'am. I believe he's in his room.'

'Thank you.'

She thought of the scene at the table, with Peggy's bruised face. *'What happened?' 'I bumped into a door . . .'* How could she have put up with it all this time? Kendall went upstairs and knocked on the door to Woody's room. There was no answer. 'Woody?'

She opened the door and stepped inside. A bitter-almond smell permeated the room. Kendall stood there a moment, then moved toward the bathroom. She could see Woody through the open door. He was heating heroin on a piece of aluminum foil. As it began to liquify and evaporate, she watched Woody inhale

293

the smoke from a rolled up straw he held in his mouth.

Kendall stepped into the bathroom. 'Woody . . . ?'

He looked around and grinned. 'Hi, Sis!' He turned and inhaled deeply again.

'For God's sake! Stop that!'

'Hey, relax. You know what this is called? Chasing the dragon. See the little dragon curling up in the smoke?' He was smiling happily.

'Woody, please let me talk to you.'

'Sure, Sis. What can I do for you? I know it's not a money problem. We're billionaires! What are you looking so depressed about? The sun is out, and it's a beautiful day!' His eyes were glistening.

Kendall stood there looking at him, filled with compassion. 'Woody, I had a talk with Peggy. She told me how you got started on drugs at the hospital.'

He nodded. 'Yeah. Best thing that ever happened to me.'

'No. It's the most terrible thing that ever happened to you. Do you have any idea what you're doing with your life?'

'Sure I do. It's called living it up, Sis!'

She took his hand and said, earnestly, 'You need help.'

'Me? I don't need any help. I'm fine!'

'No, you aren't. Listen to me, Woody. This is your life we're talking about, and it's not only *your* life. Think of Peggy. For years you've put her through a living hell, and she stood for it because she loves you so much. You're not only destroying your life, you're destroying hers. You've got to do something about this *now,* before it's too late. It's not important how you got started on drugs. The important thing is that you get off them.'

Woody's smile faded. He looked into Kendall's eyes and started to say something, then stopped. 'Kendall . . .'

'Yes?'

He licked his lips. 'I . . . I know you're right. I want to stop. I've tried. God, how I've tried. But I can't.'

'Of *course,* you can,' she said fiercely. 'You can do it. We're going to beat this together. Peggy and I are behind you. Who supplies you with heroin, Woody?'

He stood there, looking at her in astonishment. 'My God! You don't know?'

Kendall shook her head. 'No.'

'Peggy.'

Chapter Twenty-seven

Simon Fitzgerald looked at the gold locket for a long time. 'I knew your mother, Julia, and I liked her. She was wonderful with the Stanford children, and they adored her.'

'She adored them, too,' Julia said. 'She used to talk to me about them all the time.'

'What happened to your mother was terrible. You can't imagine what a scandal it created. Boston can be a very small town. Harry Stanford behaved very badly. Your mother had no choice but to leave.' He shook his head. 'Life must have been very difficult for the two of you.'

'Mother had a hard time. The awful thing was that I think she still loved Harry Stanford, in spite of everything.' She looked at Steve. 'I don't understand what's happening. Why doesn't my family want to see me?'

The two men exchanged a look. 'Let me explain,' Steve said. He hesitated, choosing his words carefully. 'A short time ago, a woman showed up here, claiming to be Julia Stanford.'

'But that's impossible!' Julia said. 'I'm . . .'

Steve held up a hand. 'I know. The family hired a private detective to make sure she was authentic.'

'And they found out that she wasn't.'

'No. They found out that she *was*.'

Julia looked at him, bewildered. '*What?*'

'This detective said he found fingerprints that the woman had taken when she got a driver's license in San Francisco when she was seventeen and they matched the prints of the woman calling herself Julia Stanford.'

Julia was more puzzled than ever. 'But I . . . I've never been in Indiana.'

Fitzgerald said, 'Julia, there may be an elaborate conspiracy going on to get part of the Stanford estate. I'm afraid you're caught in the middle of it.'

'I can't believe it!'

'Whoever is behind this can't afford to have two Julia Stanfords around.'

Steve added, 'The only way the plan can work successfully is to get you out of the way.'

'When you say "out of the way . . ."' She stopped, remembering something. 'Oh, no!'

'What is it?' Fitzgerald asked.

'Two nights ago I talked to my roommate, and she was hysterical. She said a man came to our apartment with a knife and tried to attack her. He thought she was me!' It was difficult for Julia to find her voice. 'Who . . . who's doing this?'

297

'If I had to guess, I'd say it's probably a member of the family,' Steve told her.

'But . . . *why*?'

'There's a large fortune at stake, and the will is going to be probated in a few days.'

'What does that have to do with me? My father never even acknowledged me. He wouldn't have left me anything.'

Fitzgerald said, 'As a matter of fact, if we can prove your identity, your share of the overall estate is more than a billion dollars.'

She sat there, numb. When she found her voice, she said, 'A billion dollars?'

'That's right. But someone else is after that money. That's why you're in danger.'

'I see.' She stood there looking at them, feeling a rising panic. 'What am I going to do?'

'I'll tell you what you're *not* going to do,' Steve told her. 'You're not going back to a hotel. I want you to stay out of sight until we find out what's going on.'

'I could go back to Kansas until . . .'

Fitzgerald said, 'I think it would be better if you stayed here, Julia. We'll find a place to hide you.'

'She could stay at my house,' Steve suggested. 'No one will think of looking for her there.'

The two men turned to Julia.

She hesitated. 'Well . . . yes. That will be fine.'

'Good.'

Julia said slowly, 'None of this would be happening if my father hadn't fallen off his yacht.'

'Oh, I don't think he fell,' Steve told her. 'I think he was pushed.'

They took the service elevator to the office building garage and got into Steve's car.

'I don't want anyone to see you,' Steve said. 'We have to keep you out of sight for the next few days.'

They started driving down State Street.

'How about some lunch?'

Julia looked over at him and smiled. 'You always seem to be feeding me.'

'I know a restaurant that's off the beaten path. It's an old house on Gloucester Street. I don't think anyone will see us there.'

L'Espalier was an elegant nineteenth-century townhouse with one of the finest views in Boston. As Steve and Julia walked in, they were greeted by the captain.

'Good afternoon,' he said. 'Will you come this way, please? I have a nice table for you by the window.'

'If you don't mind,' Steve said, 'we'd prefer something against the wall.'

The captain blinked. 'Against the wall?'

'Yes. We like privacy.'

'Of course.' He led them to a table in a corner. 'I'll send your waiter right over.' He was staring at Julia, and his face suddenly lit up. 'Ah! Miss Stanford. It's a pleasure to have you here. I saw your picture in the newspaper.'

Julia looked at Steve, not knowing what to say.

Steve exclaimed, 'My God! We left the children in the car! Let's go get them!' And to the captain, 'We'd like two martinis, very dry. Hold the olives. We'll be right back.'

'Yes, sir.' The captain watched the two of them hurry out of the restaurant.

'What are we doing?' Julia asked.

'Getting out of here. All he has to do is call the press, and we're in trouble. We'll go somewhere else.'

They found a little restaurant on Dalton Street and ordered lunch.

Steve sat there, studying her. 'How does it feel to be a celebrity?' he asked.

'Please don't joke about that. I feel terrible.'

'I know,' he said contritely. 'I'm sorry.' He was finding it very easy to be with her. He thought about how rude he had been when they first met.

'Do you . . . do you really think I'm in danger, Mr Sloane?' Julia asked.

'Call me Steve. Yes. I'm afraid you are. But it will be for only a little while. By the time the will is probated, we'll know who's behind this. In the meantime, I'm going to see to it that you're safe.'

'Thank you. I . . . I appreciate it.'

They were staring at each other, and when an

300

approaching waiter saw the looks on their faces, he decided not to interrupt them.

In the car, Steve asked, 'Is this your first time in Boston?'

'Yes.'

'It's an interesting city.' They were passing the old John Hancock Building. Steve pointed to the tower. 'You see that beacon?'

'Yes.'

'It broadcasts the weather.'

'How can a beacon . . . ?'

'I'm glad you asked. When the light is a steady blue, it means the weather is clear. If it's a flashing blue, you can expect clouds to be near. A steady red means rain ahead, and flashing red, snow instead.'

Julia laughed.

They reached the Harvard Bridge. Steve slowed down. 'This is the bridge that links Boston and Cambridge. It's exactly three hundred, sixty-four point four Smoots and one ear long.'

Julia turned to stare at him. 'I beg your pardon?'

Steve grinned. 'It's true.'

'What's a Smoot?'

'A Smoot is a measurement using the body of Oliver Reed Smoot, who was five feet seven inches. It started as a joke, but when the city rebuilt the bridge, they kept the marks. The Smoot became a standard of length in 1958.'

She laughed. 'That's incredible!'

As they passed the Bunker Hill Monument, Julia exclaimed, 'Oh! That's where the battle of Bunker Hill took place, isn't it?'

'No,' Steve said.

'What do you mean?'

'The battle of Bunker Hill was fought on Breed's Hill.'

Steve's home was in the Newbury Street area of Boston, a charming two-storey house with comfortable furniture and colorful prints hanging on the walls.

'Do you live here alone?' Julia asked.

'Yes. I have a housekeeper who comes in twice a week. I'm going to tell her not to come in for the next few days. I don't want anyone to know you're here.'

Julia looked at Steve and said warmly, 'I want you to know I really appreciate what you're doing for me.'

'My pleasure. Come on, I'll show you your bedroom.'

He led her upstairs to the guest room. 'This is it. I hope you'll be comfortable.'

'Oh, yes. It's lovely,' Julia said.

'I'll bring in some groceries. I usually eat out.'

'I could –' she stopped. 'On second thought, I'd better not. My roommate says my cooking is lethal.'

'I think I'm a fair hand at a stove,' Steve said. 'I'll do some cooking for us.' He looked at her and said slowly, 'I haven't had anyone to cook for for a while.'

Back off, he told himself. *You're way off base. You couldn't keep her in handkerchiefs.*

'I want you to make yourself at home. You'll be completely safe here.'

She looked at him a long time, then smiled. 'Thank you.'

They went back downstairs.

Steve pointed out the amenities. 'Television, VCR, radio, CD player . . . you'll be comfortable.'

'It's wonderful.' She wanted to say, '*Just like I feel with you.*'

'Well, if there's nothing else,' he said awkwardly.

Julia gave him a warm smile. 'I can't think of anything.'

'Then I'll be getting back to the office. I have a lot of questions without answers.'

She watched him walk toward the door.

'Steve?'

He turned around. 'Yes?'

'Is it all right if I call my roommate? She'll be worried about me.'

He shook his head. 'Absolutely not. I don't want you to make any telephone calls or leave this house. Your life may depend on it.'

Chapter Twenty-eight

'I'm Dr Westin. Do you understand that this conversation is going to be tape-recorded?'

'Yes, doctor.'

'Are you feeling calmer now?'

'I'm calm, but I'm angry.'

'What are you angry about?'

'I shouldn't be in this place. I'm not crazy. I've been framed.'

'Oh? Who framed you?'

'Tyler Stanford.'

'*Judge* Tyler Stanford?'

'That's right.'

'Why would he want to do that?'

'For money.'

'Do you have money?'

'No. I mean, yes . . . that is . . . I could have had it. He promised me a million dollars, and a sable coat, and jewelry.'

'Why would Judge Stanford promise you that?'

'Let me start at the beginning. I'm not really Julia Stanford. My name is Margo Posner.'

'When you came in here, you insisted you were Julia Stanford.'

'Forget that. I'm really not. Look ... here's what happened. Judge Stanford hired me to pose as his sister.'

'Why did he do that?'

'So I could get a share of the Stanford estate and turn it over to him.'

'And for doing that he promised you a million dollars, a sable coat, and some jewelry?'

'You don't believe me, do you? Well, I can prove it. He took me to Rose Hill. That's where the Stanford family lives in Boston. I can describe the house to you, and I can tell you all about the family.'

'You're aware that these are very serious charges you're making?'

'You bet I am. But I suppose you won't do anything about it because he happens to be a judge.'

'You're quite wrong. I assure you that your charges will be very thoroughly investigated.'

'Good! I want the bastard locked away the same way he has me locked away. I want out of here!'

'You understand that besides my examination, two of my colleagues also will have to evaluate your mental state?'

'Let them. I'm as sane as you are.'

'Dr Gifford will be in this afternoon, and then we'll decide how we're going to proceed.'

'The sooner the better. I can't stand this damned place!'

When the matron brought Margo her lunch, the matron said, 'I just talked to Dr Gifford. He'll be here in an hour.'

'Thank you.' Margo was ready for him. She was ready for all of them. She was going to tell them everything she knew, from the very beginning. *And when I'm through,* Margo thought, *they're going to lock him up and let me go.* The thought filled her with satisfaction. *I'll be free!* And then Margo thought, *Free to do what? I'll be out on the streets again. Maybe they'll even revoke my parole and put me back in the joint!*

She threw her lunch tray against the wall. *Damn them! They can't do this to me! Yesterday I was worth a billion dollars, and today ... Wait! Wait!* An idea flashed through Margo's mind that was so exciting that it sent a chill through her. *Holy God! What am I doing? I've already proved that I'm Julia Stanford. I have witnesses. The whole family heard Frank Timmons say that my fingerprints showed that I was Julia Stanford. Why the hell would I ever want to be Margo Posner when I can be Julia Stanford? No wonder they have me locked up in here. I must have been out of my mind!* She rang the bell for the matron.

When the matron came in, Margo said excitedly, 'I want to see the doctor right away!'

'I know. You have an appointment with him in –'

'*Now*. Right now!'

The matron took one look at Margo's expression and said, 'Calm down. I'll get him.'

Ten minutes later, Dr Franz Gifford walked into Margo's room.

'You asked to see me?'

'Yes.' She smiled apologetically. 'I'm afraid I've been playing a little game, doctor.'

'Really?'

'Yes. It's very embarrassing. You see, the truth is that I was very upset with my brother, Tyler, and I wanted to punish him. But I realize now that that was wrong. I'm not upset anymore, and I want to go home to Rose Hill.'

'I read the transcript of your interview this morning. You said that your name was Margo Posner and that you were framed.'

Margo laughed. 'That was naughty of me. I just said that to upset Tyler. No. I'm Julia Stanford.'

He looked at her. 'Can you prove that?'

This was the moment Margo had been waiting for. 'Oh, yes!' she said triumphantly. 'Tyler proved it himself. He hired a private detective named Frank Timmons, who matched my fingerprints with prints I had made for a driver's license when I was younger. They're the same. There's no question about it.'

'Detective Frank Timmons, you say?'

'That's right. He does work for the district attorney's office here in Chicago.'

He studied her a moment. 'Now, you're certain of this? You're not Margo Posner – you're Julia Stanford?'

'Absolutely.'

'And this private detective, Frank Timmons, can verify that?'

She smiled. 'He already has. All you have to do is call the district attorney's office and get hold of him.'

Dr Gifford nodded. 'All right. I'll do that.'

At ten o'clock the following morning, Dr Gifford, accompanied by the matron, returned to Margo's room.

'Good morning.'

'Good morning, doctor.' She looked at him eagerly. 'Did you talk to Frank Timmons?'

'Yes. I want to be sure that I understand this. Your story about Judge Stanford's involving you in some kind of conspiracy was false?'

'Completely. I said that because I wanted to punish my brother. But everything is all right now. I'm ready to go home.'

'Frank Timmons can prove that you're Julia Stanford?'

'Absolutely.'

Dr Gifford turned to the matron and nodded. She

signaled to someone. A tall, lean black man walked into the room.

He looked at Margo and said, 'I'm Frank Timmons. Can I help you?'

He was a complete stranger.

Chapter Twenty-nine

The fashion show was going well. The models moved gracefully along the runway, and each new design received enthusiastic applause. The ballroom was packed. Every seat was occupied, and there were standees in the rear.

Backstage there was a stir, and Kendall turned to see what was happening. Two uniformed policemen were making their way toward her.

Kendall's heart began to race.

One of the policemen said, 'Are you Kendall Stanford Renaud?'

'Yes.'

'I'm placing you under arrest for the murder of Martha Ryan.'

'No!' she screamed. 'I didn't mean to do it! It was an accident! Please! Please! Please . . . !'

She woke up in a panic, her body trembling.

It was a recurring nightmare. *I can't go on like this,* Kendall thought. *I can't! I have to do something.*

She wanted desperately to talk to Marc. He had

reluctantly returned to New York. 'I have a job to do, darling. They won't let me take any more time off.'

'I understand, Marc. I'll be back there in a few days. I have to get a show ready.'

Kendall was leaving for New York that morning, but before she went there was something she felt she had to do. The conversation with Woody had been very disturbing. *He's blaming his problems on Peggy.*

Kendall found Peggy on the veranda.

'Good morning,' Kendall said.

'Good morning.'

Kendall took a seat opposite her. 'I have to talk to you.'

'Yes?'

It was awkward. 'I had a talk with Woody. He's in bad shape. He . . . he thinks that you're the one who's been supplying him with heroin.'

'He told you that?'

'Yes.'

There was a long pause. 'Well, it's true.'

Kendall stared at her in disbelief. '*What?* I . . . I don't understand. You told me you were trying to get him *off* drugs. Why would you want to keep him addicted?'

'You really *don't* understand, do you?' Her tone was bitter. 'You live in your own little goddamned world. Well, let me tell you something, Miss Famous

311

Designer! I was a waitress when Woody got me pregnant. I never expected Woodrow Stanford to marry me. And do you know why he did? So he could feel he was better than his father. Well, Woody married me, all right. And everybody treated me like dirt. When my brother, Hoop, came down for the wedding, they acted like he was some kind of trash.'

'Peggy . . .'

'To tell you the truth, I was dumbfounded when your brother said he wanted to marry me. I didn't even know if it was his baby. I could have been a good wife to Woody, but no one even gave me a chance. To them I was still a waitress. I didn't lose the baby, I had an abortion. I thought maybe Woody would divorce me, but he didn't. I was his token symbol of how democratic he was. Well, let me tell you something, lady. I don't need that. I'm as good as you or anyone else.'

Each word was a blow. 'Did you ever love Woody?'

Peggy shrugged. 'He was good-looking and fun, but then he had that bad fall during the polo game, and everything changed. The hospital gave him drugs, and when he got out, they expected him to stop taking them. One night, he was in pain, and I said, "I have a little treat for you." And after that, whenever he was in pain, I gave him his little treat. Pretty soon he needed it, whether he was in pain or not. My brother is a pusher, and I was able to get all the heroin I needed. I made Woody beg me for it. And sometimes I'd tell

312

him I was out of it just to watch him sweat and cry – oh, how Mr Woodrow Stanford needed me! He wasn't so high and mighty then! I goaded him into hitting me, and then he'd feel terrible about what he had done, and he'd come crawling back to me with gifts. You see, when Woody is off dope, I'm nothing. When he's on it, I'm the one who has the power. He may be a Stanford, and maybe I was only a waitress, but I control him.'

Kendall was staring at her in horror.

'Your brother's tried to quit, all right. When it got real bad, his friends would get him into a detox center, and I'd go visit him and watch the great Stanford suffer the agonies of hell. And each time he came out, I'd be waiting for him with my little treat. It was payback time.'

Kendall was finding it hard to breathe. 'You're a monster,' she said slowly. 'I want you to leave.'

'You bet! I can't wait to get out of this place.' She grinned. 'Of course, I'm not leaving for nothing. How much of a settlement will I get?'

'Whatever it is,' Kendall said, 'it will be too much. Now get out of here.'

'Right.' Then she added with an affected tone, 'I'll have my lawyer call your lawyer.'

'She's really leaving me?'

'Yes.'

'That means . . .'

'I know what it means, Woody. Can you handle it?'

He looked at his sister and smiled. 'I think so. Yes. I think I can.'

'I'm sure of it.'

He took a deep breath. 'Thanks, Kendall. I would never have had the courage to get rid of her.'

She smiled. 'What are sisters for?'

That afternoon, Kendall left for New York. The fashion showing would be in one week.

Clothing is the single biggest business in New York. A successful fashion designer can have an effect on the economy all around the world. A designer's whim has a far-flung impact on everyone from cotton pickers in India to Scottish weavers to silkworms in China and Japan. It has an effect on the wool industry and the silk industry. The Donna Karans and Calvin Kleins and Ralph Laurens are a major economic influence, and Kendall had arrived in that category. It was rumored that she was about to be named the Women's Wear Designer of the Year by the Council of Fashion Designers of America, the most prestigious award a designer could receive.

Kendall Stanford Renaud led a busy life. In September she looked at large assortments of fabrics, and in October she selected the ones she wanted for her new designs. December and January were devoted to designing the new fashions, and February to refining them. In April, she was ready to show her fall collection.

Kendall Stanford Designs was located at 550 Seventh Avenue, sharing the building with Bill Blass and Oscar de la Renta. Her next showing was going to be at the Bryant Park tent, which could seat up to a thousand people.

When Kendall arrived at her office, Nadine said, 'I've got good news. The showing is completely booked!'

'Thank you,' Kendall said absently. Her mind was on other things.

'By the way, there's a letter marked *urgent* for you on your desk. It was just delivered by messenger.'

The words sent a jolt through Kendall's body. She walked over to her desk and looked at the envelope. The return address was *Wild Animal Protection Association, 3000 Park Avenue, New York, New York*. She stared at it for a long time. There was no 3000 Park Avenue.

Kendall opened the letter with trembling fingers.

> *Dear Mrs Renaud,*
>   *My Swiss banker informs me that he has not yet received the million dollars that my association requested. In view of your delinquency, I must inform you that our needs have been increased to 5 million*

*dollars. If this payment is made, I promise
we will not bother you again. You have
fifteen days to deposit the money in our
account. If you fail to do so, I regret that
we shall have to communicate with the
appropriate authorities.*

It was unsigned.

Kendall stood there in a panic, reading it over and over, again and again. *Five million dollars! It's imposs- ible,* she thought. *I can never raise that kind of money that quickly. What a fool I was!*

When Marc came home that night, Kendall showed him the letter.

'Five million dollars!' he exploded. 'That's ridicu- lous! Who do they think you are?'

'They know who I am,' Kendall said. 'That's the problem. I've got to get hold of some money quickly. But how?'

'I don't know . . . I suppose a bank would loan you money against your inheritance, but I don't like the idea of . . .'

'Marc, it's my life I'm talking about. *Our* lives. I'm going to see about getting that loan.'

George Meriwether was the vice president in charge of the New York Union Bank. He was in his forties and had worked his way up from a junior teller. He was an ambitious man. *One day I'll be on the board of directors,* he thought, *and after that . . . who knows?* His thoughts were interrupted by his secretary.

'Miss Kendall Stanford is here to see you.'

He felt a small *frisson* of pleasure. She had been a good customer as a successful designer, but now she was one of the wealthiest women in the world. He had tried for several years to get Harry Stanford's account, without success. And now . . .

'Show her in,' Meriwether told his secretary.

When Kendall walked into his office, Meriwether rose and greeted her with a smile and a warm handshake.

'I'm so pleased to see you,' he said. 'Do sit down. Some coffee, or something stronger?'

'No, thanks,' Kendall said.

'I want to offer my condolences on the death of your father.' His voice was suitably grave.

'Thank you.'

'What can I do for you?' He knew what she was going to say. She was going to turn her billions over to him to invest . . .

'I want to borrow some money.'

He blinked. 'I beg your pardon?'

'I need five million dollars.'

He thought rapidly. *According to the newspapers, her share of the estate should be more than a billion dollars. Even with taxes . . .* He smiled. 'Well, I don't think there will be any problem. You've always been

317

one of our favorite customers, you know. What security would you like to put up?'

'I'm an heir in my father's will.'

He nodded. 'Yes. I read that.'

'I'd like to borrow the money against my share of the estate.'

'I see. Has your father's will been probated yet?'

'No, but it will be soon.'

'That's fine.' He leaned forward. 'Of course, we'd have to see a copy of the will.'

'Yes,' Kendall said eagerly. 'I can arrange that.'

'And we would have to have the exact amount of your share of the inheritance.'

'I don't know the exact amount,' Kendall said.

'Well, the banking laws are quite strict, you know. Probates can take some time. Why don't you come back after the probate, and I'll be happy to –'

'I need the money now,' Kendall said desperately. She wanted to scream.

'Oh, dear. Naturally, we want to do everything we can to accommodate you.' He raised his hands in a helpless gesture. 'But unfortunately, our hands are tied until –'

Kendall rose to her feet. 'Thank you.'

'As soon as . . .'

She was gone.

When Kendall returned to the office, Nadine said excitedly, 'I have to talk to you.'

She was in no mood to hear Nadine's problems.
'What is it?' Kendall asked.

'My husband called me a few minutes ago. His company is transferring him to Paris. So, I'll be leaving.'

'You're go . . . going to Paris?'

Nadine beamed. 'Yes! Isn't that wonderful? I'll be sorry to leave you. But don't worry. I'll stay in touch.'

So it was Nadine. But there's no way to prove it. First the mink coat and now Paris. With five million dollars, she can afford to live anywhere in the world. How do I handle this? If I tell her that I know, she'll deny it. Maybe she'll demand more. Marc will know what to do.

'Nadine . . .'

One of Kendall's assistants came in. 'Kendall! I have to talk to you about the bridge collection. I don't think we have enough designs for –'

Kendall could bear no more. 'Excuse me. I don't feel well. I'm going home.'

Her assistant looked at her in amazement. 'But we're in the middle of . . .'

'I'm sorry . . .'

And Kendall was gone.

When Kendall walked into her apartment, it was empty. Marc was working late. Kendall looked around at all the beautiful things in the room, and thought, *They'll never stop until they take everything. They're going to bleed me dry. Marc was right. I should have gone to the police that night. Now I'm a criminal. I've*

319

got to confess. Now, while I have the courage. She sat there, thinking about what this was going to do to her, to Marc, and to her family. There would be lurid headlines, and a trial, and probably prison. It would be the end of her career. *But I can't go on like this*, Kendall thought. *I'll go crazy.*

Almost in a daze, she got up and walked into Marc's den. She remembered that he kept his typewriter on a shelf in the closet. She took it down and put it on the desk. She rolled a sheet of paper into the platen and began to type.

> *To Whom It May Concern:*
> *My name is Kendall*

She stopped. The letter E was broken.

Chapter Thirty

'Why, Marc? For God's sake, why?' Kendall's voice was filled with anguish.

'It was your fault.'

'No! I told you. It was an accident! I . . .'

'I'm not talking about the accident. I'm talking about *you*! The big successful wife who was too busy to find time for her husband.'

It was as though he had slapped her. 'That's not true. I . . .'

'All you ever thought about was yourself, Kendall. Everywhere we went, you were always the star. You let me tag along like a pet poodle.'

'That's not fair!' she said.

'Isn't it? You go off to your fashion shows all over the world so you can get your picture in the papers, and I'm sitting here alone, waiting for you to return. Do you think I liked being "Mr Kendall?" I wanted a wife. Don't worry, my darling Kendall. I consoled myself with other women while you were gone.'

Her face was ashen.

'They were real flesh-and-blood women, who had

time for me. Not some damned made-up empty shell.'

'Stop it!' Kendall cried.

'When you told me about the accident, I saw a way to become free of you. Do you want to know something, my dear? I enjoyed watching you squirm when you read those letters. It paid me back a little for all the humiliation I've gone through.'

'That's enough! Pack your bags and get out of here. I never want to see you again!'

Marc grinned. 'There's very little chance of that. By the way, do you still plan to go to the police?'

'Get out!' Kendall said. *'Now!'*

'I'm leaving. I think I'll go back to Paris. And, darling, I won't tell if you won't. You're safe.'

An hour later, he was gone.

At nine o'clock in the morning, Kendall put in a call to Steve Sloane.

'Good morning, Mrs Renaud. What can I do for you?'

'I'm returning to Boston this afternoon,' Kendall said. 'I have a confession to make.'

She was seated across from Steve, looking pale and drawn. She sat there frozen, unable to begin.

Steve prompted her. 'You said you had a confession to make.'

'Yes. I . . . I killed someone.' She began to cry. 'It was an accident, but . . . I ran away.' Her face was a mask of anguish. 'I ran away . . . and left her there.'

'Take it easy,' Steve said. 'Start at the beginning.'

She began to talk.

Thirty minutes later, Steve looked out his window, thinking about what he had just heard.

'And you want to go to the police?'

'Yes. It was what I should have done in the first place. I . . . I don't care what they do to me anymore.'

Steve said thoughtfully, 'Since you're giving yourself up voluntarily and it was an accident, I think the court will be lenient.'

She was trying to control herself. 'I just want it over with.'

'What about your husband?'

She looked up. 'What about him?'

'Blackmail is against the law. You have the number of the account in Switzerland where you sent the money he stole from you. All you have to do is press charges and –'

'No!' Her tone was fierce. 'I don't want anything more to do with him. Let him go on with his life. I want to get on with mine.'

Steve nodded. 'Whatever you say. I'm going to take you down to police headquarters. You may have to spend the night in jail, but I'll have you bailed out very quickly.'

Kendall smiled wanly. 'Now I can do something I've never done before.'

'What's that?'
'Design a dress in stripes.'

That evening, when he got home, Steve told Julia what had happened.

Julia was horrified. 'Her own husband was blackmailing her? That's terrible.' She studied him for a long moment. 'I think it's wonderful that you spend your life helping people in trouble.'

Steve looked at her and thought, *I'm the one in trouble.*

Steve Sloane was awakened by the aroma of fresh coffee and the smell of cooking bacon. He sat up in bed, startled. *Had the housekeeper come in today?* He had told her not to. Steve put on his robe and slippers, and hurried down to the kitchen.

Julia was in there, preparing breakfast. She looked up as Steve entered.

'Good morning,' she said cheerfully. 'How do you like your eggs?'

'Uh . . . scrambled.'

'Right. Scrambled eggs and bacon are my specialty. As a matter of fact, my one specialty. I told you, I'm a terrible cook.'

Steve smiled. 'You don't have to cook. If you wanted to, you could hire a few hundred chefs.'

'Am I really going to get that much money, Steve?'

'That's right. Your share of the estate will be over a billion dollars.'

She found it difficult to swallow. 'A billion . . . ? I don't believe it!'

'It's true.'

'There's not that much money in the world, Steve.'

'Well, your father had most of what there was.'

'I . . . I don't know what to say.'

'Then may I say something?'

'Of course.'

'The eggs are burning.'

'Oh! Sorry.' She quickly took them off the stove. 'I'll make another batch.'

'Don't bother. The burned bacon will be enough.'

She laughed. 'I'm sorry.'

Steve walked over to the cabinet and took out a box of cereal. 'How about a nice cold breakfast?'

'Perfect,' Julia said.

He poured some cereal into a bowl for each of them, took the milk out of the refrigerator, and they sat down at the kitchen table.

'Don't you have someone to cook for you?' Julia asked.

'You mean, am I involved with anyone?'

She blushed. 'Something like that.'

'No. I was in a relationship for two years, but it didn't work out.'

'I'm sorry.'

'What about you?' Steve asked.

She thought of Henry Wesson. 'I don't think so.'

He looked at her, curious. 'You aren't sure?'

'It's difficult to explain. One of us wants to get married,' she said tactfully, 'and one of us doesn't.'

'I see. When this is over, will you be going back to Kansas?'

'I honestly don't know. It seems so strange, being here. My mother talked to me so often about Boston. She was born here, and loved it. In a way, it's like coming home. I wish I could have known my father.'

No, you don't, Steve thought.

'Did you know him?'

'No. He dealt only with Simon Fitzgerald.'

They sat there talking for more than an hour, and there was an easy camaraderie between them. Steve filled Julia in on what had happened earlier – the arrival of the stranger who called herself Julia Stanford, the empty grave and Dmitri Kaminsky's disappearance.

'That's incredible!' Julia said. 'Who could be behind this?'

'I don't know, but I'm trying to find out,' Steve assured her. 'In the meantime, you'll be safe here. Very safe.'

She smiled, and said, 'I feel safe here. Thank you.'

He started to say something, then stopped. He

looked at his watch. 'I'd better get dressed and get down to the office. I have a lot to do.'

Steve was meeting with Fitzgerald.

'Any progress yet?' Fitzgerald asked.

Steve shook his head. 'It's all smoke. Whoever planned this is a genius. I'm trying to trace Dmitri Kaminsky. He flew from Corsica to Paris to Australia. I spoke to the Sydney police. They were stunned to learn that Kaminsky is in their country. There's a circular out from Interpol, and they're looking for him. I think Harry Stanford signed his own death warrant when he called here and said he wanted to change his will. Someone decided to stop him. The only witness to what happened on the yacht that night is Dmitri Kaminsky. When we find him, we'll know a lot more.'

'I wonder if we should bring our police in on this?' Fitzgerald suggested.

Steve shook his head. 'What we know is all circumstantial, Simon. The only crime we can prove is that someone dug up a body – and we don't even know who did that.'

'What about the detective they hired, who verified the woman's fingerprints?'

'Frank Timmons. I've left three messages for him. If I don't hear back from him by six o'clock tonight, I'm going to fly to Chicago. I believe he's deeply involved.'

'What do you suppose was meant to happen to the shares of the estate that the impostor was going to get?'

'My hunch is that whoever planned this had her sign her share over to them. The person probably used some dummy trusts to hide it. I'm convinced that we're looking for a member of the family . . . I think we can eliminate Kendall as a suspect.' He told Fitzgerald about the conversation he had had with her. 'If she were behind this, she wouldn't have come forth with a confession, not at this time, anyway. She would have waited until the estate was settled and she had the money. As far as her husband is concerned, I think we can eliminate Marc. He's a small-time blackmailer. He isn't capable of setting up anything like this.'

'What about the others?'

'Judge Stanford. I talked to a friend of mine with the Chicago Bar Association. My friend says everyone thinks very highly of Stanford. In fact, he's just been appointed chief judge. Another thing in his favor: Judge Stanford was the one who said that the first Julia who appeared was a fraud, and he was the one who insisted on a DNA test. I doubt he'd do something like this. Woody interests me. I'm pretty sure he's on drugs, and that's an expensive habit. I checked on his wife, Peggy. She isn't smart enough to be behind this scheme. But there's a rumor she has a brother who's bad business. I'm going to look into it.'

Steve spoke to his secretary on the intercom. 'Please

get me Lieutenant Michael Kennedy of the Boston police.'

A few minutes later, she buzzed Steve. 'Lieutenant Kennedy is on line one.'

Steve picked up the phone.

'Lieutenant. Thank you for taking my call. I'm Steve Sloane with Renquist, Renquist, & Fitzgerald. We're trying to locate a relative in the matter of the Harry Stanford estate.'

'Mr Sloane, I'd be glad to help if I can.'

'Would you please check with the New York City police to see if they have any files on Mrs Woodrow Stanford's brother. His name is Hoop Malkovich. He works in a bakery in the Bronx.'

'No problem. I'll get back to you.'

'Thanks.'

After lunch, Simon Fitzgerald stopped by Steve's office.

'How's the investigation going?' he asked.

'Too slow to suit me. Whoever planned this covered his or her tracks pretty thoroughly.'

'How is Julia holding up?'

Steve smiled. 'She's wonderful.'

There was something in the tone of his voice that made Simon Fitzgerald take a closer look at him.

'She's a very attractive young lady.'

'I know,' Steve said wistfully. 'I know.'

* * *

An hour later, the call came in from Australia.

'Mr Sloane?'

'Yes.'

'Chief Inspector McPhearson here from Sydney.'

'Yes, Chief Inspector.'

'We found your man.'

Steve felt his heart jump. 'That's wonderful! I'd like to arrange immediate extradition to bring him . . .'

'Oh, I don't think there's any hurry. Dmitri Kaminsky is dead.'

Steve felt his heart sink. *'What?'*

'We found his body a little while ago. His fingers had been chopped off, and he had been shot several times.'

'The Russian gangs have a quaint custom. First they chop off your fingers, then they let you bleed, and then they shoot you.'

'I see. Thank you, inspector.'

Dead end. Steve sat there, staring at the wall. All his leads were disappearing. He realized how heavily he had been counting on Dmitri Kaminsky's testimony.

Steve's secretary interrupted his thoughts. 'There's a Mr Timmons for you on line three.'

Steve looked at his watch. It was 5:55 P.M. He picked up the telephone. 'Mr Timmons?'

'Yes . . . I'm sorry I couldn't return your calls earlier. I've been out of town for the past two days. What can I do for you?'

330

A lot, Steve thought. *You can tell me how you faked those fingerprints.* Steve chose his words carefully. 'I'm calling about Julia Stanford. When you were in Boston recently, you checked out her fingerprints and . . .'

'Mr Sloane . . .'

'Yes?'

'I've never been in Boston.'

Steve took a deep breath. 'Mr Timmons, according to the register at the Holiday Inn, you were here on . . .'

'Someone has been using my name.'

Steve listened, stunned. It was the final dead end, the last lead. 'I don't suppose you have any idea who it is?'

'Well, it's very strange, Mr Sloane. A woman claimed that I was in Boston and that I could identify her as Julia Stanford. I'd never seen her before in my life.'

Steve felt a surge of hope. 'Do you know who she is?'

'Yes. Her name is Posner. Margo Posner.'

Steve picked up a pen. 'Where can I reach her?'

'She's at the Reed Mental Health Facility in Chicago.'

'Thanks a lot. I really appreciate this.'

'Let's keep in touch. I'd like to know what's going on myself. I don't like people going around impersonating me.'

'Right.' Steve replaced the receiver. Margo Posner.

* * *

When Steve got home that evening, Julia was waiting to greet him.

'I fixed dinner,' she told him. 'Well, I didn't exactly fix it. Do you like Chinese food?'

He smiled. 'Love it!'

'Good. We have eight cartons of it.'

When Steve walked into the dining room, the table was set with flowers and candles,

'Is there any news?' Julia asked.

Steve said cautiously, 'We may have gotten our first break. I have the name of a woman who seems to be involved in this. I'm flying to Chicago in the morning to talk with her. I have a feeling we may have all the answers tomorrow.'

'That would be wonderful!' Julia said excitedly. 'I'll be so glad when this is over.'

'So will I,' Steve told her. *Or will I? She'll be a real part of the Stanford family – way out of my reach.*

Dinner lasted two hours, and they were not even aware of what they were eating. They talked about everything and they talked about nothing, and it was as though they had known each other forever. They discussed the past and the present, and they carefully avoided talking about the future. *There is no future for us,* Steve thought unhappily.

Finally, reluctantly, Steve said, 'Well, we'd better go to bed.'

She looked at him with raised eyebrows, and they both burst out laughing.

'What I meant . . .'

'I know what you meant. Good night, Steve.'

'Good night, Julia.'

Chapter Thirty-one

Early the following morning, Steve boarded a United flight for Chicago. From Chicago's O'Hare Airport he took a taxi.

'Where to?' the driver asked.

'The Reed Mental Health Facility.'

The driver turned around and looked at Steve. 'Are you okay?'

'Yes. Why?'

'Just asking.'

At Reed, Steve approached the uniformed security guard at the front desk.

The guard looked up. 'Can I help you?'

'Yes. I'd like to see Margo Posner.'

'Is she an employee?'

That had not occurred to Steve. 'I'm not sure.'

The guard took a closer look at him. 'You're not sure?'

'All I know is that she's here.'

The guard reached in a drawer and took out a roster with a list of names. After a moment, he said, 'She doesn't work here. Could she be a patient?'

'I . . . I don't know. It's possible.'

The guard gave Steve another look, then reached into a different drawer and pulled out a computer printout. He scanned it, and in the middle, he stopped. 'Posner. Margo.'

'That's right.' He was surprised. 'Is she a patient here?'

'Uh-huh. Are you a relative?'

'No . . .'

'Then I'm afraid you can't see her.'

'I *have* to see her,' Steve said. 'It's very important.'

'Sorry. I have my orders. Unless you've been cleared beforehand, you can't visit any of the patients.'

'Who's in charge here?' Steve asked.

'I am.'

'I mean, in charge of the hospital.'

'Dr Kingsley.'

'I want to see him.'

'Right.' The guard picked up the telephone and dialed a number. 'Dr Kingsley, this is Joe at the front desk. There's a gentleman here who wants to see you.' He looked up at Steve. 'Your name?'

'Steve Sloane. I'm an attorney.'

'Steve Sloane. He's an attorney . . . right.' He replaced the receiver and turned to Steve. 'Someone will be along to take you to his office.'

Five minutes later, Steve was ushered into the office

of Dr Gary Kingsley. Kingsley was a man in his fifties, but he looked older and careworn.

'What can I do for you, Mr Sloane?'

'I need to see a patient you have here. Margo Posner.'

'Ah, yes. Interesting case. Are you related to her?'

'No, but I'm investigating a possible murder, and it's very important that I talk to her. I think she may be a key to it.'

'I'm sorry. I can't help you.'

'You *have* to,' Steve said. 'It's . . .'

'Mr Sloane, I couldn't help you even if I wanted to.'

'Why not?'

'Because Margo Posner is in a padded cell. She attacks everyone who goes near her. This morning, she tried to kill a matron and two doctors.'

'*What?*'

'She keeps changing her identity and screaming for her brother, Tyler, and the crew of her yacht. The only way we can quiet her is to keep her heavily sedated.'

'Oh, my God,' Steve said. 'Do you have any idea when she might come out of it?'

Dr Kingsley shook his head. 'She's under close observation. Perhaps in time she'll calm down, and we can reevaluate her condition. Until then . . .'

Chapter Thirty-two

At six A.M., a harbor patrol boat was cruising along the Charles River, when one of the policemen aboard spotted an object floating in the water ahead.

'Off the starboard bow!' he called. 'It looks like a log. Let's pick it up before it sinks something.'

The log turned out to be a body, and even more startling, a body that had been embalmed.

The policemen stared down at it and said, 'How the hell did an embalmed body get into the Charles River?'

Lieutenant Michael Kennedy was talking to the coroner. 'Are you sure of that?'

The coroner replied, 'Absolutely. It's Harry Stanford. I embalmed him myself. Later, we had an exhumation order, and when we dug up the coffin . . . Well, you know, we reported it to the police.'

'Who asked to have the body exhumed?'

'The family. They handled it through their attorney, Simon Fitzgerald.'

337

'I think I'll have a talk with Mr Fitzgerald.'

When Steve returned to Boston from Chicago, he went directly to Simon Fitzgerald's office.

'You look beat,' Fitzgerald said.

'Not beat – beaten. The whole thing is falling apart, Simon. We had three possible leads: Dmitri Kaminsky, Frank Timmons, and Margo Posner. Well, Kaminsky is dead, it's the wrong Timmons, and Margo Posner is locked away in an asylum. We have nothing to –'

The voice of Fitzgerald's secretary came over the intercom. 'Excuse me. There's a Lieutenant Kennedy here to see you, Mr Fitzgerald.'

'Send him in.'

Michael Kennedy was a rugged-looking man with eyes that had seen everything.

'Mr Fitzgerald?'

'Yes. This is my associate Steve Sloane. I believe you two have spoken on the phone. Sit down. What can we do for you?'

'We just found the body of Harry Stanford.'

'What? Where?'

'Swimming in the Charles. You ordered his body dug up, didn't you?'

'Yes.'

'May I ask why?'

Fitzgerald told him.

When Fitzgerald was finished, Kennedy said, 'You

338

have no idea who it was that posed as this investigator, Timmons?'

'No. I talked to Timmons. He has no idea, either.'

Kennedy sighed. 'It gets curiouser and curiouser.'

'Where is Harry Stanford's body now?' Steve asked.

'They're keeping him at the morgue for the present. I hope he doesn't disappear again.'

'I do, too,' Steve said. 'We'll have Perry Winger run a DNA test on Julia.'

When Steve called Tyler to tell him that his father's body had been found, Tyler was genuinely shocked.

'That's terrible!' he said. 'Who could have done a thing like that?'

'That's what we're trying to find out,' Steve told him.

Tyler was furious. *That incompetent idiot, Baker! He's going to pay for this. I have to get this settled before it gets out of hand.* 'Mr Fitzgerald, as you may be aware, I've been appointed chief judge of Cook County. I have a very heavy caseload, and they're pressuring me to return. I can't delay much longer. I'd appreciate it if you could do something to get the probate finished quickly.'

'I put in a call this morning,' Steve told him. 'It should be closed within the next three days.'

'That will be fine. Keep me informed, please.'

'I'll do that, judge.'

* * *

Steve sat in his office reviewing the events of the past few weeks. He recalled the conversation he had had with Chief Inspector McPhearson.

'*We found his body a little while ago. His fingers had been chopped off and he had been shot several times.*'

But wait, Steve thought. *There's something he didn't tell me.* He picked up the telephone and put in another call to Australia.

The voice on the other end of the telephone said, 'This is Chief Inspector McPhearson.'

'Yes, inspector. This is Steve Sloane. I forgot to ask you a question. When you found Dmitri Kaminsky's body, were there any papers on him? . . . I see . . . that's fine. Thank you very much.'

When Steve hung up the phone, his secretary's voice came over the intercom. 'Lieutenant Kennedy holding on line two.'

Steve punched the phone button.

'Lieutenant. Sorry to keep you waiting. I was on an overseas call.'

'The NYPD gave me some interesting information on Hoop Malkovich. He seems to be quite a slippery character.'

Steve picked up a pen. 'Go ahead.'

'The police believe that the bakery he works for is a front for a drug ring.' The lieutenant paused, then continued. 'Malkovich is probably a drug pusher. But he's clever. They haven't been able to nail him yet.'

'Anything else?' Steve asked.

'The police believe the operation is tied into the French mafia with a connection through Marseilles. If I learn anything else, I'll call.'

'Thanks, Lieutenant. That's very helpful.'

Steve put down the phone and headed out the office door.

When Steve arrived home, filled with anticipation, he called, 'Julia?'

There was no answer.

He began to panic. 'Julia!' *She's been kidnapped or killed,* he thought, and he felt a sudden sense of alarm.

Julia appeared at the top of the stairs. 'Steve?'

He took a deep breath. 'I thought . . .' He was pale. 'Are you all right?'

'Yes.'

She came down the stairs. 'Did things go well in Chicago?'

He shook his head. 'I'm afraid not.' He told her what had happened. 'We're going to have a reading of the will on Thursday, Julia. That's only three days from now. Whoever is behind this has to get rid of you by then or his – or her – plan can't work.'

She swallowed. 'I see. Do you have any idea who it is?'

'As a matter of fact . . .' The telephone rang. 'Excuse me.' Steve picked up the telephone. 'Hello?'

'This is Dr Tichner in Florida. Sorry I didn't call earlier, but I've been away.'

'Dr Tichner. Thank you for returning my call. Our firm represents the Stanford estate.'

'What can I do for you?'

'I'm calling about Woodrow Stanford. I believe he's a patient of yours.'

'Yes.'

'Does he have a drug problem, doctor?'

'Mr Sloane, I'm not at liberty to discuss any of my patients.'

'I understand. I'm not asking this out of curiosity. It's very important . . .'

'I'm afraid I can't . . .'

'You *did* have him admitted to the Harbor Group Clinic in Jupiter, didn't you?'

There was a long hesitation. 'Yes. That's a matter of record.'

'Thank you, doctor. That's all I needed to know.'

Steve replaced the receiver and stood there a moment. 'It's unbelievable!'

'What?' Julia asked.

'Sit down.'

Thirty minutes later, Steve was in his car headed for Rose Hill. All the pieces had finally fallen into place. *He's brilliant. It almost worked. It could still work if anything happened to Julia,* Steve thought.

At Rose Hill, Clark answered the door. 'Good evening, Mr Sloane.'

'Good evening, Clark. Is Judge Stanford in?'

'He's in the library. I'll tell him you're here.'

'Thank you.' He watched Clark walk off.

A minute later, the butler returned. 'Judge Stanford will see you now.'

'Thank you.'

Steve walked into the library.

Tyler was sitting in front of a chess board, concentrating. He looked up as Steve walked in.

'You wanted to see me?'

'Yes. I believe the young woman who came to see you several days ago is the real Julia. The other Julia was a fake.'

'But that's not possible.'

'I'm afraid it's true, and I've found out who's behind all this.'

There was a momentary silence. Then Tyler said slowly, 'You have?'

'Yes. I'm afraid this is going to shock you. It's your brother, Woody.'

Tyler was looking up at Steve in amazement. 'Are you saying that Woody is responsible for what's been happening?'

'That's right.'

'I . . . I can't believe it.'

'Neither could I, but it all checks out. I talked to his doctor in Hobe Sound. Did you know your brother is on drugs?'

'I . . . I've suspected it.'

'Drugs are expensive. Woody isn't working. He

needs money, and he was obviously looking for a bigger share of the estate. He's the one who hired the fake Julia, but when you came to us and asked for a DNA test, he panicked and had your father's body removed from the coffin because he couldn't afford to have that test made. That's what tipped me off. And I suspect that he sent someone to Kansas City to have the real Julia killed. Did you know that Peggy has a brother who's tied into the mob? As long as Julia's alive and there are two Julias around, his plan can't work.'

'Are you sure of all this?'

'Absolutely. There's something else, judge.'

'Yes?'

'I don't think your father fell off his yacht. I believe that Woody had your father *murdered*. Peggy's brother could have arranged that too. I'm told he has connections with the Marseilles mafia. They could easily have paid a crew member to do it. I'm flying to Italy tonight to have a talk with the captain of the yacht.'

Tyler was listening intently. When he spoke, he said approvingly, 'That's a good idea.' *Captain Vacarro knows nothing.*

'I'll try to be back by Thursday for the reading of the will.'

Tyler said, 'What about the real Julia? . . . Are you sure she's safe?'

'Oh, yes,' Steve said. 'She's staying where no one can find her. She's at my house.'

344

Chapter Thirty-three

The gods are on my side. He could not believe his good fortune. It was an incredible stroke of luck. Last night, Steve Sloane had delivered Julia into his hands. *Hal Baker is an incompetent fool,* Tyler thought. *I'll take care of Julia myself this time.*

He looked up as Clark came into the room.

'Excuse me, Judge Stanford. There's a telephone call for you.'

It was Keith Percy. 'Tyler?'

'Yes, Keith.'

'I just wanted to bring you up to date on the Margo Posner matter.'

'Yes?'

'Dr Gifford just called me. The woman is insane. She's carrying on so badly that they have to have her locked away in the violent ward.'

Tyler felt a sharp sense of relief. 'I'm sorry to hear that.'

'Anyway, I wanted to ease your mind and let you know that she's no longer any danger to you or your family.'

'I appreciate that,' Tyler said. And he did.

Tyler went to his room and telephoned Lee. There was a long delay before Lee answered.

'Hello?' Tyler could hear voices in the background. 'Lee?'

'Who is this?'

'It's Tyler.'

'Oh, yeah. Tyler.'

He could hear the tinkling of glasses. 'Are you having a party, Lee?'

'Uh-huh. Do you want to join us?'

Tyler wondered who was at the party. 'I wish I could. I'm calling to tell you to get ready to go on that trip we talked about.'

Lee laughed. 'You mean, on that great big white yacht to St Tropez?'

'That's right.'

'Sure. I can be ready anytime,' he said mockingly.

'Lee, I'm serious.'

'Oh, come off it, Tyler. Judges don't have yachts. I have to go now. My guests are calling me.'

'Wait a minute!' Tyler said desperately. 'Do you know who I am?'

'Sure, you're –'

'I'm Tyler Stanford. My father was Harry Stanford.'

There was a moment of silence. 'Are you kidding me?'

'No. I'm in Boston now, settling up the estate.'

'My God! You're *that* Stanford. I didn't know. I'm sorry. I . . . I've been hearing stuff on the news, but I didn't pay much attention. I never figured it was you.'

'That's all right.'

'You really meant it about taking me to St Tropez, didn't you?'

'Of course I did. We're going to do a lot of things together,' Tyler said. 'That is, if you want to.'

'I certainly do!' Lee's voice was suddenly filled with enthusiasm. 'Gee, Tyler, this is really great news . . .'

When Tyler replaced the receiver, he was smiling. Lee was taken care of. *Now,* he thought, *it's time to take care of my half sister.*

Tyler went into the library where Harry Stanford's gun collection was kept, opened the case, and removed a mahogany box. From a drawer below the case, he took out some ammunition. He put the ammunition in his pocket and carried the wooden box upstairs to his bedroom, locked the door behind him and opened the box. Inside were two matching Ruger revolvers, Harry Stanford's favorites. Tyler removed one, carefully loaded it, and then placed the extra ammunition and the box containing the other revolver in his bureau drawer. *One shot will do it,* he thought. They had taught him to shoot well at the military school his father had sent him to. *Thank you, Father.*

Next, Tyler picked up a telephone directory and looked for Steve Sloane's home address.

280 Newbury Street, Boston.

Tyler made his way to the garage, where there were half a dozen cars. He chose the black Mercedes as being the least conspicuous. He opened the garage door and listened to see if the noise had disturbed anyone. There was only silence.

On the drive to Steve Sloane's house, Tyler thought about what he was about to do. He had never physically committed a murder before. But this time he had no choice. Julia Stanford was the last obstacle between him and his dreams. With her gone, his problems would be over. *Forever,* Tyler thought.

He drove slowly, careful not to attract attention. When he reached Newbury Street, Tyler cruised past Steve's address. A few cars were parked on the street, but no pedestrians were around.

He parked the car a block away and walked back to the house. He rang the doorbell and waited.

Julia's voice came through the door. 'Who is it?'

'It's Judge Stanford.'

Julia opened the door. She looked at him in surprise. 'What are you doing here? Is anything wrong?'

'No, not at all,' he said easily. 'Steve Sloane asked me to have a talk with you. He told me you were here. May I come in?'

'Yes, of course.'

Tyler walked into the hall and watched Julia close

the door behind him. She led the way into the living room.

'Steve isn't here,' she said. 'He's on his way to San Remo.'

'I know.' He looked around. 'Are you alone? Isn't there a housekeeper or someone to stay with you?'

'No. I'm safe here. May I offer you something?'

'No, thanks.'

'What did you want to talk to me about?'

'I came to talk about you, Julia. I'm disappointed in you.'

'Disappointed . . . ?'

'You should never have come here. Did you really think you could walk in and try to collect a fortune that doesn't belong to you?'

She looked at him a moment. 'But I have a right to –'

'You have a right to nothing!' Tyler snapped. 'Where were you all those years when we were being humiliated and punished by our father? He went out of his way to hurt us every chance he got. He put us through hell. You didn't have to go through any of that. Well, we did, and we deserve the money. Not you.'

'I . . . what do you want me to do?'

Tyler gave a short laugh. 'What do I want you to do? Nothing. You've done it already. You damned near spoiled everything, do you know that?'

'I don't understand.'

'It's really quite simple.' He took out the revolver. 'You're going to disappear.'

She took a step back. 'But I . . .'

'Don't say anything. Let's not waste time. You and I are going on a little trip.'

She stiffened. 'What if I won't go?'

'Oh, you'll be going. Dead or alive. Suit yourself.'

In the moment of silence that followed, Tyler heard his voice boom out from the next room. *'Oh, you'll be going. Dead or alive. Suit yourself.'* He whirled around. 'What . . . ?'

Steve Sloane, Simon Fitzgerald, Lieutenant Kennedy, and two uniformed policemen stepped into the living room. Steve was holding a tape recorder.

Lieutenant Kennedy said, 'Give me the gun, judge.'

Tyler froze for an instant, then he forced a smile. 'Of course. I was just trying to scare this woman into getting out of here. She's a fraud, you know.' He put the gun in the detective's outstretched hand. 'She tried to claim part of the Stanford estate. Well, I wasn't about to let her get away with it. So I . . .'

'It's over, judge,' Steve said.

'What are you talking about? You said Woody was responsible for . . .'

'Woody wasn't up to planning anything as clever as this, and Kendall was already very successful. So I started checking up on you. Dmitri Kaminsky was killed in Australia, but the Australian police found *your* telephone number in his pocket. You used him

350

to murder your father. You're the one who brought in Margo Posner and then insisted she was an impostor to throw suspicion off yourself. You're the one who insisted on the DNA test and arranged to have the body removed. And you're the one who put in the phony call to Timmons. You hired Margo Posner to impersonate Julia, then had her committed to a psychiatric ward.'

Tyler looked around the room, and when he spoke, his voice was dangerously calm. 'And a *phone number* on a dead man is your evidence? I can't believe this! You set up your pitiful little trap based on *that*? You don't have a shred of proof. My telephone number was in Dmitri's pocket because I thought my father might be in danger. I told Dmitri to be careful. Obviously, he wasn't careful enough. Whoever killed my father probably killed Dmitri. That's who the police should be looking for. I called Timmons because I wanted him to find out the truth. Someone impersonated him. I have no idea who. And unless you can find him and tie him to me, you have nothing. As far as Margo Posner is concerned, I really believed that she was our sister. When she suddenly went crazy, going on a buying spree and threatening to kill us all, I persuaded her to go to Chicago. Then I arranged to have her picked up and committed. I wanted to keep all this out of the press to protect the family.'

Julia said, 'But you came here to kill me.'

Tyler shook his head. 'I had no intention of killing

351

you. You're an impostor. I just wanted to scare you away.'

'You're lying.'

He turned to the others. 'There's something else you might consider. It's possible that none of the family is involved. It could be some insider who's manipulating this, someone who put in an impostor and planned to convince the family she was genuine and then split a share of the estate with her. That didn't occur to any of you, did it?'

He turned to Simon Fitzgerald. 'I'm going to sue you both for slander, and I'm going to take away everything you've got. These are my witnesses. Before I'm through with you, you'll wish you had never heard of me. I control billions, and I'm going to use them to destroy you.' He looked at Steve. 'I promise you that your last act as a lawyer will be the reading of the Stanford will. Now, unless you want to charge me with carrying an unlicensed weapon, I'll be leaving.'

The group looked at one another uncertainly.

'No? Well, good evening, then.'

They watched helplessly as he walked out the door.

Lieutenant Kennedy was the first one to find his voice. 'My God!' he said. 'Do you believe that?'

'He's bluffing,' Steve said slowly. 'But we can't prove it. He's right. We need proof. I thought he would crack, but I underestimated him.'

Simon Fitzgerald spoke. 'It looks like our little plan

backfired. Without Dmitri Kaminsky or the testimony of the Posner woman, we have nothing but suspicions.'

'What about the threat on my life?' Julia protested.

Steve said, 'You heard what he said. He was just trying to scare you because he thought you were an impostor.'

'He wasn't just trying to scare me,' Julia said. 'He intended to kill me.'

'I know. But there isn't a thing we can do. Dickens had it right: "The law is a ass . . ." We're right back where we started.'

Fitzgerald frowned. 'It's worse than that, Steve. Tyler meant what he said about suing us. Unless we can prove our charges, we're in trouble.'

When the others had left, Julia said to Steve, 'I'm so sorry about all this. I feel responsible in a way. If I hadn't come . . .'

'Don't be silly,' Steve said.

'But he said he's going to ruin you. Can he do that?'

Steve shrugged. 'We'll have to see.'

Julia hesitated. 'Steve, I'd like to help you.'

He looked at her, puzzled. 'What do you mean?'

'Well, I'm going to have a lot of money. I'd like to give you enough so you can –'

He put his hands on her shoulders. 'Thank you, Julia. I can't take your money. I'll be fine.'

'But . . .'

'Don't worry about it.'

She shuddered. 'He's an evil man.'

'It was very brave of you to do what you did.'

'You said there was no way to get him, so I thought if you sent him here, that could be the way to trap him.'

'It looks as though we're the ones who fell into the trap, doesn't it?'

That night, Julia lay in her bed, thinking about Steve and wondering how she could protect him. *I shouldn't have come,* she thought, *but if I hadn't come, I wouldn't have met him.*

In the next room, Steve lay in bed, thinking about Julia. It was frustrating to think that she was lying in her bed with only a thin wall between them. *What am I talking about? That wall is a billion dollars thick.*

Tyler was in an exuberant mood. On the way home, he thought about what had just taken place, and how he had outwitted them. *They're pygmies trying to fell a giant,* he thought. And he had no idea that these were once his father's thoughts.

When Tyler reached Rose Hill, Clark greeted him. 'Good evening, Judge Tyler. I hope you're well this evening.'

'Never better, Clark. Never better.'

'Can I get you anything?'

'Yes. I think I'd like a glass of champagne.'

'Of course, sir.'

It was a celebration, the celebration of his victory. *Tomorrow I'll be worth over two billion dollars.* He said the phrase lovingly over and over. 'Two billion dollars . . . two billion dollars . . .' He decided to call Lee.

This time Lee recognized his voice immediately.

'Tyler! How are you?' His voice was warm.

'Fine, Lee.'

'I've been waiting to hear from you.'

Tyler felt a little thrill. 'Have you? How would you like to come to Boston tomorrow?'

'Sure . . . but what for?'

'For the reading of the will. I'm going to inherit over two billion dollars.'

'Two . . . that's fantastic!'

'I want you here at my side. We're going to pick out that yacht together.'

'Oh, Tyler! That sounds wonderful!'

'Then you'll come?'

'Of course, I will.'

When Lee replaced the receiver, he sat there saying lovingly over and over, 'Two billion dollars . . . two billion dollars.'

Chapter Thirty-four

The day before the reading of the will, Kendall and Woody were seated in Steve's office.

'I don't understand why we're here,' Woody said. 'The reading is supposed to be tomorrow.'

'There's someone I want you to meet,' Steve told them.

'Who?'

'Your sister.'

They were both staring at him. 'We've already met her,' Kendall said.

Steve pressed a button on the intercom. 'Would you ask her to come in, please?'

Kendall and Woody looked at each other, puzzled.

The door opened, and Julia Stanford walked into the office.

Steve stood up. 'This is your sister, Julia.'

'What the hell are you talking about?' Woody exploded. 'What are you trying to pull?'

'Let me explain,' Steve said quietly. He spoke for fifteen minutes, and finished by saying, 'Perry Winger confirmed that her DNA matches your father's.'

When he was through, Woody said, 'Tyler! I can't believe it!'

'Believe it.'

'I don't understand. The other woman's fingerprints prove that *she* is Julia,' Woody said. 'I still have the fingerprint card.'

Steve felt his pulse pounding. 'You do?'

'Yeah. I kept it as kind of a joke.'

'I want you to do me a favor,' Steve said.

At ten o'clock the next morning, a large group was gathered in the conference room of Renquist, Renquist & Fitzgerald. Simon Fitzgerald sat at the head of a table. In the room were Kendall, Tyler, Woody, Steve, and Julia. In addition, there were several strangers present.

Fitzgerald introduced two of them. 'This is William Parker and Patrick Evans. They're with the law firms that represent Stanford Enterprises. They've brought with them the financial report on the company. I'll discuss the will first, then they can take over the meeting.'

'Let's get on with it,' Tyler said impatiently. He was sitting apart from the others. *I'm not only going to get the money, but I'm going to destroy you bastards*.

Simon Fitzgerald nodded. 'Very well.'

In front of Fitzgerald was a large file marked HARRY STANFORD – LAST WILL AND TESTAMENT. 'I'm going to give each of you a copy of the will so it won't be necessary to wade through all the technicalities. I've already told you that Harry Stanford's children will equally inherit the estate.'

Julia glanced over at Steve, a look of bemusement on her face.

I'm glad for her, Steve thought. *Even though it puts her way out of my reach.*

Simon Fitzgerald was going on. 'There are a dozen or so bequests, but they're all minor.'

Tyler was thinking, *Lee will be here this afternoon. I want to be at the airport to meet him.*

'As you were told earlier, Stanford Enterprises has assets of approximately six billion dollars.' Fitzgerald nodded toward William Parker. 'I'll let Mr Parker take it from here.'

William Parker opened a briefcase and spread some papers out on the conference table. 'As Mr Fitzgerald said, there are six billion dollars in assets. However . . .' There was a pregnant pause. He looked around the room. 'Stanford Enterprises is in debt in excess of fifteen billion dollars.'

Woody was on his feet. 'What the hell are you saying?'

Tyler's face turned ashen. 'Is this some kind of macabre joke?'

'It has to be!' Kendall said hoarsely.

Mr Parker turned to one of the men in the room. 'Mr Leonard Redding is with the Securities and Exchange Commission. I'll let him explain.'

Redding nodded. 'For the last two years, Harry Stanford was convinced that interest rates were going to fall. In the past, he had made millions by betting on that. When interest rates started to rise, he was still convinced they would drop again, and he kept leveraging his bets. He did massive borrowing to buy long-term bonds, but the interest rates went up and his borrowing costs jumped, while the value of the bonds tumbled. The banks were willing to do business with him because of his reputation and his vast fortune, but when he tried to recoup his losses by starting to invest in high-risk securities, they began to get worried. He made a series of disastrous investments. Some of the money he borrowed was pledged by securities he had bought with borrowed money as collateral for further borrowing.'

'In other words,' Patrick Evans interjected, 'he was pyramiding his debts, operating illegally.'

'That is correct. Unfortunately for him, interest rates underwent one of the steepest climbs in financial history. He had to keep borrowing money to cover the money he had already borrowed. It was a vicious circle.'

They sat there, hanging on Redding's every word.

'Your father gave his personal guarantee to the company's pension plan and illegally used that money to buy more stock. When the banks began to question what he was doing, he set up decoy companies and provided false records of solvency and fake sales of his properties to drive up the value of his paper. He was committing fraud. In the end, he was counting on a consortium of banks to bail him out of trouble. They refused. When they told the Securities and Exchange Commission what was happening, Interpol was brought into the picture.'

Redding indicated the man seated next to him. 'This is Inspector Patou, with the French Sûreté. Inspector, would you explain the rest of it, please?'

Inspector Patou spoke English with a slight French accent. 'At the request of Interpol, we traced Harry Stanford to St-Paul-de-Vence, and I sent three detectives there to follow him. He managed to elude them. Interpol had put out a green code to all police departments that Harry Stanford was under suspicion and should be watched. If they had known the extent of his crimes, they would have circulated a red code, or top priority, and we would have apprehended him.'

Woody was in a state of shock. '*That's* why he left us his estate. Because there was nothing in it!'

William Parker said, 'You're right about that. You were all in your father's will because the banks refused to go along with him and he knew that, in essence, he was leaving you nothing. But he spoke to René Gautier at Crédit Lyonnais, who promised to help him. The moment Harry Stanford thought that he was solvent again, he planned to change his will to cut you out of it.'

'But what about the yacht, and the plane, and the houses?' Kendall asked.

'I'm sorry,' Parker said. 'Everything will be sold to pay off part of the debt.'

Tyler sat there, numb. It was a nightmare beyond imagining. He was no longer Tyler Stanford, Multibillionaire. He was merely a judge.

Tyler got up to leave, shaken. 'I . . . I don't know what to say. If there's nothing else . . .' He had to get to the airport quickly to meet Lee and try to explain what had happened.

Steve spoke up. 'There is something else.'

He turned. 'Yes?'

Steve nodded to a man standing at the door. The door opened, and Hal Baker walked in.

'Hi, judge.'

The breakthrough had come when Woody told Steve that he had the fingerprint card.

'I'd like to see it,' Steve told him.

Woody had been puzzled. 'Why? It just has the woman's two sets of fingerprints on it, and they matched. We all checked it.'

'But the man who called himself Frank Timmons took the fingerprints, right?'

'Yes.'

'Then if he touched the card, *his* fingerprints will be on it.'

* * *

Steve's hunch had proved to be right. Hal Baker's prints were all over the card, and it had taken less than thirty minutes for the computers to reveal his identity. Steve had telephoned the district attorney in Chicago. A warrant was issued, and two detectives had appeared at Hal Baker's house.

He was in the yard playing catch with Billy.

'Mr Baker?'

'Yes.'

The detectives showed their badges. 'The district attorney would like to talk to you.'

'No. I can't.' He was indignant.

'May I ask why?' one of the detectives asked.

'You can see why, can't you? I'm playing ball with my son!'

The district attorney had read the transcript of Hal Baker's trial. He looked at the man seated in front of him and said, 'I understand you're a family man.'

'That's right,' Hal Baker said proudly. 'That's what this country is all about. If every family could –'

'Mr Baker.' He leaned forward. 'You've been working with Judge Stanford.'

'I don't know any Judge Stanford.'

'Let me refresh your memory. He put you on parole. He used you to impersonate a private detective named Frank Timmons, and we have reason to believe he also asked you to kill a Julia Stanford.'

'I don't know what you're talking about.'

362

'What I'm talking about is a sentence of ten to twenty years. I'm going to push for the twenty.'

Hal Baker turned pale. 'You can't do that! Why, my wife and kids would . . .'

'Exactly. On the other hand,' the district attorney said, 'if you're willing to turn state's evidence, I'm prepared to arrange for you to get off very lightly.'

Hal Baker was beginning to perspire. 'What . . . what do I have to do?'

'Talk to me.'

Now, in the conference room of Renquist, Renquist & Fitzgerald, Hal Baker looked at Tyler, and said, 'How are you, judge?'

Woody looked up and exclaimed, 'Hey! It's Frank Timmons!'

Steve said to Tyler, 'This is the man you ordered to break into our offices to get you a copy of your father's will, to dig up your father's body, and to kill Julia Stanford.'

It took a moment for Tyler to find his voice. 'You're crazy! He's a convicted felon. No one is going to take his word against mine!'

'No one has to take his word,' Steve said. 'Have you seen this man before?'

'Of course. He was tried in my court.'

'What's his name?'

'His name is . . .' Tyler saw the trap. 'I mean . . . he probably has a lot of aliases.'

363

'When you tried him in your courtroom, his name was Hal Baker.'

'That . . . that's right.'

'But when he came to Boston, you introduced him as Frank Timmons.'

Tyler was floundering. 'Well, I . . . I . . .'

'You had him released into your custody, and you used him to try to prove that Margo Posner was the real Julia.'

'No! I had nothing to do with that. I never met that woman until she showed up here.'

Steve turned to Lieutenant Kennedy. 'Did you get that, Lieutenant?'

'Yes.'

Steve turned back to Tyler. 'We checked on Margo Posner. She was also tried in your courtroom and released into your custody. The district attorney in Chicago issued a search warrant this morning for your safe-deposit box. He called a little while ago to tell me that they found a document giving you Julia Stanford's share of your father's estate. The document was signed five days before the supposed Julia Stanford arrived in Boston.'

Tyler was breathing hard, trying to regain his wits. 'I . . . I . . . This is preposterous!'

Lieutenant Kennedy said, 'I'm placing you under arrest, Judge Stanford, for conspiracy to commit murder. We'll arrange for extradition papers. You'll be sent back to Chicago.'

Tyler stood there, his world collapsing around him.

'You have the right to remain silent. If you choose to give up this right anything you say can and will be used against you in a court of law. You have the right to talk to a lawyer and have him present with you while you are being questioned. If you cannot afford to hire a lawyer, one will be appointed to represent you before any questioning, if you wish one. Do you understand?' Lieutenant Kennedy asked.

'Yes.' And then a slow triumphant smile lit his face. *I know how to beat them!* he thought happily.

'Are you ready, judge?'

He nodded and said calmly, 'Yes. I'm ready. I'd like to go back to Rose Hill to pick up my things.'

'That's fine. We'll have these two policemen accompany you.'

Tyler turned to look at Julia, and there was so much hatred in his eyes that it made her shudder.

Thirty minutes later, Tyler and the two policemen reached Rose Hill. They walked into the front hall.

'It will take me only a few minutes to pack,' Tyler said.

They watched as Tyler went up the staircase to his room. In his room, Tyler walked over to the bureau containing the revolver and loaded it.

The sound of the shot seemed to reverberate forever.

Chapter Thirty-five

Woody and Kendall were seated in the drawing room at Rose Hill. Half a dozen men in white overalls were taking down paintings from the walls and starting to dismantle the furnishings.

'It's the end of an era,' Kendall sighed.

'It's the beginning,' Woody said. He smiled. 'I wish I could see Peggy's face when she finds out what her half of my fortune is!' He took his sister's hand. 'Are you okay? About Marc, I mean.'

She nodded. 'I'll get over it. Anyhow, I'm going to be very busy. I have a preliminary hearing in two weeks. After that, I'll see what happens.'

'I'm sure everything will be all right.' He rose. 'I have an important telephone call to make,' Woody told her. He had to break the news to Mimi Carson.

'Mimi,' Woody said apologetically, 'I'm afraid I'm going to have to go back on our deal. Things haven't worked out as I had hoped they would.'

'Are you all right, Woody?'

'Yes. A lot has been going on here. Peggy and I are finished.'

There was a long pause. 'Oh? Are you coming back to Hobe Sound?'

'Frankly, I don't know what I'm going to do.'

'Woody?'

'Yes?'

Her voice was soft. 'Come back, please.'

Julia and Steve were out on the patio.

'I'm sorry about the way things turned out,' Steve said. 'About your not getting the money, I mean.'

Julia smiled at him. 'I don't really need a hundred chefs.'

'You're not disappointed that your trip here was wasted?'

She looked up at him. 'Was it wasted, Steve?'

They never knew who made the first move, but she was in his arms, and he was holding her, and they were kissing.

'I've been wanting to do this since the first time I saw you.'

Julia shook her head. 'The first time you saw me, you told me to get out of town!'

He grinned. 'I did, didn't I? I don't ever want you to leave.'

And she thought of Sally's words. *'Don't you know if the man proposed?'* 'Is that a proposal?' Julia asked.

He held her tighter. 'You bet it is. Will you marry me?'

'Oh, yes!'

Kendall came out to the patio. She was holding a piece of paper in her hand.

'I . . . I just got this in the mail.'

Steve looked at her, worried. 'Not another . . . ?'

'No. I've been named Women's Wear Designer of the Year.'

Woody and Kendall and Julia and Steve were seated at the dining-room table. All around them workmen were moving chairs and couches, and carrying them off.

Steve turned to Woody. 'What are you going to do now?'

'I'm going back to Hobe Sound. First, I'm going to check in with Dr Tichner. Then a friend of mine has a string of ponies that I'm going to ride.'

Kendall looked at Julia. 'Are you going back to Kansas City?'

When I was a little girl, Julia thought, *I wished that someone would take me out of Kansas and bring me to a magical place where I would find my prince.* She took Steve's hand. 'No,' Julia said. 'I'm not going back to Kansas.'

They watched two men take down the huge portrait of Harry Stanford.

'I never did like that picture,' Woody said.

Bloodline
Sidney Sheldon

A daughter of privilege: Elizabeth Roffe possessed beauty, intelligence, youth, the adored daughter of a rich and powerful father.

At his death she had to obey his behest and take command of his mighty global empire. It made Elizabeth the richest girl in the world. But someone, somewhere, was determined that she must die . . .

In this story that spans three continents, Sidney Sheldon spins a hypnotic, exotic web – of love and ambition, of danger and death.

'Sheldon is a writer working at the height of his power . . . powerful enough to drag us along with him. I hung on till the very end.'   *New York Times*

ISBN 0 00 617501 5

Rage of Angels
Sidney Sheldon

At the heart of the story stands the woman who is Sheldon's most unforgettable creation . . .

Jennifer Parker is brilliant, beautiful and indomitable – the most glamorous lawyer in America and one of the most successful.

Her life is shadowed by two men. Both of them powerful and both drawn irresistibly to her.

One is the politician, destined for greatness who fathers her son. The other is the Mafia boss, her only ally when crisis strikes and the man who brings her world crashing down . . .

'The fast moving plot . . . with new surprises on every page . . . will keep his fans enthralled.' *Publishers Weekly*

The Doomsday Conspiracy
Sidney Sheldon

A devastatingly topical novel from
the world's master storyteller

Robert Bellamy of US naval intelligence, a disillusioned man
recovering from a broken marriage, is despatched on a top
secret mission. A weather balloon, he is told, carrying
sensitive military information, has crashed in Switzerland
and Bellamy must locate the ten witnesses to the incident.
But when he arrives in Switzerland he discovers that it wasn't
a weather balloon that crashed after all, but a UFO with two
dead aliens aboard, whose remains have since vanished . . .
As the story unfolds, Bellamy gradually discovers the full,
terrible nature of Operation Doomsday, a conspiracy of such
magnitude as to threaten the destruction of the earth's
environment. He also rebuilds his own shattered life, finding
true love and hope for the future again.

ISBN 0 00 647208 7

The Other Side of Midnight
Sidney Sheldon

The magnificent novel of scorching sensation and shimmering evil that became a triumphant screen sensation.

A beautiful French actress whose craving for passion and vengeance took her from the gutters of Paris to the bedroom of a millionaire . . . a dynamic Greek tycoon who never forgot an insult, never forgave an injury . . . a handsome war hero drawn from his wife to a woman none could resist . . . and a girl whose dream of love was transformed into a nightmare of fear . . .

Paris and Washington, Hollywood and the islands of Greece are the settings for a dramatic narrative of four star-crossed lives enmeshed in a deadly ritual of passion, intrigue and corruption where the punishment will always exceed the crime . . .

'Gripping, glamorous, memorable, heart-stopping.'

Irving Wallace

ISBN 0 00 617931 2

The Stars Shine Down
Sidney Sheldon

A magnificent story of passion, intrigue, ambition and revenge – Sidney Sheldon at his compelling, provocative best.

Lara Cameron seems to possess everything that life has to offer. Young, beautiful, a self-made tycoon, she has outshone her competitors to reach the pinnacle of international fortune and renown. But the real Lara is a lonely figure, driven by a childhood obsession, trying, at all costs to bury the ghosts of her terrible past . . .

With her glittering marriage to a world-famous concert pianist, Lara is sure she has fulfilled her destiny. But what she cannot foresee is that terrifying, uncontrollable forces from her secret past are bent on destroying everything she has created, everything she values in life . . .

'Sheldon shines again . . . a compelling read'   *Today*

ISBN 0 00 617871 5